DATE			
6-15	4C		
2/12	3C	13cop	10/11

At college, and perhaps for a year afterwards, they had believed in literature, had believed in Beauty and in personal expression as an absolute end. When they lost this belief, they lost everything.

— NATHANAEL WEST, *Miss Lonelyhearts*

Not to be onto something is to be in despair.

— WALKER PERCY, *The Moviegoer*

MY AMERICAN UNHAPPINESS

Books by Dean Bakopoulos

Please Don't Come Back from the Moon

My American Unhappiness

MY AMERICAN UNHAPPINESS

Dean Bakopoulos

HOUGHTON MIFFLIN HARCOURT

BOSTON • NEW YORK

2011

For information about permission to reproduce selections from this book,
write to Permissions, Houghton Mifflin Harcourt Publishing Company,
215 Park Avenue South, New York, New York 10003.

www.hmhbooks.com

Library of Congress Cataloging-in-Publication Data
Bakopoulos, Dean.
My American unhappiness /Dean Bakopoulos.
p. cm.
ISBN 978-0-15-101344-9
1. Young men—Fiction. 2. Mate selection — Fiction. I. Title.
PS3602.A593M9 2010
813'.6 — dc22
2010025837

Book design by Linda Lockowitz

Printed in the United States of America

DOC 10 9 8 7 6 5 4 3 2 1

This book is for my friend Steve Myck,
and in memory of his late partner, Mark Gates, Book Whisperer.

And for Amanda, Lydia, and Amos:
My happiness!

SPRING 2008

1

Zeke Pappas is off to the Rotary Club luncheon.

NINE YEARS AGO, in the summer of 1999, I was hired to be the director of the Great Midwestern Humanities Initiative (GMHI), a federally funded program designed "to foster a greater sense of community, increase public literacy, and strengthen levels of civic engagement in the American heartland." The program was typical of the projects launched at the end of that optimistic and high-rolling decade, as its founders believed it could cease or at least slow the brain drain that was occurring in that region of the country, both the crumbling Rust Belt and the blighted Grain Belt. I was raised in Madison, Wisconsin, and I still live there, a city full of transplants where everybody's optimism about the heartland seems to outpace the reality of our condition: we are dying.

People have been leaving the Midwest for decades and they still are many decades later and nobody is particularly surprised. From the streets of Cleveland and Detroit and Gary, to the fertile fields of Wisconsin and Iowa and southern Indiana, the young people flee. They go south and west, to the newly cosmopolitan and sprawling cities like Atlanta and Orlando and Salt Lake; they deal with the heat—it's worth it to them. I can imagine them sweating, those exiles, in newly purchased summer suits of linen and seersucker, in dresses that bare their still pale and overly broad shoulders. Some of the exiles head west to the great mountains and the deserts and the outdoorsy, freestyling existence that such places as Boulder and Bozeman and Tucson seem to promise. They go to sunny and arid places with high-tech corridors and solar energy projects. Some go directly to the coasts: to San Francisco or New York, those hubs of artistry and commerce with their diverse and teeming neighborhoods, the magnetic bustle of business and action, the sounds of foreign music and unknown spices wafting out of the windows and into the sky and streets. They do not stay here in the Midwest with its sagging and empty auto plants, steel factories running at half power, and farms plagued by unprofitable hogs, underpriced grain, silos in sore need of repair.

The founders of the Great Midwestern Humanities Initiative included a gaggle of congressional leaders, led by Wisconsin Republican Quince Leatherberry, an anti-immigration conservative from the state's wealthy Fifth District, who, despite his constant sermons on self-reliance and hard work, has never held a job outside of Capitol Hill and has lived, largely, on the fat of his father's land. Leatherberry, an unlikely ally for public humanities funding, was joined by H. M. Logan, a business leader and the chair of GMHI, as well as an odd alliance of advocates, vigorously paid lobbyists, and oft-bewildered but generous businessmen who believed that in order to slow our regional brain drain, young Midwesterners simply needed to know the hallowed heritage of their homeland, to read the rich literature of their own region, and to understand the blessed uniqueness of their landscape and culture. Then they might stay!

It was also believed, by the founders, that the study of the humanities, in the broader sense, might enlighten the work force of the Midwest, ignite a wildfire of innovation and experimentation in the private sector, from automotives to agriculture, economic combustion engines fueled by the bright minds of Michigan and Wisconsin and Iowa and Minnesota and Ohio and Nebraska, digesting and ruminating upon the works of our own undervalued sons and daughters: Willa Cather and F. Scott Fitzgerald and Sinclair Lewis. If only the music of our own famous musicians and composers—John Alden Carpenter, Benny Goodman, Miles Davis, Bob Dylan—were lodged forever in our internal melodies; if only we allowed the images of John Steuart Curry and Grant Wood to enliven our vision of place; if only we realized that we share the prairie with the same lines, light, and landscapes that inspired Frank Lloyd Wright and moved Aldo Leopold—if only, if only, then our engineers in Detroit and our productivity managers in Cleveland and our logistics coordinators in South Bend would discover new ideas and revolutionary technologies.

It was, as Representative Leatherberry said, "a real win-win."

"Oh, the humanities!" once exclaimed benefactor Howard Morgan Logan, after a particularly rousing Governor's Lecture in the Humanities by the visiting critic Stanley Fish. Logan, a retired oil man and closeted homosexual originally from Kenosha, turned to a harrumphing Congressman Leatherberry and whispered, tears in his eyes, "Oh, life!"

I was barely twenty-four the year I took this job, armed with a self-designed bachelor's degree in "The Narrative Text and Social Movements" from the University of Michigan, and I believed in many things, including the noble and mind-boggling mission of the GMHI: *To encourage and advance civic engagement, commercial initiative, economic development, and regional pride in the American Midwest through the study and promotion of the humanities disciplines.*

I was charismatic then, I worked out every day, and my eyes shone with the sort of confidence I think we all gleaned from our silver-haired president in that decade: no conflict too deep to resolve, no domestic issue too muddy to clarify, no potential lover too distant or risky to bed, no humanities discipline too abstract to define. In fact, I'd been the one who'd written the successful vision statement that had landed us ten million dollars in federal money—an earmark added to a domestic spending bill sponsored, for some unknown reason, by Representative Leatherberry, which, he claimed on the House floor, would somehow help the United States clamp down on illegal immigrants. And so the newly incorporated board of GMHI, chaired by H. M. Logan and supported by letters of proclamation from the governors of thirteen Midwestern states, chose Madison, Wisconsin, as the project's headquarters, appointed me as the executive director, and then pretty much left me alone except for twice-a-year meetings that very few board members ever attended. I'd been working part-time at a small, erudite independent bookstore near campus, where H. M. Logan was a loyal customer and, to all appearances, had no small crush on me. The job was mine, most likely, for no reason other than this: he wanted to spend more time with me.

Today, nearly a decade later, the economy is in shambles, the nation is at war, and my own job is precariously perched on a list of the luxuries we can no longer afford. I am sitting at a banquet table in the corner of a reception room at the Marriott on the far west side of the city, picking at a rubbery piece of pork loin smothered in a raspberry barbecue sauce. The West Side Rotarians are about to commence their weekly meeting, and I am, courtesy of H. M. Logan, guest speaker, an honor I accepted because it is widely known that Rotarians are often insurance brokers and lawyers and bankers and have the ability to be philanthropists. The GMHI is now in dire need of philanthropy.

The club's president calls the meeting to order with a gavel. All of the Rotarians stand at once. There is a short prayer, led by a man in a blue suit with neatly parted white hair. Just as I manage to mumble my "Amen," the crowd turns abruptly to the left, where a large American flag stands on a raised platform on a golden pole. The Rotarians begin to recite the Pledge of Allegiance, something I have not done since sixth grade. For a moment, I place my left hand over my right breast, but by the time the crowd is pledging to the republic for which it stands, I have the correct hand in the correct position, and I am hoping nobody noticed my very unpatriotic *faux pas*. At "justice for all," I sit down, but when I realize everyone else has remained standing, I get back to my feet.

Logan looks over at me and gives me a thin-lipped, embarrassed smile. Even after all these years, he is still a bit smitten by me, even if I can't quite say a convincing Pledge of Allegiance; he confesses secrets to me that he can't tell to any of his other friends. I am an avowed liberal, and, as a dedicated neo-con, H. M. believes that I have lax moral standards of some sort, but the truth of the matter is that I do not condone married men, with four children and nine grandchildren, hiring high-priced male prostitutes (for instance), as H. M. does when he is in Washington, DC.

H. M. smiles and nods in my direction as I hear the club president say something about a song book, and then the Rotary Club of Madison's West Side begins to sing "America the Beautiful," not in the lilting, halfhearted, heads-down manner of schoolchildren, but in a bellowing chorus dominated by forceful tenors and hearty basses. There are women in the audience, but you cannot hear them singing and I think some of them are simply mouthing the words.

The singing is what truly flusters me, I suppose: So much earnestness! So much blessed assurance! This sort of social confidence, the sort of bravado that allows men in suits to sing in public, always makes me squirm. Even after 9/11, when earnestness seemed to be appropriate and easy, I still felt uncomfortable, almost disheartened, anytime members of Congress and other power brokers began singing patriotic hymns at public events. There are many of us who love our country, who have spent decades examining its complex woes and its noble ways, and simply cannot bring ourselves to be the sort of highly visible cheerleaders our media demand. The spirit of critical inquiry and constant reflection is too bright within us. I wonder how many capable, smart, and worthy public servants might shy away from office simply because they are not comfortable with such outward displays of emotional patriotism.

This particular afternoon, however, I have at least one red, white, and blue ace up my sleeve, a patriotic credential that is legitimate, that is the opposite of the empty gestures so often trotted out for the sake of media events. My brother, Cougar, was killed while serving overseas in Iraq. I mention this at the beginning of my talk. I say, "It does my heart good to hear such patriotic voices this afternoon. I can't hear those words without thinking of my brother, whom everybody called Cougar and who died while serving our nation in Iraq."

This generates some polite applause and the collective gasp of concern that always accompanies this announcement. I feel a little guilty using my dead brother like this, but I do not think Cougar would mind if he were alive. I was a generous and warm-hearted older brother who had helped him in many ways over the years. We grew distant and our relationship contentious before he died, but I like to believe that if his spirit has any sort of eternal state, he would say, to whatever angelic neighbors he has on his lonely cloud, that I was a good brother.

Thus, I stop short of mentioning that his final e-mail message to me informed me that I was being "a self-righteous, conceited, washed-up, elitist, cowardly little puss." This characterization was in response to a picture of me that our mother had just sent him. I was marching up State Street in an antiwar protest, shouting and holding a sign that said, "Regime change begins at home." I was also wearing a T-shirt that sported the Canadian maple leaf, which I insisted, vainly to my mother, was not intended as any sort of statement or symbol. (Like many of my peers, I have a drawer full of T-shirts that mean nothing: Drink Orange Crush. Be a Pepper. Do the Dew.)

8

"Why did you send that e-mail to Cougar?" I'd asked her. This was before he was dead, when the war was still new and people like me believed we could end it with T-shirt slogans and halfhearted chanting. "Why on earth?"

"How can you hate your own country?" my mother had sobbed.

"I don't," I said. "I swear."

Despite the sympathy card I play early in my speech, in short, my talk to the Madison West Side Rotary Club does not go well: whatever is on the minds of these upright citizens gathered before me, it is not the public humanities—that much is certain. Once I notice this, I'm flustered and have a difficult time making my main points, and several of the suited men in the audience start to fiddle with their BlackBerries, as if urgent, potentially million-dollar e-mails are attempting to vibrate their way into consciousness. Even a rather zippy little joke about whether Brett Favre would make a comeback attempt falls flat, and so about ten minutes into my prepared remarks, I pause and say, "Well, I am sure that many of you have specific questions about the work that we do, so maybe I'll stop there and take a few. Anybody?"

Did you have anything to do with the funding of Mapplethorpe and that cross in urine?

Do you fund religious organizations, or is there a bias against Christianity in the work you do?

Do you fund individuals? I am working on a history of my grandfather's company, a shipping outfit that once graced the shores of Lake Superior. Would you be interested in funding that?

For instance.

And then, this, from a gray-haired, pocket-eyed man at the far back table: *Why didn't you sing with more conviction? Where was your gusto? I watched you singing; your singing was pathetic.*

I left the podium. Exactly! Where *is* my gusto?

2

Zeke Pappas needs a triple shot of gusto.

I FLEE THE SUBURBAN blight of Madison's far west side and retreat downtown to Nick's for a quick vodka tonic and a chat with Gus, the Greek who runs the place with his brother, George. There is no Nick anymore, not to my knowledge, though I have never asked, not really, as the subject of death is one I avoid at all costs. I have never attended a funeral. I have skipped the funerals of several people whom I knew rather well, including one whom I, in my own way, loved (my father); one I truly loved, in my own way, but never admitted that love (my brother); and one whom, in my own way, I deeply loved (her name was Valerie and, briefly, she was my wife). This has provided an opportunity for others to judge me but I feel no reason to defend myself. I will not attend a funeral, and when I die I do not want one. I want my survivors, whoever they may be, to dispose of my remains in the most efficient, inexpensive, and eco-friendly way possible.

"*Ti kanis?*" Gus asks me. He cannot believe that I have a Greek father yet know no Greek.

"*Kala,*" I answer, which means "Fine," and which is one of the only words I know.

"So how have you been?" I ask Gus.

"Busy," he says. "Very busy. You?"

"Oh, okay. Not that busy," I say.

I finish my cocktail in awkward silence. Gus and George are good men, but they are not the kind of men I am particularly good at making conversation with—they are hulking, hard-working, with no time for the intellectual sparring that dominates conversation in my social circle. I should say my waning social circle. Nine years ago, there was a pack of us who spent a great deal of time at Nick's, discussing weighty books and foreign films, drinking can after can of Miller High Life in ironic appreciation for the cheap things in life. I was there almost nightly. But most of those friendships have faded in this decade. A few of my friends—the bravest, in my humble opinion—have gone off to New York where they live interesting, mildly erotic lives in tiny, shared apartments. The rest have married and settled into a quiet life on the near west side of Madison with their children, whom they wheel around the city in mammoth, brightly colored strollers. I see them sometimes as I drive, jogging behind those strollers, faces twisted as if they are still perplexed by the routines of domestic life. Sometimes I see one of them squat down, hand encased in plastic bag, and pick up a steaming pile of dog shit while his wife, his strollered children, and his impatient labs wait for him to perform the gross but righteous act of a good citizen. Some days, as I pass in my car or on the soft seat of a city bus, I laugh at him, the poor sap, bent over the smoldering turd; but lately when I see these friends, attacked by sticky fingers in a loud family restaurant near the Hilldale mall or struggling to change a diaper in the Borders bathroom, I feel not superiority and the tickle of my ample freedom but a searing feeling of envy and loss. I want that, I think. That's what I want.

"Anything else?" Gus asks.

"Nope. Nope, I'm good then," I say, savoring the sensation of a faint buzz at midday. I put a five-dollar bill on the counter. The cocktail is three-fifty. I tip fairly well for a Midwesterner. "Thanks for the drink!"

"That's it?" he says.

"Yes," I say. "It's a bit early for a second one, don't you think?"

"No lunch? Tuna melt special today."

"I do like tuna melts," I say. "But I just needed a drink."

"Take it easy," Gus says.

"You also," I say. "Don't be so busy!"

In recent weeks, I have begun to answer the standard "How're you doing?" with the phrase "Not that busy." I've taken to doing this because so many people reflexively answer, "Busy." Especially academics, activists, and artists, who should have at least some free time each day to spend daydreaming and thinking big thoughts. *How are you? Busy.* How did we get so busy? If you think about it, busyness is decidedly not one of the ideals of Midwestern culture (see GMHI Book Discussion Series #13: *Big Business or Big Busyness?*). Hard work, perseverance, determination, yes—but busyness? No. It smacks too loudly of self-importance and futility. So, now, when asked, I always say I am "not that busy." Because I am not and that is perfectly okay; it says nothing about my intellectual might or social standing. In fact, one might argue that being busy is a very common, as in pedestrian, thing to be.

Before I head back to my office, I decide to stop by Starbucks on the Capitol Square, not so much because I want a cup of coffee—in fact, I worry that any caffeine might prematurely end the minor buzz of a midday cocktail—but because I want to see Minn, full name Minerva Koltes, who is twenty-nine years old and the assistant manager of this Starbucks. Minn is one of those service industry professionals with a competence and friendliness that are rare. I enjoy my midafternoon caffeine jolt so much, partly because she is the one who serves it to me.

We are not really friends, Minn and I, not yet. In fact, we have never had a conversation in which we were not separated by the merchandise-cluttered counter of the Starbucks, exchanging quips and pleasantries over a folk rock compilation CD and a small stand of roasted almonds and chocolate-covered espresso beans.

I have friends, beset by liberal guilt, who refuse to set foot inside a Starbucks, despite my assurances that the store has decent, and rapidly improving, business practices and geopolitical stances. I also happen to prefer their coffee's hearty richness and their homogenized and nationalized standards of quality control; so be it. But I go there, ultimately, because of Minn, with her dark hair and her blue eyes, and the smile that twitches when she shows her teeth, the freckles barely visible on her high, olive cheeks. When she serves me my usual drink, a tall, triple-shot roomy Americano, she never charges me for the third shot, which is technically an extra shot and should cost me eighty-five cents.

I'm just saying.

"Hi, Zeke," she says.

"Hello," I say. I glance at her left ring finger. Her diamond engagement ring is still there. It's one small thing I take note of each day. I do not know her fiancé's name; I do not know who he is or what he does. I know nothing of Minn's life outside the walls of this warmly lit national chain. This is fine. Such relationships, based on the ancient economic principle of supply and demand, are one of the most sacred elements of our social contract in America.

"Do you have time to play the Starbucks Challenge?" she asks. Brightly, she smiles.

"I do," I say. I smile back.

The Starbucks Challenge is a game I invented one day, publicly sharing a gift I had long held private. I was feeling particularly bold and confident, perhaps somewhat inspired by the way Minn had her dark hair, shorter than usual, held out of her eyes with a small pink barrette.

A new customer walks into the coffee shop, and Minn and I

share a quick, knowing glance. Her smile is the sort of smile that seems secretive, and her posture can only be described as sheepish, as if she always is hanging on to an inside joke. In this case, she is.

"You can take care of this gentleman first," I say, stepping aside and motioning to the man who has just come into the store. He is doughy, tall, with a buzz cut; he wears pleated khakis and a red golf shirt with a country club insignia on the left breast. I glance at him—former college athlete now making a go of it in sales. Far from home, a long drive ahead of him, he wants a special treat, an acceptable vice until he goes home to his wife and children. He's marginally in love with his wife; she sort of detests him. His kids, he adores. Only on the golf course does he feel truly comfortable. If I turned to him and asked, "Why are you unhappy?" he would tell me all of these things.

Instead, I wave him ahead of me in line.

"Thanks," he says.

I stop him. "I have this game I like to play," I say. "Might I guess what you are going to order?"

"Huh?"

"I like to guess what people are going to order just by looking at their faces," I say.

"He's quite good," Minn says. "I'm always amazed."

The man gives Minn a flirty smile. It occurs to me that she could come work for me someday and add energy and dazzle to my days.

"Yeah? Okay, go ahead," the man says, giving Minn a wink as if to say, *Hey, dollface, who's this clown? Should we humor him?*

I turn my back, while Minn hands the man a Post-it notepad and has him write down his order.

"Okay," Minn says.

"Caramel Frap, extra whip. And a toffee bar," I say, still facing away from the counter.

The man looks around the shop, as if he expects to be flanked by cameras.

"Holy shit," the man says. "That's amazing. How did you do that?"

I turn toward him.

"I'm remarkably intuitive about other people's emotional landscapes. Especially strangers. I'm much better with strangers. The less I know you, the better. Starbucks is a source of simple pleasure, an acceptable and fulfilling vice, if you will. I like to look at people, measure the hardness of their day, their circumstances—the general crumminess they feel in their hearts—and decide what sort of beverage, and perhaps snack, could remedy their misery for a while. It's my belief that you are happy only on the golf course, but for now, this infusion of fat and sugar—and there is a great deal of it in the combination that you ordered—is akin to temporary salvation for you."

A line has formed behind the man.

Minn takes his money and hands him a small brown bag that holds his toffee bar, and her fellow baristas finish making his drink.

The man walks away from me, bewildered and hollow. He is too disarmed, and I am too right, for him to be angry.

"Do mine," says the next customer in line. She has overheard the entire exchange. I look at her. She is in a black business suit, mildly attractive unless you focus on her face for too long, and then you see the badly drawn lines of her mouth, a permanent frown as if she is in chronic pain. She is an uninteresting woman—she feels that in her bones—but wants desperately to be interesting. Minn hands her the notepad. And I turn my back.

"Vanilla skinny latte," I say. "Extra shot."

She looks wildly enthusiastic.

"Wow. Wow. Do you do this a lot?"

"Fairly often," I say.

"He's incredible," Minn says. "I love this guy."

The woman in the black suit is really beaming now. "Seriously?" she asks Minn.

"Seriously?" I ask. Does Minn mean "I love this guy" the way you talk about an odd and eccentric weirdo—*Dude, I love that homeless guy who plays the kazoo all day on State Street*—or does she mean, you know, that she *loves* this guy, me?

It turns out the woman with the vanilla skinny latte, extra shot, is a reporter for Channel 3. She wants to do a segment on me, maybe on Minn, too, about how I guess drinks at Starbucks every afternoon.

"Well, I don't do this every afternoon," I say. "Only when the café is slow—for example, we never play this game in the morning rush—and only when I am feeling particularly intuitive."

"It's amazing," the reporter says.

"It always makes our day," says Tammy, another barista who is working the milk steamer.

Minn just smiles at me. She never seems to not be smiling; she may be the only genuinely happy person I know.

"Anyway," I tell the reporter, "media attention would simply negate the subversive pleasure I get from this little game. People would come in to deliberately throw me off. Imitating guessers would crop up all over town, plaguing cafés with such guessing games. But, anyway, you were debating getting a pack of trail mix. You should get it. But in truth, I think you really wanted a pumpkin scone. But there's your diet to consider, especially given your profession."

Minn is laughing so hard tears come down her face.

The TV reporter gives me her card as she exits. Her name is Kathy Simon. The trail mix comment has left her dazed, as if I have plumbed an intimate region of her psyche. She is a bit more attractive now, smiling. Her gray eyes look almost blue, but no, they are gray. Her skin is pale, too, and in midwinter it will turn to gray. Soon, her hair will be gray; it's possible that she will be all gray soon. A gray woman.

"Do you have a gray cat?" I ask her as she nears the exit.

Now she just leaves, wide-eyed, near tears. Minn helps a few other customers and I go to the washroom. When I come back, Minn has my triple-shot ready.

"On me," she says.

"Many thanks," I say.

"You have a dark edge to you today," Minn says. "A sort of harsh subtext to your guessing."

"It's a gift. A useless one, but interesting: I've studied unhappiness for a long time and now I can sort of guess everybody's unhappiness before they speak. And I also note, at least among a certain well-educated demographic, Starbucks is a ritual—costly and mildly unhealthy as it is—meant to mitigate our day-to-day unhappiness."

"It's like this very focused sort of ESP, don't you think?"

"Funny thing is this: if I know the person at all, I can never guess what they'll order."

I hear my name being called, boisterously, across the room.

"Zeke!"

I nod at Minn, mumble "Thanks," and go over to the waving, suited man. H. M. Logan has obviously followed his Rotary meeting with cocktails, too, many more than the one I had, and now is trying to sober up at a corner table before heading back to his office, a palatial suite on the thirteenth floor of the U.S. Bank building from which he runs the Dorothy Logan Memorial Foundation, named after his mother. "You were terrible today," he says. "What were you thinking? You embarrassed me in front of the Rotarians!"

"Sorry, H. M. I really am, but it wasn't an ideal audience," I say. "It was like giving a lecture about cooking with bacon at a PETA conference."

"What are you talking about?"

"You can't have an attentive audience without a receptive one," I say.

H. M. is drooling a little. "What are you talking about?"

"How much did you have to drink today?" I ask.

"Look," he says, "I got a call from somebody in Washington yesterday. Apparently, my name is the contact name in their database for GMHI. I told them to call you."

"Okay."

"Why would they call me?" H. M. asks.

"I don't know. Because you're the chair of the board?" I say.

"It makes me nervous, federal bureaucrats calling me on the phone."

"It's probably nothing. Maybe Lara forgot to turn in a form," I say, which I know would never happen, as Lara is an amazingly organized assistant, but I just want to assure H. M. that nothing is wrong. He has gotten sweaty and visibly anxious, though that may be the cocktails and whatever prescription anxiety drugs he is on this week. Still, he is my major benefactor, and such a relationship requires, above all, that I offer a pleasant smile and listen to everything he says, no matter how absurd it's getting.

"I just don't like people nosing around in my business," he says. "Especially not the federal government."

The stranger H. M.'s private sexual escapades get, the more paranoid he becomes.

"Well, I'll go back to the office, right now, and find out what is going on. We'll handle it."

"Just don't let them call me anymore. I don't want anything to do with them."

"H. M.," I say, "it's not a big deal."

"I have things—as you know—that would be very embarrassing, should, you know, they come out in the press. I trusted you with my secrets, Zeke!"

"They're safe with me, H. M. Besides, I've done my best to forget them, and anyway, I don't think they're interested in your personal decisions."

"What if they inquire into my travel activities?"

H. M. uses a GMHI credit card for many of his personal expenses, but he always reimburses the organization double. Lara and

I know enough to turn the other way when the card has a questionable expense. JJ'S FULL SERVICE, for example, for three hundred dollars. Or THE PINK ROOM for four hundred fifty-six dollars. We know who pays our salary these days, and we quietly pay the bill so that H. M.'s wife, who handles the family finances, does not see it. And a few days later, a "donation" always arrives from H. M. for double the amount of his charges.

"Not to worry," I say, and I believe it.

It's—most likely—simply some bureaucratic quest for job-justifying information. Lara and I take such calls from the federal government at least once a week as of late. Well, mostly Lara takes them. Washington has become vigilant in all the wrong places: they chase errant nickels while billions of dollars are squandered by corporate greed and excess. I say something to this effect to H. M. and he just grunts and waves a dismissive hand at me.

I leave him sighing and staring out the window.

When I turn around, Minn is dealing with six men in suits, all of them ordering very involved beverages, and so I simply give her a brief wave and head back to the office. But en route I check my watch and discover how close it is to three in the afternoon. The girls are home from school, and I decide to head home too.

3

Zeke Pappas is on his way home.

GENERATIONS FROM NOW, I believe that historians will assess the first decade of the twenty-first century and declare that these years turned out to be a time of colossal bad luck and almost unbelievable failure. On a microscopic level, nowhere was this more evident than in the life of my own family, the Pappases of Madison, Wisconsin, though it's doubtful historians will remember us at all. Still, it is worth noting, as a rather inaccurate *Wisconsin State Journal* tearjerking feature story by George Hessenfessen did during the previous holiday season, that in recent years, my family has endured a series of the most incredible and relentless heartaches imaginable.

While it'd be hard to say that we were a family who subsisted wholly on mirth and joy in the years before our tragedies, let us begin here: On September 12, 2001, my father died of a massive heart attack outside the Oscar Mayer plant where he worked, an untimely death, my mother insisted to George Hessenfessen, caused by his patriotic grief over the terrorist attacks that had occurred the day before. He had stayed up all night long, as so many of us did, watching the news, alternating between weeping and thirsting for blood.

(And while it is poetic to think his heart stopped out of woe and rage and uninhibited sorrow, I blame his enlarged heart and a prediabetic condition, fueled by endless cigarettes and a diet that consisted, almost exclusively, of frozen pizzas, Funyuns, and chocolate ice cream, all of it usually consumed after ten in the evening.)

But fathers die, often from heart attacks and often in conjunction with national news events. This alone did not make my family's woe legendary. This was not the extent of my family's misfortune. It grew deeper: a little over two years after my father's death, my brother, Cougar, died while serving with his National Guard unit in the Iraq war, the victim of sniper fire near Fallujah; he had enlisted the day after my father's funeral, with my mother's blessing and against my advice. This is what I said: "Don't do it. You'll die."

I now regret my armchair prophecy.

Even so, soldiers do die, and while tragic to the nation and excruciating to the soldier's family, it is not wholly unexpected. No, what happened next, this, this is what catapulted our family's grief from the tragic to the epic: three months after my brother's death, his fiancée and the mother of his children, a beautiful but often unstable woman named Melody Leeds, drank just a tad too much wine at what was intended to be a spirit-lifting dinner party thrown by some old high school friends. Melody ended up hitting a patch of late March black ice and dying in a one-car accident on a rural road northwest of Madison. At the time, her home was in foreclosure and she was self-medicating, with limited success, her understandable depression.

Melody was a good, kind woman, a caring mother when she was sober but, if I may be blunt, an emotional wreck when she was not. My mother and I always played a somewhat stabilizing role in her life—often cleaning her house, cooking her meals, running errands for her, not to mention baby-sitting for her. My mother, in fact, seemed to have two full-time jobs—assistant manager at the east side Old Country Buffet, and nanny to her two young granddaughters.

After Melody's death, caring for Cougar and Melody's twin daughters, my nieces, two-year-old girls named April and May, fell to my mother, Violet, who excelled as a grandmother, but who was terrified at the prospect of being the sole means of support—financial, emotional, and spiritual—for such bright, energetic, and needy orphans. Although April and May—so named because the former had been born on April 30 at 11:58 P.M. and the latter had arrived on May 1 at 12:01 A.M.—received survivor's benefits from both the Social Security Administration and the military, my mother was quickly overwhelmed, on an emotional and financial level, by her charges. In particular, her new duties as a primary caregiver made her unable to continue to work the fifty or sixty hours a week she was used to working as a salaried employee at the Old Country Buffet. By necessity, she went down to an hourly wage, slashed her hours by nearly sixty percent, and was forced, by a rather crippling amount of debt left behind by Melody, to move in with me and become a part of my household. I am a generous man, and think very little of hoarding wealth, and was in fact quite happy to become the financial provider for this new and loving, if fragmented, family.

I suppose it could be said that my mother had had a harder time accepting my generosity than I had extending it. But she needed help, quickly. There was no time to explore options. She sold her house, paid off all the debts (hers and Melody's) that she could, and arrived along with a large moving truck from Smitty's Specialty Movers. It was not a joyful day for her, but she could see that the twins loved their Uncle Zeke, and ever since that move-in day, I have ended my evenings by telling three bedtime stories to the girls. My mother, often exhausted by the twins' eight o'clock bedtime, always seems to sigh with relief when I am home from work.

That is how, despite my mother's objections to the Kerry-Edwards sign that I'd posted on my lawn, my mother and two nieces moved in with me in the fall of 2004. We celebrated Christmas together that year in our shared living room, my once spacious and spare rooms of Ikea-esque clarity now cluttered with the happy detritus of life with children: toys, dolls, gift wrapping, and small discarded half-empty bags of dried fruit snacks. A fresh-cut Fraser fir looked remarkable all lit up and festive against the backdrop of oak built-in bookcases.

Shortly after my mother and the twins moved in, I went with my mother to see her pastor one afternoon, in the hope that she would see that I had a respect for her beliefs and that she would soon show the same respect for mine. In truth, I suppose I didn't have respect for her faith—she'd begged me to come along, despite my well-known unbelief—and her new pastor, Revered Ty Willis of the New Promise Church, which has usurped my mother's Catholic faith, encouraged us to read the book of Job. I'm not sure if my mother read it—to her, church, in her post-Catholic phase, was a bit of a social club more than anything—but I did, and I was less than comforted. The horror of the Lord engaging in high-stakes bets with Satan, and the absolute lack of comfort that Job's so-called friends bring to his grief, did change my view of God. The book made me feel as though God, if he existed, was sort of capable of being a major, reckless dick. Christians in the Midwest are fond of saying, "Everything happens for a reason." The book of Job illustrates, I think, that that's not the case at all.

I have never been a dutiful son, nor have I ever fit in particularly well with my family. As a boy, I spent long stretches of time alone, in a small basement room that I had cleaned out and furnished with garage sale items and called my "study." My father thought of me as a sort of freak. My brother, though younger than me, considered me to be a boy of great weaknesses and useless pursuits, a spineless, though kind and generous, sad sack. My mother took most of my actions personally, as a judgment of her parenting and moral character, especially when, graduating early at the age of seventeen, I turned down a scholarship to the University of Wisconsin, in my own backyard, and headed "out east" as my father liked to say, to the

University of Michigan, which I did because I desperately wanted to do something that my family did not understand in a place they had never been.

Years later, lighting that Christmas tree for the first time with my mother and the twins, I felt as if I finally belonged to the Pappas clan, now severely decimated by tragedy. My mother looked at me, playing with my nieces, and I think she felt it too: I, her only remaining son, am not a bad man. And, I must admit, she is not a bad mother.

I told her that after the tree was lit, and the girls had fallen asleep underneath it. I brought her a cup of Constant Comment tea and poured myself a small tumbler of bourbon. And then I looked at my mother and said, "You're amazing. The girls are lucky to have you."

My mother turned to me, almost pale, as if she was in utter shock. And then she began to tear up on the sofa, and I put on George Winston's *December* CD, which I knew she loved and which I once, on a more cynical Christmas years ago, disparaged. I sat with her on the sofa, and we stared at the lights, listening to the tinkling piano. Soon, she too was asleep, and eventually it sounded as if she murmured my name, but I couldn't make out the rest. On the floor, the twins twitched a bit under the afghan I'd spread over their bare legs, and I watched my dreaming family and felt, well, something akin to happiness.

I'd like to tell you that my family has maintained this domestic bliss on a consistent basis since that Christmas season, but no family finds such bliss sustainable. Still, I am always somewhat happy to come home from the office, which I suppose is more than the breadwinner in a traditional domestic situation can often say.

Approaching our house after my rather eventful coffee break with Minn and H. M., I can already see that April and May are in the front yard, playing some sort of game with a long yellow jump rope. Today is the sort of sunny afternoon in which a soul goes reeling.

On one hand, before us is the sheer and dazzling beauty of spring's golden light, the leaves attempting to burst through their buds. And on the other hand we know winter is not gone for good—we know that in seven months, maybe less, we will have to deal, once again, with the endless snow, the days that go dim at four o'clock, and the icy, painful winds.

Such dualities—pleasure and pain, contentment and longing—plague us in the Midwest. Everything is beautiful; everything is fleeting. Everything warm eventually cools and bitters.

This afternoon, as I walk toward April and May, their blond hair absolutely magnificent in the waning light, two teenagers, both driving modest American two-doors, race up and down Commonwealth Avenue, engaged in some sort of vehicular flirtation. The first time they come tearing down the block, I ignore them, though I am aware that up the street, April and May have put down their jump rope and April is now creating enormous bubbles with a bubble wand that I bought her at the dollar store. The second time the two vehicles, a blue Geo and a green Neon, appear on Commonwealth, going faster now, chasing each other, I notice that May is dancing after the bubbles, precariously close to the curb. Soon, two doors away from my home, the two speeding cars reappear, on their third lap, and I scream, at the top of my lungs, "Freeze!"

April and May stop and stare at me as I sprint after the racing Geo. I find a rock on the ground and hurl it. The Geo stops and does a U-turn and I run to the car window, screaming at the teen-aged driver who is also screaming at me, a litany of obscenities between us. The kid, this punk, is wearing a black baseball cap with a logo I don't recognize. Some team of sorts, an expansion team I've never heard of from some league I don't follow. At first, he is smirking at me from underneath a weak caterpillar of a mustache, but once I snarl at him, his face grows sober, and his defiant expression fades. My anger is fierce, and I lean into his open window and hiss in his face, "If you ever drive like this on my street again, asshole, I will cut you from your privates to your throat. I will bleed you out right here."

It's a variation of a line I remember from the movie *Young Guns*, which I watched many times as a teenager, and it suddenly comes to me, but it is sufficiently creepy to scare the young punk, who apologizes and drives off. As a man of average size and limited physical prowess, I have long ago learned that insanity is far more intimidating than size or strength. Nobody, if you will, fucks with a crazy man.

The street once again safe for my nieces, I head toward my front yard. April and May hug me as we stand in front of the Obama yard sign (my mother also disapproves of this one, though the political rage she showed in 2004 has mellowed, replaced by hopelessness) and begin showing me their various tricks. I look up at the front porch, where my mother is sitting in a chair, smiling. My chest is still heaving and my guts are watery with adrenaline. I shake my hands as if drying them; a jittery wave of electricity still pulses in my fingertips.

"Zeke," she says, "I didn't know you had that in you."

I shrug and go back to watching April and May craft enormous bubbles with their bubble wands, my heart still racing as the adrenaline begins to subside. Frankly, I sort of surprised myself, but the image of those speeding cars, careening recklessly so near the spot where my nieces were playing, well, I couldn't help but think, what if, what if something happened to them right now that was irrevocable and tragic? Suddenly, it is as if they were the most important things in the whole world to me, as if losing them would stop time and shatter everything.

And then I realize this: they are and it would.

That night, we eat dinner at six thirty, like we always do, and my mother is serving what she always serves on Wednesday nights: spaghetti. It has been this way since Cougar and I were young boys, spaghetti and garlic bread, six o'clock Wednesdays. It used to be my father's favorite night of the week, solely for this reason, I think, although my father once slyly intimated to me that Wednesday was also a weekly sex night for him and my mother, though I have tried to forget that for the obvious reasons.

Tonight, my mother hardly eats a thing, though at least she sits down with us. As of late, she's taken to lying on the couch soon after she serves dinner, falling into a soft nap, and my nieces and I eat together, discussing both the intricacies of my day at a marginal cultural nonprofit, and their days as the only set of twins in the second grade. I might tell them about a grant application I am submitting to a private foundation, and, smiling at each other because they find me so unbelievably boring, they might start to giggle.

"What?" I'll ask, making my eyes look huge and incredulous. "You're not interested in the programmatic evaluation techniques used by federally funded nonprofits?"

The girls will giggle harder.

Eventually, they'll tell me a story about how Miles Gregorson lost three teeth playing floor hockey in gym class, or they'll regale me with details of Marnie Finn's family vacation to Disney World and I will take absolute delight in their storytelling. Watching them build to a narrative climax, trading off the revelation of details, finishing each other's sentences, is really one of the finest moments of my day. When I am away for work, on the road overnight, or even when I am out with friends, I am always cognizant of the fact that I am missing April's and May's stories.

Tonight, my mother is reading a copy of *Simply You* as we eat, and she interrupts April's story about Brett Wilson's missing dog and begins to read to us aloud: "Listen to this, Zeke," my mother says. "*Does it seem like you're ready for marriage, but you don't have any prospects on the horizon? Well, just like any good business executive knows the importance of cultivating contacts and nurturing networks, any woman who wants to find Mr. Right knows that she must do the same thing. Follow these simple steps, and you might just be head over heels (or engaged!) by the end of the summer.*"

"Mom," I say, "April was talking."

"What does that mean?" April says. "What is head over heels?"

"I don't get it," May says.

"Well," my mother says, "it's the sort of quiz that might explain why Uncle Zeke is not married."

"Aw, come on, Ma," I say. "It's for women."

My mother continues reading.

"Are you getting married, Uncle Zeke?" April says.

"Oh, oh, you totally should," May says.

"*Attractiveness, real attractiveness,*" my mother says, "*lasting attractiveness, doesn't really set in until you get to know somebody, until you admit that you're open to the possibility of a lasting relationship with somebody.*"

"Mom," I say, "enough!"

My mother smiles. "Okay, maybe this isn't a good time," she says.

"It's not," I say.

"Always so moody," my mother says.

The meal falls into silence for a moment, the only sound the clinking of silverware and china together, the same awkward dinnertime cacophony that often plagued my own childhood as the soundtrack for my father's virulent disapproval. When he was mad at me, as he often was, he gave me the silent treatment. If he was disappointed in a sweatshirt I wore, or a paper I'd written, or a comment I'd made, or my failure to get him a birthday card, he could pretend, for weeks on end, as if I didn't exist.

After supper, my mother wants to rest on the couch as usual. She takes her magazine to the living room, and soon I hear her asthmatic wheeze of a snore from the next room. It is not easy, I'm sure, to be the primary caregiver for two seven-year-olds when one is sixty-three. My mother, it seems, will never have time that is truly her own, though I've never heard her complain about it.

April and May help me with the dishes that evening, and then they go upstairs to bathe and brush their teeth and dress in their pajamas while I mop up the vast puddles they have created on the kitchen floor. April and May are remarkably self-sufficient, as orphans almost always are. By the time I come upstairs, they are under the covers of the double bed they share, each of them reading a library book, their Ikea bedside lamps—a present from me, as I was always a before-bed reader—lighting their faces in a soft yellow glow. April is looking at a book called *Amazing Aquatic Creatures* and May is looking at one about a young boy and a terrible, horrible, no-good day.

"You guys want a story tonight?" I ask, and, neither of them looking up from their books, they mumble, "No, thanks." I go back downstairs to finish cleaning the kitchen, and when I return, no more than ten minutes later, they are asleep. I take their books and stack them on the desk in the corner of the room. I kiss both of them on the forehead, smelling the toothpaste on their breaths, then I turn off the bedside lamps, and, as is my habit of late, I stand there in the dark and listen to their breathing. Only when I am sure, completely sure, that their breaths are steady and normal and without distress do I leave the room and shut the door.

My mother is still asleep in the living room. The girls have worn her out. On Wednesdays and weekends, when she works her longs shifts (five to five) at the Old Country Buffet on the east side of town (she does this mainly for the health insurance), she seems less tired than she does after an afternoon with the energetic twins. I go out to the porch to sit and enjoy the breeze of the evening. My mother comes out onto the porch fifteen minutes or so later, wrapped in her robe, holding two mugs of tea. She sits next to me on the porch swing, and we sway there, me staring out ahead at nothing, she huddled over her steaming tea for warmth.

"You should have woken me up," she says.

"You need to rest," I say. "That's a long day of work."

"Say, can I bring the girls to your office tomorrow afternoon?" my mother asks. "After school? I have a doctor's appointment at four."

"Everything okay?"

"Yeah, yeah. Just need an asthma checkup. My doctor had one open appointment all month. Can you believe it? This was it."

"No sweat. Bring them by anytime."

"I know you must be busy at work," she says.

"Not that busy actually," I say.

We sit in the dark a while longer. My mother lights a cigarette, her only vice, the worst one an asthmatic can have. I've often tried to turn her on to the joys of alcohol, its uncomplicated sorrow and numbing joy, but she prefers to smoke. She will drink with me on occasion, but frankly, I doubt she likes the strange numbness drinking provides. She is a woman who is often at the helm—of family, of a problem, of a shortage of roast beef in the Sunday afternoon buffet—and I suppose it feels unnatural to her to deaden any impulse or instinct.

Across the street, in the Mendelsohns' big stone house, I can see the Mendelsohns gathered around the television, watching something that is apparently hilarious, as all four teenagers, as well as the parents, have silly smiles on their faces.

"They seem like a happy family," my mother says. "Don't they?"

"Everybody seems happy through a window. Do you think it's weird that we're sitting here watching them?"

"No," she says. "I think it's weird they don't pull the drapes."

"Good point."

"Zeke, I'm sorry I dropped that quiz on you at dinner," she says. "I just thought it would be amusing. I think it ruffled your feathers a bit."

"I know. I'm sorry if I overreacted," I say. "I just was uncomfortable discussing such things in front of the girls."

"I suppose," she says.

We swing in the breeze a bit more, the chains squeaking with marginal protest. Since we've moved in together, my mother and I are exceedingly polite to each other. We know, deep down, that we disagree vehemently on many political and social issues, but we are the only family the girls have now, save for Melody's twin sister, the girls' Aunt Harmony, a real estate agent in Livonia, Michigan, with whom they spend two weeks each summer and two weeks each winter. And so we do what we can to keep the peace with each other, avoiding any topics that would arouse passions.

"I suppose I was just trying to get information from you," she says. "You're so secretive. You always were."

"Uh-huh," I say. I let the passive aggressiveness slide.

"Just tell me, Zeke. Satisfy an old woman's curiosity. Is there anyone you're interested in at all? Are you seeing anybody?"

"When would I have time to date?" I ask. "I work all day, I'm home with you all in the evenings, and I watch the girls all weekend while you work."

"I'm home by five thirty on Saturdays and Sundays," she says.

"Well, then there's dinner to cook, and dishes to wash, and baths to give, and bedtime stories to read."

"Well, you don't need to do that. You don't have to be home every night. And we could get a sitter on the weekend, if you wanted one. Sharon Loy's daughter, Maya, she is a great babysitter."

"She's fourteen!" I say. "I wouldn't trust her. I see her trolling the neighborhood a lot. She runs with hoods."

My mother smiles. "Well, how about Cathy Pettijohn? She could always baby-sit."

"Mrs. Pettijohn was crazy when I was a kid and she seems crazier now. I ran into her at Whole Foods last week. She's on a raw food diet."

"So?"

"So, that sort of betrays a kind of inner instability, don't you think?"

"I'm not even sure what a raw food diet is, Zeke," my mother says. "The truth is, I think you're afraid to leave the girls with a babysitter."

"If I had need for one, I would find one."

"Aw, come on, Zeke. You must know of at least one woman you'd like to date. The article calls them *prospects*. Do you have any prospects? Let's make a list. Just for fun!"

"Are you worried that I'm gay?" I ask. "Is that what this is about?"

"No!" she says. "I worry that you're lonely. That you'll be lonely."

"I see."

"You're not gay, are you?"

It occurs to me that the only way to end this thread of conversation is to give my mother some nugget of information that proves to her I am neither an asexual nor a homosexual human being.

"There is a woman, at the coffee shop," I say, "but I think she has a boyfriend. She must. She wears an engagement ring of sorts."

"Does she know you're interested?"

"I suppose. I go there every day. That might be a clue."

"What's her name?"

"Mother, the fact is, there are probably dozens and dozens of sad sacks like me whom she smiles for every day. She has to be pleasant. It's a corporate ethic. A mandate."

"What about the girl at your office? Lara?" my mother says. "I know she's divorced and has those two children, but, well, you're at the age when . . ."

"Mom! She is my employee. That would be very unprofessional. And she's not 'the girl at the office.' We don't call them girls anymore. She is an administrative specialist."

"Always so sensitive, Zeke."

"Jesus, Mother."

"Well, why don't you ask the coffee shop girl to go to the movies?" my mother says. "I know. I can call Hadley French. The girls can go over to play with Lily and Winnie next Saturday and maybe spend the night . . ."

"Hadley French is a strumpet," I say. "That's no place for April and May to spend the night."

My mother groans. "You're hopeless."

"Besides, you don't just ask a barista for a date. It's creepy."

"What's a barista?" my mother asks.

"Look, I'm taking my hopeless self for a walk," I say. "Don't lock the side door. I may be gone for a while."

We live, the four of us, on the near west side of Madison, in a neighborhood of professors, nonprofit workers, artists, and graduate students. Our house is a Sears bungalow with an added rear dormer, all assembled right here on Commonwealth Avenue in 1925. It is a neat and tidy house (despite an unruly garden of prairie flowers — and, shamefully, invasive species — that flanks the front porch) and is complete with hardwood floors, original woodwork, four bedrooms, and two full baths. My mother and the twins have the upstairs rooms and bath, and I have the two bedrooms and the bath on the first floor. The back bedroom on the first floor is large enough to contain my king-size bed and a dresser and nightstand, no more. You cut through my small bathroom to get to the front bedroom, which has three large windows that overlook the garden. This is my office, and the books and piles of manuscripts and news clippings and magazines make the room a musty maze of intellectual distractions. It is my favorite place on earth, quite frankly.

As I walk through the neighborhood this evening, I can't help but consider my mother's question: *Don't you have any prospects, Zeke?* The truth of the matter, I want to tell my mother, is that I do not. Now that I'm in my thirties, I have found it difficult to find romantic partners in Madison. In Madison, everybody seems to be already partnered up. Domestic bliss is a sort of matter of civic pride; unhappy families and single people do not play much of a role in Madison's social fabric.

Yet, although one doesn't get the sense that there is a great deal of unhappiness behind the closed doors of Madison, especially in the Dudgeon-Monroe neighborhood, I know the truth. Some of my neighbors have sat for interviews for my current professional project: *An Inventory of American Unhappiness.* I have heard, in stark and trenchant detail, the long woes and worries of their lives.

On Fox Avenue, for instance, there is a man who wants to be a woman. On Keyes, there is a young computer programmer whose equally young wife is sleeping with a sixty-eight-year-old butcher. On West Lawn, a thirty-seven-year-old piano teacher, addicted to online poker, has lost everything and faces foreclosure. His garden rots in a state of moldy neglect, high with thistles and pigweed.

On Gregory Street, a financial analyst for the Credit Unions of North America, a man who urinates off his back deck each and every night as an assertion of some buried wildness and freedom, contemplates suicide every Sunday evening as he prepares his clothes for the workweek. This man said to me, "The logistics of living wear me out—paying bills, dropping off the dry cleaning, making sure there is butter in the house. I can't seem to ever have butter or eggs in the house when I need them. I can't take it. It's too much."

As I wander past these houses, my own loneliness seems a small problem, and, as is the case most of the time, I return from a walk in the neighborhood restored and settled.

When I get to our driveway, I see my neighbor Elizabeth Vandeweghe sitting at her patio table by candlelight, her feet propped on a chair across from hers. I go over to say hello, and she doesn't move. Elizabeth Vandeweghe has a long, lean runner's body, and her legs, wrapped in Lycra running tights, shine up at me. It appears as if she is dozing. She wears a black hooded sweatshirt, unzipped to show the top of a white men's sleeveless undershirt, and a pair of brown Ugg boots. A paperback novel has fallen onto the flagstone below her chair, and her head is slumped forward, so that I can see the back of her long, exquisite neck. Quickly, I go inside my house, pour two tumblers of Irish whiskey, and meet my sleeping neighbor in her backyard. We have, on occasion lately, shared some Jameson's on the porch, and it is always a highly pleasurable exchange for me.

I sit down across from her.

"Elizabeth," I say.

She wakes, looks around, dazed. "Zeke," she says. "Sorry. My God."

"Don't be sorry," I say. "I brought out some whiskey."

"I guess I fell asleep," she says.

"It's lovely," I say. I hand her a glass of whiskey and she smiles.

"Thanks," she says.

"You're very welcome," I say.

Elizabeth has three children, three blond girls, very spirited and amusing. They often play in my yard with the twins, and so we have developed the easy silence that sometimes exists between neighbors as they sit and watch children play, or cars pass, or snow fall.

"Can't refuse one of these," she says. "It's been a long day."

"Wednesdays are tough," I say. "Cheers."

We drink.

"Anyway," she says, "Rod is here and so I just wanted to hide out somewhere and read."

"What are you reading?"

"*Blood Meridian.*"

"Cormac McCarthy?"

"I'm feeling sort of dark, lately. It's rather cathartic. All of that blood, all of that grimness."

"Rod?" I ask, and she nods.

Rod is Elizabeth's estranged husband and the father of her three kids. He lives in a rented room near campus; they are not, yet, technically divorced. Rod's rented room is so small that he visits his children in their own home, every Wednesday, and he cooks them dinner.

"I hoped nobody would bother me back here," she says.

"Oh, I'm sorry," I say.

"No. Not you!" she says. "The kids! Rod!"

"Right," I say.

We drink for a while in silence.

"Shall I let you go back to your book?" I say.

"What?" she says. "Oh, no, it's okay."

"How've you been?" I say.

"We're good," she says, and then she seems to retract that statement. "We're okay," she says.

There's a scream from the inside of the house, one of the Vandeweghe girls. Another of the girls is now crying. Then we hear the sound of Rod yelling and then Rod Vandeweghe comes out the back door of what used to be his own home, holding a spatula. "Can you come in here, please?" he says, exasperated.

"Rod," I say, nodding.

"Hi, Zeke," Rod says, but fails to make eye contact with me.

Rod stands there staring at Elizabeth, who has not moved. She kicks off her Uggs and puts her feet back into the chair next to me, as if to tell Rod, *Not now, pal, I'm quite comfortable.* Her bare feet are lovely and clean, in the seat next to mine. I am not a foot fetish sort of guy, but her feet strike me as immensely sexy. I would not be beyond defiling them.

"I'll be right there," Elizabeth finally says. "Let me finish my drink," she says, shooing Rod back into the house.

We finish our cocktails in silence. Without thinking, I sort of touch her foot, and then squeeze it. She looks at me, awkwardly, but she does not shriek.

"I'm sorry," I say. "I don't know why I did that."

"I don't either," she says.

"It was just, they were there and you sounded so sad, and I, well, it was like squeezing a child's shoulder when they are scared or something."

"Okay," she says. "It was sort of weird. But not all that terrible. My feet were in your face, after all."

"Nonsense," I say. "I get dreamy in the evenings. I do things, without thinking. The loss of light or something."

When she stands, I resist the urge to help her into her Uggs.

And then the beautiful and lithe Elizabeth Vandeweghe mutters, looking at the ground, "I hate my life."

Before I can say anything, she is gone.

Elizabeth is someone I always thought quite lovely, but I certainly never had any serious designs on her previously. She seemed happily married, firmly entrenched in a middle-class domesticity that so mirrored the one I myself longed for, and the idea of even attempting to pull her from that fertile ground seemed insane. Thus, she was lovely, but not someone I lusted after with any real intentions.

But last spring, on one of the first warm nights of the season, I was sitting outside, in my boxer shorts, in complete darkness, my chair up against the back of the house. I was drinking a small bottle of chilled white wine, sans glass, and I was admiring the moon, when I heard a door slam. I heard the jingle of keys. And then I heard Elizabeth Vandeweghe, trying not to yell, saying, through what sounded like gritted teeth, "Where the fuck are you going?"

And Rod Vandeweghe hissed, "I'm leaving until you calm down."

At this moment I slipped inside my house, quiet as a mouse, and, in the darkness, found my way to the twins' bedroom upstairs, where there is a window that looks out at Rod and Elizabeth's driveway. The window, because of the warmth, was already open, and I sat in the shadows beyond it, watching and listening.

Elizabeth looked gorgeous in the evening, wearing a white slip, one spaghetti strap falling off of her shoulder. Her voice sounded hoarse, and from the window I could see, when she turned to the porch light near the garage, that her nipples were hard. Men notice such things, no matter what trauma is going on around us.

I could hear parts of their conversation and surmised that they had had a huge fight, and that Rod had been caught having an affair with a young graduate student who interned at the Department of Natural Resources where Rod worked as a wildlife biologist.

"This isn't fatal," Rod had said. "We can work through this."

"You fucked her outside, didn't you?" Elizabeth had said.

"Elizabeth," Rod had said. "Jesus."

"You did. You fucked her on that prairie, under the stars."

"Elizabeth, don't do this to yourself."

"Tell me if you fucked her there, Rod."

"Why?"

"Don't be a coward."

"Fine. We fucked outside, Elizabeth."

"We've never fucked outside, Rod. Not once!"

Rod was trying to whisper something to her, he came close, and she smacked his face. Three times.

Then Rod drove off, and I watched from my window as Elizabeth went back into the house. I could hear her sobbing. It was eerily beautiful.

A few weeks later, Rod Vandeweghe moved out of the house.

And now, with my mother pressing me about my *prospects* for marriage, and with Elizabeth suddenly so, well, available, it is hard not to think lustily of Elizabeth as I enter the side door of my own house.

My intent is to retire with another small cocktail to my home office and work, but my mother is still up, wrapped in an afghan in the living room. The television is off, there is no book beside her, and she stares at the wall as if somebody's image is displayed there, as if somebody that I can't see is talking to her. I think I know this look.

It is the look of grief. She is thinking about Cougar. Or my father. Or Melody.

"Ma?" I say. "Are you okay?"

"Well, Zeke," she says, "I'm going to die someday."

I look at her and see from the sunken state of her eyes that she is terrified.

"What?" I say. "What are you talking about?"

She stares at the wall a moment longer, then stands up, quickly, and begins folding the afghan.

"Someday," she adds. "I'm going to die someday."

"Well, of course you are," I say. "I mean, you are a superb grandmother. That's for sure. But I've always assumed you were a mortal being."

She smiles. And then moves to the kitchen. I follow.

"Ma," I ask. "Why now? What made you say that?"

"Have you ever even thought of getting married?" she says, rummaging in the fridge.

"Not this again," I say.

"I just don't know," she says, "if it's in your plans. You never tell me anything. You never did. A mother just wants her children to be settled, you know. And it would be good for the girls, too. An aunt. Somebody young and energetic, not old like me."

"They have Aunt Harmony," I say.

"She lives so far away," my mother says. She closes the fridge empty-handed.

"It's hard to plan for marriage," I say, "without having any idea of whom you might marry. It's doubly hard to plan for marriage with seven-year-old twin orphans factoring into the equation."

"Zeke," she says. "Please."

"Zeke what?" I say. "Please what?"

"I'm just curious."

"You're being judgmental of my bachelorhood."

"Now you're just being silly," she says.

39

"Silly?"

"You know what I mean," she says. She goes to the sink, takes the skillet I've already washed, and begins rewashing it vigorously.

"I'm afraid I don't," I say.

The skillet drops into the sink with a clang. She stalks off, leaving the water running. I shut off the faucet, and I do not follow my mother, not even later, when I hear her in her room, maybe, perhaps, crying.

4

Zeke Pappas is weary.

THE NEXT MORNING Wisconsin dips into that beautiful period of transition from spring to summer, and in the newly warmed air, one senses that, up and down the block, good-looking couples are shedding their lightweight, moisture-resistant pullovers and Smart-Wool socks after a brisk and vigorous run, and making happy love while their children doze soundly upstairs. I imagine them then sitting around, still naked, drinking fair-trade coffee and eating tamari almonds and figs from the Willy Street Co-op. They'd shower, the children would wake, and the father would read a story aloud—something like an African folk tale in a bright, colorful picture book recently featured on NPR—as the mother prepared breakfast. This is precisely the carefree, sweaty, and familiar intimacy I long for in my own life, and there it is, all around me, plain as day.

As I think I've said, Madison is not an easy town for those of us who are single. It is not conducive to, or particularly tolerant of, the sort of melancholy that accompanies solitude. Like most college towns, Madison has all of the same brightness that comes with young bodies and rich minds. And I don't just mean the bared limbs and midriffs, the display of flesh and hipbone, but also the bubbling optimism of life at a Big Ten school: the expectation that your team will win, that life will offer you much, that you will have choices upon choices set out before you like a feast, and all you have to do is choose the kind of happiness you would like to pursue. It makes a man want his own fight song!

This morning, however, still shaken a bit by my mother's inquiries from the night before, those probing questions into my potential loneliness, I am faced with the realization that I, for the most part, am a solitary creature. And under the burden of this realization, I find that the friendliness of everybody in Madison suddenly strikes me as a problem. And when I hear my friend Mack Fences, the book salesman, calling my name from half a block away (he must be en route to his partner's bookshop), I pretend not to hear him and walk briskly in the opposite direction. Around the corner, I break into a brief sprint to increase the distance between us, even though now I hear him yelling my name.

Some mornings you simply have no desire to make conversation. You long for a reflective stroll, in which you amble along the sidewalk, gazing here and there at one of the city's lakes. Still, you see people you know everywhere—neighbors, baristas, colleagues from the university, past grant recipients, and potential grant applicants. It is difficult to see so many people you know, so many busy and active people, if, frankly, you don't care how somebody's novel, thesis, art, job, marriage, life is going, not because you are heartless or cruel, but because you simply don't have the energy to hear about other people's struggles and triumphs. Your own joys and woes are exhausting enough, aren't they? And in Madison, where everybody is supercharged by yoga, organic food, locally roasted coffee, microbrewed beer, biking to work, and classes at the Monkey Bar Gym, the energy and optimism in the air can make one weary. What is it that the Old Testament prophets say? Do not *grow faint*? Well, I realize that I have done just that on this fine morning: I have grown faint.

I enter the vestibule of the GMHI offices, where the sole remaining staff member of GMHI (other than me), Ms. Lara Callahan, is typing away at the reception desk. I am not quite sure what she is typing, but she is typing rather furiously. There is no reason for such a breakneck pace; there is not that much to do here. The phone rarely rings and the mail—other than junk mail—slowed to a one-envelope-a-day trickle, usually a form from the federal government, which she completes and I sign.

The days are slow for her. The ten million dollars we received from the federal government is mostly gone: with a rubber stamp from the board of directors, I have generously awarded grants, hired promising scholars, assisted rural libraries and urban community centers in building campaigns, and I have run the ship aground, so to speak, by giving generously and enthusiastically to worthy causes. I believe there is about twenty thousand dollars in federal money left, a few months of operating expenses at best. The truth is, this is *exactly* what I was supposed to do: give away federal money. But the second part of my charge was to raise significant private funds that would make the GMHI a sustainable endeavor. On that front, I have failed.

Frankly, I probably do not need Lara's assistance anymore, but I keep her on the payroll because she is thirty-six and is the single mother of two. And, if I may admit this without sounding like a misogynist, I enjoy the sexual energy she brings to the office—her shapely, smooth legs, the faint scent of lavender, the glistening dampness on her forehead when she returns from a vigorous lunchtime walk. When my mother brought Lara up as a potential *prospect,* she was not voicing a thought that I haven't considered many times myself.

With the generous federal funding, I am able to pay her forty-six thousand dollars a year plus benefits, and she knows she will not be able to make that kind of money elsewhere. She is very bright, a wonderful receptionist, an excellent writer of correspondence, and she keeps the books tidily and brilliantly, even alerting me, weekly, to the fact that I have spent nearly all of our money and cash reserves. She is a few inches taller than me. Her skin is fair, in the way of those milky Irish lasses I so love to see in movies, and her hair is short and dark, and I would gladly spend a week of my life kissing her extravagant legs, hips to toes.

Certainly, her legs are one of the main reasons to make her, as my mother urges, one of my *prospects:* her intelligence, bluntness, efficiency, and grace are other reasons. I see her five days a week, and she sees me. We are both lonely. Some days, I am sure, that is enough. In truth, it's hard for me to think of anybody on earth who knows me better than Lara. But isn't it hard to tell with coworkers, especially those you supervise, how much of the extended kindnesses and smiles and tender gestures are intended as deference and how much of them come from a real and deep well of friendship?

Never mind. It is better, as I have told my mother, not to mix work and love. My work is, and always has been, the dominant actor on my life's stage.

I breeze by Lara's desk with the ease and purpose of a busy man.

"Good morning," I mutter, a tight smile on my lips, and walk briskly to my office and shut the door.

I hear her say, "What's the matter with you?" as I walk past her, but I do not acknowledge it. Normally, I greet her with a bit of chatter, so much so, in fact, that once she asked me to limit my morning conversation with her to fifteen minutes.

At this moment, as I wait out the last of the GMHI funds, I am still working, with great passion and discipline, I assure you, on a project that, though this may sound trite, may actually, in truth, be my life's work (if you will pardon the dramatic weight of that old phrase): *An Inventory of American Unhappiness.* This project has become the sole focus of the GMHI. It is my hope to finish this project before the money that funds the GMHI runs out, and then use the amazingly strong critical and public reception of my project as a catalyst to raise more funds. At this date, however, the mountain of work atop my desk is high; the balance remaining in my federal grant is low.

The thinking, the rationale, the philosophy, behind my project is this: Americans are fundamentally unhappy, and they are fundamentally unhappy because they suffer from institutional addiction. If you consider the comfort (for most), the wealth (relative), and opportunities (many) with which Americans have matured, it is mind-boggling to consider that anybody here could be unhappy. But everywhere I go, I can see it, such unhappiness, such an overwhelming need to be drugged and distracted, lest a moment of silent, melancholy self-reflection pierce our fragile hearts!

We are, at our heart, a nation of rugged individualists. Not in the absurd, capitalistic manner of an Ayn Rand protagonist or a blue-blooded intern at the American Enterprise Institute, but certainly in the manner of our philosophical forefathers—Emerson, Thoreau, Jefferson, Paine. These men all advocated a nation, a way of living, where men and women are free to march to the beat of their own drummer, empowered by self-reliance, by an abundance of practical skills, and by an economic and political system that champions pluck and innovation over size and institution.

How quickly has such an American ideal faded! Now, we are all slaves to institutions. Educated in them from the age of five, or younger, and often imprisoned within them, accumulating piles of debt, until we are pushing thirty. At the end of our educational process, we know what? How to plant a garden? Build a home? Repair and maintain machines? Hunt? Fish? Camp?

Hardly. Rather, we leave these institutions with only one small skill—trading commodities, analyzing prose, ceramics, welding widget A to widget B—and we immediately need to find another institution to take us in: General Motors, Yale, the Federal Reserve, the UAW, Target, any place that will allow us to put food on the table.

Once food is on the table, we must find shelter, often for a growing family, and instead of having any idea of how to build a shelter, we must buy a shelter, and because the costs of shelter are so absurdly prohibitive in comparison with actual wages, we must move immediately into the debtor system Thoreau likened to slavery. We must move into a home that is owned by an institution—Bank of America, Countrywide, CitiFinancial—and we must make ourselves adhere to a payment schedule. We must then secure health care coverage from a large institution, finance transportation through a large institution, deficit-spend based on the leverage of a large institution, worship the Lord at an approved institution, and then, one morning, our children enter a federally mandated pre-K program or a twenty-five-thousand-dollar-a-year private preschool. And the cycle begins again. You can almost hear the tiny hearts of America's children breaking as they gather around the story circle or line up for a carton of milk. Slaves!

Thus, for most Americans, life becomes a series of debts and dependencies on entities much larger, and much more powerful, than ourselves.

The paradox is this: in the middle of such indebtedness and dependence, we are bombarded with an apparent array of choices, are we not? Walk into a Walmart, surf Amazon, pull off at the Des Plaines Oasis, and you instantly are given the illusion of freedom. You can buy anything you want! Read anything you want! Eat anything you want! What a country!

But in our quietest moments, these very choices become so bewilderingly superficial that they bring with them insurmountable gloom. The fact is, by the time we are old enough to comprehend the magic and bounty offered by the wider world, we are so indebted to institutions, financially, spiritually, and otherwise, that we have no real choices. *Listen,* the internal memo bellows from our soul's central office: *You have no options. You won't start that business, you won't open that café, you won't live in Costa Rica, you won't come out of the closet, you won't write that novel, and you won't ever have a threesome.*

And this is the epiphany, the realization that makes us so alarmingly unhappy. I am not the first to editorialize about my generation's abundant choices, or its accompanying debt, but few people, if any, have expounded on this troubling irony: throughout our lives we will have many choices but little by way of means. By the time the average American is able to grasp the choices and opportunities that Jefferson and Paine and his ilk so desperately fought for and advocated, they will not have any means or freedom with which to pursue them.

But, I'd argue, our sadness goes even deeper, punctuated by a crippling lack of the time, space, silence, energy, and/or capacity for critical self-reflection that life in the twenty-first century has brought upon us. In this culture, one discovers an alarmingly high rate of unhappiness. Some of this unhappiness is chronic; one finds some subjects to be wholly unhappy. For many, many others, most of my subjects, in fact, the breakneck pace of change in the past eight years, coupled with national leadership that is fumbling, frustrating, and frightening, has made them absolutely terrified of reflection. Pausing to think—i.e., unplugging the computer, the phones, the Black-Berry, the Facebook—is horrifying. When one does such a thing, one is visited by unhappy images, thoughts of doom and woe, the thumping footsteps of melancholy, and the assurance of global tragedy and destruction. Quickly, the self-reflection impulse is stifled. And that lack of self-reflection makes it nearly impossible for us to find our authentic selves and our true callings, especially ones unfettered from institutional hierarchies and dependence. Thus, we sit, like scores of drug-addled teens with distant parents, inundated with college catalogs and ineligible for financial aid.

I have many other secondary hypotheses about our unhappiness—it stems from constant war, environmental degradation, chemical toxicities and food additives, the underfunding of cultural programs, the student loan industry, et cetera. The companion essay for the oral history project was supposed to be a five-page overview but has become a three-hundred-and-sixteen-page document titled *Why So Vague?: An Introduction to the American Unhappiness Project*. *Why so vague* is a question I once heard a man ask the author Charles Baxter at a fiction reading (GMHI mini-grant #02-898: *Surprised by Joy: The Unhappy Midwest of Charles Baxter*). The open-ended obtuseness of the question has always stayed with me: yes, so much malaise, so much heartache, a mountain of woe—but who can define it? Why so vague? Indeed!

I suppose the idea for my project came to me shortly after college, when I was rather absent-mindedly thumbing through a copy of *The Portable Chekhov*, during a register shift at the bookshop where I once worked. Rereading the story "Gooseberries," I came across these lines: "There ought to be behind the door of every happy, contented man some one standing with a little hammer continually reminding him with a tap that there are unhappy people; that however happy he may be, life will show him her laws sooner or later, trouble will come for him—disease, poverty, losses, and no one will see or hear, just as now he neither sees nor hears others."

It was during a time in my life when I wanted to do something revolutionary, or at least vital. I wanted to serve some greater purpose, to create something that changed the way humankind viewed itself. Having also just finished reading a slim volume called *Let Your Life Speak* by Parker Palmer, I was quite open to signs and symbols; I was sort of anticipating an epiphany about what I would do with my life's work. And there, buried in one of Chekhov's masterpieces, was my calling. I would be that little man with a hammer, constantly tapping away on a happy nation's door.

In subsequent years, *An Inventory of American Unhappiness* has led to my interviewing over five hundred Americans about the nature and rubrics of their discontent. I've also collected thousands of e-mail responses to the question *Why are you so unhappy?* In my grandest moments, I imagine it will eventually be a seminal work that helps us understand our culture in a new and promising way, something along the lines of Studs Terkel's *Working* and Rachel Carson's *Silent Spring.*

Lara tells me that the project is a brilliant one and she has worked countless hours transcribing my interviews and editing video. Yet, she is an optimistic woman—the sort of person who ends a phone call with the phrase *Make it a great day*—and her one complaint is that my questions often steer the conversations off into depressing places. Well, of course they do! She feels that perhaps it is I, the anonymous interviewer, who might be convincing my subjects of their unhappiness. Of course! I know that happens! But there is no malice at work here. It is more like Michelangelo, I tell her, when he was asked how he managed to carve the beautiful figure of David from a towering piece of marble over eighteen feet high.

It was already there, he said. *I just chipped away the excess.*

Yes! It is already there, so much woe. I want to distill it for the world to see.

Why are you so unhappy?

That is the simple question I ask after a very brief introduction. And certainly some people say, "I'm not." Or "What do you mean?" Or "I gotta get back to work." But so many people, triggered by such a direct and probing question, tell me everything.

Some recent responses:

Abigail H., 41, medical software trainer, Verona, WI:
Unhappy? Well, I suppose I am. I suppose it has something to do with, well, work. Actually, in all seriousness, I've been unhappy since I was about nine. One day, this gray, damp January day, I remember waking up and getting upset

because I had to go to fourth grade that day. And then, in one of those *bizarre* flash-forward moments you sometimes get as a kid, I saw the older version of myself, me, now, and I thought, there I am, getting up for work, going somewhere I don't want to go. And at that moment I realized that there was my life, all of it, and almost every day of my life I would have to get up and go somewhere I didn't really want to go. And now, the other morning, I was dropping off my daughter, Zoe, she's four, at preschool, and I was like, oh, look at this, here we go again, her too. God.

Seth S., 30, bike messenger, New York, NY:
Cars, the great American automobile, pal, that's what has me down. Not only do I come close to getting clipped once an hour by some cell-phone-talking prick in a Land Rover, but I have to breathe all that shit we put into the air. When my son Silver inherits this earth, it's gonna be totally fucked. There. Sorry you asked?
    [*Interviewer: No. No it's okay.*]
    You said this is going to be on NPR?
    [*Interviewer: Perhaps. I said perhaps.*]
    All right. Cool. Check this: www.cararmageddon.org!

Simms P., 39, retail clerk, Cleveland, OH:
Well, if you mean, why am I so depressed, look around you. Food courts. Shitty fast-food places posing as Asian-fusion and Latin-fusion bistros. ATM surcharges. That rent-a-cop hitting on that high school girl. The Pretzel Peddler, where I just had lunch. Think of it: I'm almost forty, I'm on my lunch break from a place called Famous Footwear. And where did I eat lunch? The fucking Pretzel Peddler, man? I eat pretzels with fake cheese dip for lunch. And you want to know what makes me unhappy? Me. I make me miserable.

Josh F., 45, government analyst, Washington, DC:
I'm wondering if you have any idea how much federal money goes into this project, which, in my view, is a deliberate attempt to *cynicize* the nation?

And so on.

5

Zeke Pappas is Bloody Married.

LAPTOP SLUNG OVER my shoulder, I slip out to lunch a bit early, around eleven, for an omelet and a Bloody Mary or two at Nick's. George and Gus throw in a third Bloody Mary on the house, as Gus remarks that I look "weary with the weight of the world." How perceptive good bartenders can be! How they know exactly what a regular client needs! I work away on my laptop at the bar, firing off e-mails, then I change my Facebook status, pay the tab, tipping generously, and walk back to the office, abuzz and enlivened.

Having spent much of the morning, and much of my lunch hour, poring over responses to my unhappiness inventory, I come back from lunch in a kind of intellectual fog; I plunk down on the small sofa in our reception area and find myself staring at Lara as she works. This goes on for some time and I find myself still wondering about my mother's inquiry from the night before. Don't I have any prospects? Haven't I even considered the fact that it is time for me to get married, find a wife?

Finally, Lara stops typing for a moment, looks up at me, and slides her delicate reading glasses down her nose, lifting her eyes to meet mine. She points her small chin right at my heart.

"Are you okay, Zeke?"

"A bit of reverie," I say. "Lost in a bit of a reverie."

She pauses and now removes her reading glasses.

"What?"

"I'm afraid I was staring."

"I didn't notice," she says.

"Yes, well," I say, "often one can't help it."

"Who kept calling this morning?" she says.

"Pardon?" I say.

"Your direct line's been ringing all day. It must have rung fifty times!"

"Did it?"

"You didn't hear it?"

"I suppose not. I was working on my project."

"What's wrong with you?"

"You know I have an amazing ability to tune out distractions when I am engaged in my project."

"Have you been drinking?" she asks.

"No," I say. "Jesus."

She gazes at me for a minute, but I say nothing else.

"Have you been crying?" she asks.

"That's extremely doubtful," I say.

"Your eyes are all red."

"Are they?"

"Yes."

"Seasonal allergies. Spring! The rise of leaves and vegetation, so ripe with pollen and lust!"

"I thought I heard weeping."

"What?"

"Earlier this morning, when you first came in."

"You did not!"

"It's unsettling to hear your boss weeping in this economy," she says. "Did something happen?"

"Lara! Stop!"

"Are you okay? Did you eat lunch?"

"Yes," I say.

"Did you drink?"

"I had a drink. Just one."

"You said you didn't drink," she says.

"These hardly seem to be the sort of questions an executive director should have to answer after a long lunch. I was meeting with some potential donors, if you must know, and then I was checking my e-mail, and there was a great deal of e-mail that needed my attention."

"How did the lunch go?"

"Fine."

"Are you sure you were not crying?"

"I do not recall, Lara," I say. "I was in my office all morning, engaged in my work, and that is an emotional trance for me. I do not remember what the trance led to, but usually there is some sort of spiritual epiphany or emotional catharsis of some magnitude. While you were away from your desk, in the powder room or whatnot, I went out, laptop in hand, for a bite to eat. A working lunch."

"You should eat something else. You seem unsteady. I've got half a sub from Fraboni's in the mini-fridge."

"That's kind of you, but I am quite satiated at present."

"Okay, Zeke."

I have been trying to speak less formally of late, particularly with Lara. As I navigate the superior-subordinate relationship we share, I have a tendency to speak in long sentences and say things like "quite satiated" and "at present" instead of "full" and "right now." It's as if I haven't quite mastered the easy social interaction that coworkers should have after so many years.

"Did you get that solicitation letter written this morning?" Lara says. "Because if you want to get that mailed out—and we could use some cash infusions right now—I need the text today. Remember, I'm off next week. Your last letter brought in just enough to get through the summer. Maybe you can get us through the fall as well."

"Right," I say. "Sure. I'll get to it this afternoon."

"E-mail it to me when you're done and I'll merge it and print the envelopes."

"I may prefer to dictate it, if you don't mind."

"You're the boss," she says. "Whatever."

"If it's unpleasant for you . . ." I say.

"It's neither pleasant nor unpleasant," she says, now gone back to the keyboard. "It is simply my job."

"You know I don't care for that attitude," I say. "I want you to like the work. But I prefer to dictate."

"I love it. I love my job. I've been here eight years, haven't I?"

"You sound unconvincing."

"Do I?" she says, and she offers me a smile—a small one.

I retreat to my office and close the door. Although I consider myself a student of human relationships, I admit that Lara is someone I can't figure out: Was what we just had flirtatious and witty banter? Or was it a tense exchange rife with latent aggression? It's not out of the realm of possibility that Lara might be attracted to me. I am a fairly good-looking man and I know it helps me get through life. I am of medium height, broad-shouldered. I have the blue eyes from my mother's Irish side coupled with black hair and skin one would describe as olive-toned, thanks to my father's Greek genes. Three years ago, I even did a brief bit of modeling for a local ad agency—a serendipitous encounter at the natural foods co-op turned into a decent part-time job. For a few months, my face was on a billboard over the Beltline Highway, smiling deliriously over the great service I received at a bank. Outside Milwaukee, above the interstate, I stood with a beautiful family, and my smile assured commuters that All-state was on their side. I drove by that billboard only a handful of times, as it was sixty miles east of Madison, but each time, that picture of me, standing next to that blond, big-eyed wife, those two beaming children, filled me with woe. I still remember how my billboard wife—Ingrid was her real name—smelled, how her hair gave off the vague scent of dandelion stems.

More about Lara: Many days, I confess, I have an urge to kiss her, and once, five years ago, at the National Humanities Conference in Omaha, we almost did kiss in the arcade room of the hotel lobby. We were both fairly intoxicated, having spent most of the evening at the hotel bar with our comrades from the Deep South Humanities Project and the Big Sky Humanities Coalition, and we had retreated to the arcade, alone. We were playing Mortal Kombat II, and she shoved me once, in real life, after my ninja destroyed her buxom, knife-wielding avatar and I shoved her back, playfully, and then she grabbed my hand, and we were there, a few inches from each other, and almost, almost!

This afternoon, weary and restless, bolstered by my three Bloody Marys, I go back out to Lara's desk and I bring up that night in Omaha, and, admittedly, it is the sort of "Do you remember that time?" kind of question you hope rekindles a spark that seems so long gone and dormant.

"I don't remember it," she says. "I don't think that's what happened, Zeke."

"What do you think would have happened," I say, "if we'd kissed?"

"Regret," she says. She is straightening her desk, ending the workday. "Wearying, gut-wrenching regret."

"Really?" I say.

"We were different then," she says. "My husband was cheating on me, my marriage was failing. And you, well, you weren't so weird. You were more vulnerable then, a young widower, not the *bon vivant* you are today!"

It's true, she struck me as enormously sad on that trip, a woman whose life was falling apart, a woman saying farewell to a future she'd imagined, and had good reason to imagine, too. This is when a woman is at her most beautiful, I think, when she is at her saddest. Show me a sad woman, and I will fall in love.

Lara laughs then, turning what could become a poignant moment into a joke. "Anyway, we should never bring that up again. Okay?"

"Weird?" I say, but she is on her way to shut down the copier. "I have not gotten weird."

She turns back toward me and sighs.

"We both have, Zeke. We both have gotten weird and middle-aged."

"We are neither weird nor middle-aged, Lara!"

"Well, maybe you're not. But I am," Lara says. "Anyway, I've got to get home and you've got two girls waiting for you in the conference room."

"Oh, no! I forgot!" I say. "Have they been here long?"

"No. Your mother dropped them off about forty minutes ago. I wasn't sure if you were in any condition to care for them, so I said you were on a conference call."

"Lara!"

"Zeke, you got drunk at lunch!"

"Please, please, Lara," I say. "Why hurl such accusations?"

"They're little angels anyway," she says. "I don't mind. They're doing an art project."

Lara smiles at me with a warmth that seems genuine. I'm not sure what to do in response to that.

Perhaps my mother is right in calling Lara a *prospect*. I don't mind that she has two children from a previous marriage; in fact, I prefer it: a ready-made family longing to welcome me into its bosom, and ready to welcome my family into theirs! I can imagine adding some fiscal advantages to the family with my solid annual income of seventy-nine thousand dollars, and also, I think, they'd welcome my good sense of humor. I would play any sort of board games the children liked to play, and I would see beauty in all of their creations. I'd be at every soccer game and dance recital; I'd hang their pictures on the fridge. I'd involve myself in their imaginative games, playing house or school or spaceship.

"Is it four o'clock already?" I say, poking my head into the conference room where April and May are coloring on the whiteboard with an array of erasable markers.

They turn to me and smile.

"We're drawing a whole city," April says.

"I'm drawing the shopping mall," May says.

"Wow," I say. "Impressive. I'd live there."

I watch them work a little while longer.

"What's that?" I ask April.

"The wastewater treatment plant."

"Wow. How do you know about that?"

"I want to be an urban planner when I grow up," April says.

"How do you even know what that means?" I ask.

"It's part of our social studies unit," May says.

"How old are you again?" I ask, feigning a dramatic incredulity.

"Seven," they both say, giggling.

"Don't seven-year-olds like to do kids' stuff? Or is it all about urban planning now?"

"We like kids' stuff," May says.

"Yeah, Uncle Zeke," April says. "We love kids' stuff too. We just like learning."

"Let's go get some mac-and-cheese?" I say. "Then some ice cream? And let's learn absolutely nothing?"

The girls whoop with glee, dropping their markers and running to the front door. As we exit, I notice Lara looking at us and smiling, and, for what it's worth, I give her a jaunty wink.

* * *

I take the girls to State Street, to the Noodles restaurant, a high-end fast-food place that has all the forced charm of an urban bistro with none of the shabby ambience. They both love the macaroni-and-cheese entrée here, as do I, a warm mush of yellow cheese, butter, and noodles, a fat-and-carbohydrate orgy that always hits my system like a drug. Everything is clean and well shined at Noodles, even at this hour, the height of the dinner rush. The ceiling seems impossibly far away, fashionably exposing ductwork painted taupe and gray. I place our orders at the counter, including a beer for myself, and then I get each of the girls a gigantic glass of orange Hi-C with ice, against all my good judgment, and find us a booth in the corner. Before I had a relationship with these nieces of mine, I never understood the immense pride and satisfaction that can come from simply being able to purchase a meal for children. My feeling as a provider to two dependent souls sustains me in dark times when, in truth, I'm not sure anything else could.

"This is gonna be sooooooo good," May croons, as we take our seats in the booth.

"I'm totally starved," April says, almost shaking with anticipation.

Just then, I see sitting at the booth opposite, nose in a book — *The Uses of Enchantment* by Heidi Julavits — Minn. A number stands on her table, meaning she's just arrived and is waiting for her food as well. Minn turns to look at us, as April and May begin to talk excitedly about what dishes they would serve if they ran a restaurant — avocados, strawberry jelly, Wheat Thins — and smiles.

"Hello, Zeke," she says.

"Hi, Minn," I say. She's wearing her Starbucks uniform but still looks different, somehow, away from the counter. More fetching, if that's possible. Accessible. I resist an impulse to leap up and embrace her.

"These are my nieces, April and May," I say. "This is Minn; she works at Starbucks down the street."

"I want to work at Starbucks someday!" April says.

"What are you doing here?" May asks. "Don't they have food there?"

"I'm on my break," Minn says. "I'm in love with the mac-and-cheese, unfortunately for my thighs."

Her thighs, which I can't help but look at given her comment, look remarkably lean and luscious in her tight black pants, but I don't remark on them. Sometimes I actually do know when to shut up.

"We love the mac-and-cheese too," April says.

"I get tomatoes on mine," May says.

"I hate tomatoes," April says.

"I'm with you," Minn says. "Never liked 'em."

May looks crestfallen.

"But I admire people who can eat 'em. That takes resolve."

May smiles. April seems confused, but she smiles too.

"Do you want to join us?" I ask Minn.

Immediately after asking the question, I feel red with embarrassment. Of course she does not want to join us, to use her thirty minutes of downtime talking with a customer and his two overzealous nieces.

"I'd love to," she says. She gets her book, her water glass, and her plastic number and slides into the booth next to me. And then she gives me this odd, wide-eyed look, as if she is suppressing a laugh. She raises her eyebrows some and I smile back. Then she turns to April and May and says, "Tell me, are you in school?"

Our food arrives and we all blow on our steaming bowls, mixing our noodles up until they are cool enough to eat.

The girls have launched into a long-winded and frenzied description of school—the names of their teachers, the bad kids in the front row, the hot lunch program, the book fair that they had last week, the state capitals, which they recite with blinding speed, alternating one with the other, and then, finally, as they slow down and May says, "Yeah, we like school, pretty much," April cries, "We love it!"

"I always did, too," Minn says. "All the way through college."

"What did you major in?" I ask.

"Anthropology," she says, "with a minor in rural sociology."

"Ah," I say.

"Very practical, right?" Minn says. "And now I work at Starbucks."

"That's so cool!" May says.

We eat a little more, all of us eating at a fairly frenzied pace. I try to think of something to say, an anecdote of sorts that might also demonstrate my romantic interest in Minn. Something about going to movies alone and a trip I might take to Brussels.

But before I can speak, Minn wipes her hands and mouth on her napkin, smiles at us, and says, "I'm sorry, I have to go back to work. My breaks are so short."

"Okay, bye," April and May shout in unison.

And then Minn looks at me and says, "Hey, Uncle Zeke, you should bring these girls in for hot chocolate or cookies one of these days."

With that, Minn turns, a bounce in her gait, hands holding a large colorful purse in front of her, and exits Noodles. April and May and I all watch her, absolutely delighted.

When I get home with the girls that night, we find my mother asleep on the couch.

I quietly send the girls up to their room and instruct them to get started on their homework.

Then I sit down at the edge of the couch and gently wake my mother, who sits up suddenly, takes a deep and violent breath, and begins coughing atrociously.

I get up and bring her some water and she sips it slowly, gradually regaining control of her spastic lungs.

"Are you okay?" I say.

"Fine, fine," she says. "I swallowed my gum or something."

"Okay," I say.

"Did you have a nice time with the girls?" she asks.

"We had a great time," I say. "We always do."

"Did they eat supper?"

"Mac-and-cheese," I say. "At Noodles."

"Good, good. Thanks for doing that."

"No sweat," I say. "What did the doctor have to say?"

"He said, 'You're old.'"

"What else, Mom?"

"He said we'd take some more tests. More tests. More money for him, more unpleasantness for me."

"What is wrong?" I ask. "What do they think it is?"

"I'm sure it's my asthma. They did a scan of my lungs today. I'll know more by the end of the week."

"They probably suggested you stop smoking," I say.

"Imagine that," she says. "They did."

"Will you?"

"I can try."

"I hope you will," I say.

"Tell me about work. What's happening there? Anything from Lara? Did you buy her flowers for her desk today? I think you should buy her flowers."

"Funny you should bring her up," I say. "She looked beautiful today. But you know who ended up eating dinner with me and the girls?"

"Who?" my mother asks. I know the twins will tell her about Minn anyway, as soon as they have a chance, so I figure I face fewer questions from my mother if I control the conversation about Minn from the outset.

"The woman from the coffee shop whom I like," I say. "Minn."

"Oh, the barista," my mother says.

"Exactly," I say, pleased that my mother has used the term.

"I'll have to find out how the girls like her."

"They seemed to love her," I say.

"How wonderful!"

"But don't get your hopes up, Mom. She might be engaged. I'm pretty sure there's an engagement ring on her left hand."

"Maybe she just likes rings?"

"Maybe," I say, "maybe. Can I make you some dinner?"

"No," she says. "Maybe a drink? Can you make us a couple of drinks?"

"A drink?" I ask. "A real one?"

"Life's too short," she says.

I drink a few gin and tonics with my mother that night and then get the girls to bed. Finally, after lying in my bed for an hour or more without falling asleep, I rise and go into my study and, half-drunk, sip tea and return to my work. I often wonder how it would feel to be an insomniac if you did not have some sort of intellectual pursuit to turn to in the wee hours. What if you worked at McDonald's or some warehouse, and you could not work from your home office at two in the morning? Could you just show up at the graveyard shift and say, like so many of my poet and painter and professor friends say when they e-mail me at 3:12 A.M.: "I couldn't sleep, so I thought I'd get some work done"? Can you imagine how your colleagues at, say, Dunkin' Donuts might react to that?

I imagine you could read or watch television, but somehow, to me, insomnia does not seem so bad when the sleeplessness is productive in some way, and, as insomnia has been a continuing battle for me these past few years, I immediately fall back into some of the work I have been doing in the middle of the night, transcribing and analyzing my unhappiness interviews in the late hours. It's amazing to me how often people answer right away. They do not stop to think, or second-guess, or resist when I ask, "Why are you so unhappy?" They just answer.

Tonight, I scroll through a sampling of these responses on my laptop, in hopes that the collective malaise detailed there might make me feel a little better. My mood has slipped into the top layer of despair, and I need a lift out of it.

Marvin H., 26, adjunct lecturer in economics, Montgomery, AL:
I suppose what really has tormented me—no, that's too strong a word—what has challenged my happiness, has been growth. I do not necessarily see growth as a good thing. For instance, when they built a new Cracker Barrel out by the highway—my mom was thrilled, she loves Cracker Barrel, I swear, it's the only reason she takes vacations. I wasn't. I mean who needs another Cracker Barrel, right? Who needs any of the shit they've been building on that edge of town? Seriously, nothing is fueled by need anymore. Everything new they come up with is an extra. They have to spend a lot of money convincing you that they need it. There's a sporting goods store the size of the Pentagon. It's crazy. I don't like it. It used to be, hey, this town needs a dry goods store or a butcher shop, so somebody opened one up and that was that. Now, now, forget about it. Oh, also, I have an old high school friend and he and his wife had a baby at twenty-two. I know, it's young, but they didn't go to college and so, anyway, they had this kid. I saw this kid a lot for the first year of its life—a beautiful, dark-haired, biracial kid. And then I go to graduate school and I get back to Montgomery and the kid is like, four. He's four. He hits, he talks back, his nose runs like a sieve, and he just won't stop growing.

Leslie J., 33, graphic designer, Ypsilanti, MI:
Unhappy? I don't know. I'm not really an unhappy person.

64

I'm not. I'm lucky that way. [*Long pause. Subject begins weeping.*]

Swanson B., 31, high school history teacher, Seattle, WA:
Lots of things. It doesn't take much to make me unhappy. I'm thirty-one. That alone makes me unhappy. But, for instance, the other day I had eaten an apple Jolly Rancher one of my students gave me. And it was pretty good. It had been years since I'd had a Jolly Rancher. But then I went over to the coffee shop for some coffee. That's the best part of my day. Double-cap, low foam. But it tasted like shit because I had just sucked on this Jolly Rancher for forty minutes. I was so disappointed. I guess disappointment makes me unhappy. And my name. I hate my name. Three months ago, my father—my mom's dead—admitted that they were eating frozen dinners in front of the TV when they came up with it. I'm named after a convenience food. That's not exactly a bright spot for me either.

Martha N., 39, cabdriver, Madison, WI:
Well, the war. The president. Lies. Liars. Secrets and lies. Most everything political. I've gone from anger to sadness about most things. Health care. Global warming. I guess that's the way you can control a population, you know? Appease their rage with products and cheap credit. Then everybody gets surrounded by stuff and crap they can't pay for and they get totally down. You want to control everything? Just make everybody really unhappy. Then put them all on the same pill.

Cory, 19, college student, Knoxville, TN:
Suffering, I guess. Is that what you mean? I don't know. This is sort of a dumb question.

Holly R., 28, editor, New York, NY:

Everything. I'm totally serious. Elevators, pigeons, that plump woman over there in stilettos? All of those things, that's a start. My boyfriend makes me unhappy most of the time. I know, I know, that sounds awful, right? Well, there you go. That's what makes me unhappy.

[*Interviewer: Do you think I could make you happy?*]

What? No. Oh, shit. You are some creep. I knew it. No.

Sara B., 28, wedding planner, Tucson, AZ:

My ankles. I hate my ankles and every day I have to engage with them and notice how fucking unattractive they are and if that makes me petty, fine. There's a lot to be unhappy about. A lot of things make me unhappy. But, that's what my predominant unhappiness is. Ankles.

God. Do you do this for a living?

Kyle, 27, waiter, Houston, TX:

Um, geez. Jay Leno, I guess. Can't stand him and if I watch it, if I get sucked into his monologue, I can't sleep the whole night. I just lie there in bed perplexed by his fame and appeal.

Wayne, 34, real estate agent, Dodgeville, WI:

Not much. I'm a pretty happy guy.

[*Interviewer: You never get unhappy?*]

No. No, I just don't. Happiness is a choice. You know? Well, good luck with your project. And make it a great day!

Larson, 32, Presbyterian minister, Ames, IA:

Faith. I know that is supposed to make you happy, right? Right? Anyway, lately, I feel like nobody is living according to Jesus's standards. I mean, how greedy can we get as a nation? How violent, how shallow, how full of selfishness?

And then here I am, believing in this guy, this god, who was on earth two thousand years ago and said, "Give away your money, turn the other cheek, judge not." Who else is listening to him, I mean, really listening to him? Am I some freak because I listen to him? I actually talk to him every morning and think he is listening. Yeah, no, seriously—having faith in God can be miserable.

Leah, 27, yoga and Pilates instructor, Austin, TX:
Oh, God, I don't know, I don't think about it so much anymore. I mean, well, a lot of things. But I'm a pretty positive person, really. Why don't you ask people what makes them happy?

[*Interviewer: That's not the aim of my project.*]

What is the aim of your project?

[*Interviewer: To uncover why so many people in our prosperous, abundant nation are unhappy.*]

Oh, that's easy. Clutter. We have too much stuff. We have too much body fat on our bodies and that messes with your energy and we have too much crap in our homes and that messes with your energy. We need to have a massive garage sale, send all our stuff to poor people in other countries. And then we need to go on a thirty-day juice fast, collectively, the whole nation. I'm serious. It'd be that easy. A mandatory cleanse. Then, worldwide peace and prosperity.

I now have over five hundred of these short interviews, compiled on my travels across the country and funded by the Great Midwestern Humanities Initiative. I do a number of these interviews in airports, where, I find, many people are feeling ill at ease and killing time and thus, some time with a man and his tape recorder is time well spent, a perfect distraction. I confess that, on occasion, I do tell my subjects that I work for National Public Radio, as a reporter for *All Things Considered.* It lends legitimacy to my claim, and, well, I like to think that my project adheres to the same professional standards as their programs. And, in theory, I could submit some of these to *All Things Considered* someday and they might do a story on my project. (In fact, often, while driving, I do pretend to be a guest on Terry Gross's *Fresh Air,* giving an interview that is warm, engaging, and witty, or on Rachel Maddow's show on Air America, where I make her laugh and laugh and later, off-mic, I say, "Oh, Rachel, you crack me up and I crack you up! Are you sure you prefer women?")

I have other interviews done by phone, some by e-mail. But the ones I have done in person are my favorites to review; often I can see myself just as I was on the day I asked the questions—what sport coat or cotton half-zip pullover I might have been wearing, what shoes—my chukkas or my slip-on loafers or my L. L. Bean walking shoes. At night, when I look through the interviews, at random, I am hoping to see that some sort of pattern is emerging. Can I illuminate our darkness? Can I find out why, over and over again, we Americans, without even being pressed, admit to a paralyzing unhappiness? I have to admit that, unless some sort of insight is gained from my inventory project, it does little for the common good. I learned that from reading the works of Studs Terkel—as individual pieces, his interviews are compelling for their voyeurism, but collectively, they are the greatest chronicles of the twentieth century ever compiled by one man. The truth is I am not unhappy. I am not unhappy at all!

6

Zeke Pappas journeys, long-day-style, into night.

THE NEXT MORNING I open the door to our office, which was an old grocery store in the days when this neighborhood was still an Italian enclave known as the Greenbush. The dark brick and large shop-style windows make it a pleasant building to work in, and I have seen pictures of what it once looked like, its windows full of bounty—meat, cheese, onions, peppers, and bread.

In the common area of the office Lara is making herself a cup of tea.

"Good morning, Lara," I say.

"Hey," she says. "I'm ready to take that letter."

"We'll get to that."

"I actually need to get it out of the way first thing if you want it done today, Zeke. I have an appointment."

"Do you?"

"Or, you could probably type it yourself, Zeke. Couldn't you?"

"I'd rather not."

"Seriously, Zeke? Come on! You know you type just as fast as me."

69

"I think better orally," I say. "I'm sorry."

I sit in the reception area of the GMHI, my feet up on the coffee table. Lara sits at her desk. From my slouched position on the sofa I have a good view of her legs. She is dressed a bit more formally than normal, a smart black suit I have never seen before with a crisp white blouse unbuttoned just enough to be both sexy and professional. The skirt is flattering to the extreme. What I wouldn't do to those legs on our wedding night! I would ravage them! I would leave no cell neglected, not one!

At this point, however, I can't say that she is behaving like a good prospect at all. She is distant and impatient.

"I'm ready," she says. "Let's go."

"Right, right," I say. "Sorry."

"Another reverie?"

"Of sorts."

"Shall I start?" she says. "The usual way? 'Dear Friend of the Humanities'?"

"Yes. Yes," I say. "Okay, *Dear Friend of the Humanities: This year, the Great Midwestern Humanities Initiative (GMHI) has embarked on an exciting new focus. You already know that, since our inception in 1999, we have funded a number of innovative public humanities projects that bring some of our region's brightest scholars into a diverse group of rural, suburban, and urban communities. From a project in which high school filmmakers chronicled the contents of their families' basements as an exercise in historical analysis to a program that brought together dozens of senior citizens to discuss the social and economic prophecies contained in the novels of native son F. Scott Fitzgerald, GMHI projects focus on the telling details of our world, in an attempt to distill the true core of our communities and culture, particularly our shared Midwestern heritage.*"

"Amazing. Off the top of your head! Shall I read it back to you so far?" Lara asks.

"No, no, I'm on a roll."

"You certainly are," she says, "A roll of BS."

I shoot her a look that is, I hope, simultaneously admonishing and flirtatious.

"*Now, our organization,*" I begin, "*is working on a major, multi-year project that will examine the peculiar and troublingly prevalent phenomenon of American unhappiness. Through a number of oral history initiatives, new media projects, public symposiums, and original scholarly research, we hope to find answers to one of the most crushing spiritual questions of our time: Why are we so unhappy?*"

"Zeke this isn't very uplifting."

"It's moving," I say. "That's what raises money. You have to move the donors."

"You're the boss," she says.

"Here, how's this: *In 1999, our national leaders understood the compelling reasons for public funding of ambitious and original humanities projects. Today, we are in a new and daunting era. Federal and state support for important programs like the GMHI is waning, if not extinct. That's why we rely, now more than ever, on visionary and generous donors like you. Please consider joining our efforts with some significant financial support. The future of humanity, or at least the humanities, depends on our culture's ability to reflect upon and connect with the overwhelming and unprecedented changes that the twenty-first century has brought and will continue to bring.*"

"Jesus," Lara says.

"What?"

"A little thick, don't you think? The future of humanity?"

"Sign it like this: *With great vision and in solidarity, Zeke Pappas.*"

"Geez."

"Geez," I say. "Done. Send it."

"Do you want me to read it back to you?"

"No," I say.

"Do you want to read a printout before I send it? It's a little long."

"Use eleven-point font. Garamond. Check for typos."

"You don't want to reread it?"

"No, no. It would sully the message. I spoke from the heart. With great passion and belief. This is how you engage donors."

"Zeke," Lara says.

"What?"

"Nothing," she says.

"Very well," I say. "Many thanks."

"Zeke," she says.

"What is it?"

"We had another midyear narrative due to the Department of the Interior's Office of Cultural Affairs on June 1, okay? Don't forget. We're late. They keep calling."

"Yes, yes, of course. I'll get right on that. Soon."

"They have a new solicitor general. He's not at all pleasant," she says. "I hate it when he calls."

"Consider it done, Lara," I say, and then add, swiftly, "My dear."

A moment later, she is back in the doorway to my office. A fine image.

"Zeke, I have a job interview today. At ten o'clock. And I am hoping you will be a good reference."

"You're kidding me."

"No. No, I'm afraid I'm not. Look at the books, Zeke. How much longer do you think you can go on paying me?"

"That is my concern," I say. "You will do nothing so foolish as to go to that interview."

"Zeke, I don't know if I trust you anymore," she says. "How can I?"

"Please shut the door," I say.

I do like having the door shut and, frankly, am glad for a moment when Lara isn't hounding me to write the narrative for this report or comply with this information request. I am always happy to have some time to work on my project by myself, without the distraction of other energies in the office. My office is in the back of the building, in the rear corner, with two bright windows and many books. There are three plants on top of my lone file cabinet, which is largely empty (I love how little need we have for paper files anymore!). Lara purchased the plants and cares for and waters them. It is a fine highlight of my day when she walks in with her watering can, smiles, walks to the corner near a window, stretches slightly, her backside to me, her calves flexing, and she waters the plants. Even describing it to you now, I tremble slightly. I have air in my palms. Some days, I'm sure she knows what the sight of her stirs in me. Some nights, I imagine coming up behind her as she waters.

But enough about Lara!

I begin by sifting through my inbox, signing several forms from the federal government which I do not read and then perusing two overdue reports from past grantees—*Kirkegaard's Labels: Multicultural Identity Politics and the End of Community* and *Flaubert's* Madame Bovary *and the Plight of American Sex Workers: A Consideration.* Once my inbox is cleared, I pick one of the many Penguin Classics off my shelf at random, as is my daily ritual, open the book to a random page, and begin reading. Today the volume chosen is Lermontov's *A Hero of Our Time,* one of the first great misanthropic novels; I confess this morning has found me feeling like quite the misanthrope myself.

After reading three pages, I check my voice mail. The only message is from Josh Farnsworth: "Hello, Mr. Pappas. We really need you to return this phone call from the Department of Departmental Compliance and Oversight. Please call my cell phone . . ."

I delete the message.

I check my e-mail. Nothing. I double-check my spam folder just to be sure no messages were accidentally filtered from my inbox. Nothing.

I dislike an empty inbox. I actually like a long queue of e-mails to return. It feels as if you're on a ship headed to port with a gaggle of admirers awaiting your arrival.

The empty office, coupled with the warm sunlight coming

through the windows, creates a pensive, reflective milieu in which to do some contemplative writing. I open the file on my computer called "The Inventory Essay 16.doc." I stare at the open file for a long time, change the font of the title to Copperplate, and add my name to the title page. After a few minutes of staring at the text, I add an epigraph, which tends to change weekly. Today, I add a quote from Salinger's *The Catcher in the Rye,* the final lines: "Don't ever tell anybody anything. If you do, you start missing everybody."

Then I hit Save and close my file.

Not in the right frame of mind for creative or intellectual work, I look over the budget reports that Lara prepared for me weeks ago. There is no good news in them, not in a plus-and-minus sort of way. We are certainly on our way to being out of money, but then again it seems as if we are no different from the entire nation in this way.

On my desk there is a copy of a report I filed last month with the Department of the Interior, the federal agency where the GMHI funding earmark came from so many years ago, as did a smaller, second earmark four years ago. On it, in red ink, is a message from Lara: *You received a call, three calls actually, from a Josh Farnsworth regarding this report. Please call him.* There is a phone number next to that note, on a separate Post-it, beginning with the area code 202.

I open the manila folder, labeled "Interim Report, Spring 2008." In it I see my handwriting on a federal form, though I barely remember writing out the report. The question: *What sort of progress has your organization made in terms of solving the initial problem you aimed to address with your federal funding? What major steps still need to be undertaken in order to achieve the quantifiable outcomes your project outlined in its initial planning phase?*

My answer: *We have made significant progress toward the elimination of ignorance, malice, and greed that plagues American culture. If one measures progress, for instance, in the same way that our current administration measures progress in, say, Iraq, then we are a deliriously successful operation at the GMHI. We simply could use a surge.*

74

I continued: *We are now embarking on a revolutionary study of American unhappiness, one that will illuminate the darkest corners of our collective psyche. In order to understand the crisis of American intellect and spirit that we are experiencing as a nation, particularly here in the American Midwest, we must first understand the peculiar nature and complexity of our own discontent. Thus, we have begun to collect a series of interviews with average Americans, which will, I have no doubt, be successful in identifying, if not solving, the sadnesses we share.*

I'm not all that aware of having written such things, but in the world of cultural nonprofits, one gets used to shoveling a certain amount of shit, usually in the form of grant applications that save one's bacon, and so I have a faint recollection of writing out my answers, with great haste, one afternoon while chatting on the phone. I think they are honest and accurate answers. I look at Josh Farnsworth's name and phone number again, scrawled in what seems to be angry handwriting from my dear Lara, and decide, well, if it's urgent, Farnsworth, you can just call me back. Nothing depresses me more than jousting with bureaucrats.

I Google Farnsworth's name and discover that he is a former staffer for Congressman Leatherberry. I also discover that he is now a bureaucrat in an obscure domestic wing of the Department of Homeland Security, which I discover because he is pictured, in some newsletter photo, in black tie, shaking the hand of Congressman Tom DeLay. I decide to call him back and start with his cell number.

"Farnsworth," he says.

"Hello, Mr. Farnsworth. It's Zeke Pappas from the Great Midwestern—"

"You finally called me back."

"Right, well, lots of calls here—some urgent issues relating to the public humanities, in fact. Sorry for the delay. What can I do for you?"

"Federal law requires me to ask you if I may record this call for quality assurance purposes."

"Aren't you on a cell phone?"

"Can I tape this phone call?" Farnsworth says, slowly, as if I am a foreigner who doesn't speak English.

"I understood your words," I say. "I just didn't quite believe them. You want to tape this phone call?"

"Yes," he says.

"Most certainly not," I say.

"Look, it's standard procedure, Mr. Pappas."

"Well, it shouldn't be!"

"It's just a precaution in case there's a question. I hate it too. You think I want to tape my methods of interrogation?"

"Interrogation? Is that what you think this is?"

"It's a line of questioning."

"Well, I don't like it."

"Do you want me to come down there and talk to you in person, Mr. Pappas? Is that what you want?"

"Are you threatening me? Is that a threat?"

Farnsworth hangs up.

And then, this afternoon, at the supposed safety of my desk, my office door shut, my enclave of my books and papers and the towering "to-be-read" desk tray overflowing with clippings and periodicals and pamphlets, I get one new response via our instant web feedback form:

Valerie, 34, self-employed, Ely, MN:
Q: Why are you so unhappy?
A: Deception, discontent, the things we've done that we
cannot take back, and loneliness. That is what makes me
so unhappy.

And, lo, there I sit, greatly unsettled in front of my screen.

7

Zeke is floored.

THE NAME IS a problem. *Valerie.*

I am not often unsettled by responses to the *American Unhappiness* website. In fact, more often than not I see them as pure data—a bit sad-making, yes, occasionally quite witty—but at their core they are raw data, field notes, tales from the front for a project that I hope someday comes to define my working life. To be a great chronicler of the social condition, one must practice a level of detachment from one's subjects. One's observations cannot lead to emotional reactions. For instance, I am a happy man, the best sort of observer of America's overwhelming unhappiness—there is no agenda to make my unhappiness the nation's unhappiness. I am, as Fox News wishes it were, fair and balanced.

But this message, from Valerie, age thirty-four, of Ely, Minnesota, is stunning in the old sense of the word. Temporarily paralyzed, I find I have to get up from my desk just to be sure I still can. It's not easy.

Valerie is the name of my late wife. We married young and our marriage was brief. I was twenty; she'd just turned twenty-one. A few months into our union, she disappeared during a canoeing adventure in the Boundary Waters with her friend and former roommate, Jeanette. The last place she was seen, by anyone other than Jeanette, was in Ely, Minnesota, a small town near the wilderness area. Today, Valerie, too, would be thirty-four.

Certainly, it is entirely within the realm of possibility in a digital age that a random and *different* woman named Valerie, age thirty-four, would live in Ely, Minnesota, and would wander to my website. But the eeriness of the coincidence, and the cryptic nature of the message, is certainly enough to derail my orderly afternoon.

I do not speak often about Valerie, not out of any sense of shame, and not because her memory is so grief-laden that it is unspeakable (though it once was, surely), but because I do not like the pity people offer when I tell them I am a young widower. Over a decade ago, I believed that I had met my soul's match, and that she and I would embark on a romantic and domestic life together to rival the world's greatest partnerships; now that she is gone—and time has softened what once felt like a fatal blow—I want to get on with my life, to try another, perhaps less intense, partnership, and resume living. Were I to tell everybody I knew about this brief chapter in my life, set in Michigan, it would inexorably change the way they see me. I do not want to be seen as a sad or damaged person. For one, nobody invites such people to dinner parties—so profound is the weight they carry that people are afraid to express mirth around them.

Valerie and I met during my junior year at the University of Michigan; she was a senior. We were both taking the impressive Shakespeare course taught by the legendary Ralph Williams, one of the university's most popular professors, who packed hundreds of undergraduates into a sprawling lecture hall. Despite the cavernous vastness of that place, Professor Williams captivated all of us as he bounced about in the front of the hall, waving his enormous hands. There was a palpable energy in the room, an almost sexual energy, and one day in early September, when a lean, fair-skinned woman with green eyes and long, dark red hair sat down next to me in that packed hall, I felt a tingling sensation coming from the skin of her forearm next to mine. I turned and smiled at her. She smiled back. *Valerie!*

Valerie again sat down next to me during the following lecture, with another big smile, and then, the next week, I sought her out. There was a young woman already sitting next to her on one side and on the other side, a massive frat brother in a white ball cap. I simply went into that aisle, approached Valerie's neighbors, and quietly but confidently said, "I'm sure this sounds ridiculous, but my ability to get through the week depends on my being allowed to sit next to this particularly fetching woman."

At the front of the stage, Professor Williams entered with a flourish. The pre-lecture talking began to fade, and the frat boy stared at me. The woman on Valerie's right said, "Sorry, I like this seat." I scowled at her rather dull face. That was, as it turned out, Valerie's roommate, Jeanette, and it was prudent of me to refrain from a snide remark. The frat brother in question, however, took pity on me, knew the inexplicable ways that lust could overtake a young man's sanity and sense of decorum on short notice, and he laughed, stood up, and moved to an empty seat in the front row, saying, "Good luck, brother."

I sat next to Valerie just as Professor Williams was calling out a good morning to all of us. "So good to see you!" he bellowed, as he always did, and I turned to Valerie and smiled and she turned to me and said, "Fetching?" in a way that betrayed how hard she was trying to resist a smile or possibly outright laughter.

Perhaps that was the fateful blessing I needed, because that night, Valerie and I went out for coffee, and we stayed up all night talking. I finally left at dawn, sun-dazed in Ann Arbor's morning light and with a terrible headache from lack of sleep. At noon we met again, and, after sharing a smoothie at a café on South U., we retreated to her place for a nap, both of us insistently referring to our fatigue.

There, in the well-lit back bedroom of her apartment, we began what still ranks as the most intense sexual and emotional afternoon of my life.

I had never seen hair that particular shade of red before; it was a deep copper color, and in the sunlight, I thought, it looked as if it were about to catch fire.

Our courtship had the feverish hunger that only college can provide—free of binding schedules, basic housekeeping standards, and the traditional time structures of the working culture, one was free to engage in all sorts of frivolity. Daytime sex, sleepless nights, drinking to excess, intellectual masturbation, creative freedom—all of these blessings heaped on our young, flawless bodies, our shiny teeth, our bright, yearning eyes. Even on Sunday mornings when we lounged about in sweatpants, unwashed and hung-over, we were beautiful.

Our semester went on in this way: we attended our Shakespeare lectures together, we studied together, wrote papers together, drank large amounts of both coffee and beer. We hung out with our good friends, a ragtag group of earnest lefties and aspiring poets and re-porters from the *Michigan Daily*, and I think they were all some-what jealous of our certainty and lust. I know Jeanette disliked me. She was a political science major, forever reading texts like *The Art of War* and *The Prince,* attempting to be, at age twenty, a serious scholar; but it was difficult in that shared apartment. Valerie and I were often behind the thin bedroom door at odd hours, in verita-ble ecstasy. We coupled at all times of day, showered or unshowered, sleepy or caffeine-buzzed, sober or drunk. We were not quiet. We had the brashness of new and young lovers: just as Americans travel-ing in Europe flaunt their American-ness, we believed we possessed something so pure and shining that anybody who could experience it even vicariously would be blessed.

And talk about Europe: Oh, Europe! On our spring break that year, we went to Paris, charging our plane tickets and our hotel on brand-new credit cards we did not have the means to pay back. All of our friends moaned. They hated us for doing something so bold. As they went off to tired beaches in Florida, ripe with STDs, or to something as earnest as a spring break service project rebuilding blighted parts of rural America, Valerie and I were off to Paris. In Paris, our love was respected. These were the Clinton years, and two young, leftist Americans in love, ambling along the Seine, were a sight to behold. We took in the knowing nods and warm smiles of the French, we acknowledged the silent accord we had with them—they would continue to provide us a place of rest and higher culture, and we would continue to come there and spend our money; we would beam all of the American earnestness and heartfelt wonder that we could muster and they could feel superior to our lack of urbanity and sophistication.

We stayed at a cheap hotel in the heart of Paris; it was near nothing famous but in the center of everything, and while the neighborhood is something I can scarcely remember, the hotel was family-owned. It was called the Hotel Cambrai and it was clean and friendly and a place to ravish each other with the sort of recklessness foreign travel brings into one's sex life. In the morning, there were bread and croissants. I drank the coffee, Valerie the hot chocolate. We returned to our room after breakfast for more love. One morning, we shattered the innocence of a young Albanian cleaning woman, having forgotten to latch our door.

On our last night, sitting in the courtyard of the closed Louvre, I decided to ask Valerie to marry me. Lacking a ring, or any preconceived ideas of a grand gesture, I led her to the edge of the fountain, and we sat there on the half wall. I said, "Valerie, I am going to ask you something and when you have an answer, please tap me on the shoulder and let me know."

She leaned in, laughing. "What is it, my sweet?"

"Will you marry me?" I said, then quickly plunged my head down into the fountain's murky water. It was cold, full of sediment.

I heard her screaming and laughing above the water's surface. Then, I felt her frantic slapping of my shoulder.

I surfaced and gasped and spit.

"Yes!" she shrieked. "God, yes, you're crazy!"

For the rest of the spring semester, we jokingly and annoyingly (to our friends) referred to each other as *Jean-Claude* and *Amelie* and drank only French wine. We did not have the money for an engagement ring, so we bought the cheapest wedding bands we could find at a Montgomery Ward that was going out of business, and we wore them on our right hands as engagement symbols. Our friends shuddered about this, too. Yuck! Fuck! But despite the strong protests of our peers, we were married at Ann Arbor's city hall during the week of final exams. I still had one year of college left, and so we decided to stay put in Ann Arbor. Our friends thought it odd, crazy, in fact, that we would, in 1995, decide to marry so young. But there was something oddly alternative about it—revolutionary. To be married young was so square and unexpected that it was cool. I felt as if we had warded off the end of the century and its inherent uncertainty. We had been *grounded*.

We rented a tiny efficiency apartment, on the third floor of an old Victorian on North Thayer Street, and we slept in a Murphy bed. We bought dishes at Goodwill, had our friends over for dinner parties, opened a joint checking account, and shared a closet. We wrote letters of lofty prose to our families, telling them what we had done. I loved the new intimacies of marriage, the shame-free birth control pills on the nightstand, the merging of morning routines and sets of towels and CDs. We each owned the Bruce Springsteen box set, for instance, so we traded one in at a used record shop and came home with Serge Gainsbourg and Edith Piaf! Aha! With marriage, we were suddenly more interesting!

Then it was summer and the apartment was sweltering. One night I went to Meijer's at two A.M. and bought us a window air conditioner. I had installed it by three and I felt so heroic as we made love in the factory-chilled air. In July, Valerie was off on her long-planned canoe trip with Jeanette. She had ignored Jeanette, somewhat, after we had married. She'd even left her holding a lease, and Jeanette had ended up with a most unpleasant subletter. I did not want Valerie to leave me for even a couple of weeks. Can you imagine that? I didn't even want the short sort of break that most spouses secretly thirst for on occasion. I'm ashamed to say that I begged her to stay, to blow off the trip and forever sever her friendship with Jeanette. I was a jealous lover. I didn't want an ounce of Valerie's love or energy to go to anybody else. But, in the end, I saw her off with my warm wishes and blessings. It was before dawn when they drove away. I stood in the third-floor window and waved. I looked at my desk. I'd been up all night. I was taking two summer classes and I was going to stay behind and work on my honors thesis. The two weeks, I assured myself, would go by quickly. But what if I had convinced her to stay there with me? My life would be so different now.

If I think of myself then, I am hard to imagine. Her, I can see her. Me? I am faded. Someone else. How was I different then? I can't say. I just know that I was different.

Today, my memories of Valerie are contained in a large plastic tote that resides in my attic. Therein lie my photographs, my letters, and a few of her personal articles. I saved a pair of underwear, cotton panties festooned with butterflies, that I had slid from her hips that first afternoon in her apartment. I saved a sketchbook she had kept for an art history class, full of small pencil drawings and cryptic notes taken during visits to the art museums of Toledo and Chicago and Detroit. I saved a stick of lip gloss and her sunglasses and an unused circle of birth control pills, her backups. They are there in my attic, though it has been years since I've allowed myself that self-indulgent gesture of what I call memory sifting. Didn't Jesus say something to the effect of "Let the dead bury the dead?" I don't recall the context in which he says that, but I think of that quote often, when I am tempted to find those sacred underpants, press them to my face, and spend a day weeping.

And now, in my office, behind the closed door, I'm alone with this e-mail, from a Valerie, age thirty-four, from the same city where my wife was last seen. I chalk it up to eerie coincidence and file the response on my hard drive.

8

Zeke Pappas considers and weighs, weighs and considers.

NORMALLY, EACH DAY at four o'clock, when Lara leaves the office, I retreat to my own office, close the door, make myself a large gin and tonic at the small wet bar I had added some years ago (with some gift funds from H. M. Logan, mind you, not federal money), and call my friend Mack Fences.

Mack, a book salesman who covers the Midwest for a major publishing company, and I have been good friends since my brief stint working in the Madison bookstore, the Pilgrim's Pages, which is owned by his partner, Joseph Simms. Mack, who often worked in the store, too, was impressed one evening by my literary taste and took me out for a martini at Paul's Club, where our bartender, a young man named Jim Meehan, instantly made us feel welcome. He was one of those rare bartenders who seem able to suspend time, so that you do not notice how much of the afternoon you are drinking away. One drink turned into several, and soon we were dining on big medium-rare steaks and mammoth plates of calamari and mushroom caps at one of Madison's better restaurants, Mack's Smith & Gallatin company credit card on the table and a bottle of white wine between us. (Mack always drinks white wine, no matter what the menu recommends. A chilled bottle of white Vendage, to Mack, is the ideal blend of comfort and elegance.)

Although he is more than two decades my senior, Mack is probably the one individual I know whom I could designate as a best friend. In truth, if I am honest about things—and I usually am—I would say he is sort of a father figure to me. He understands my work, for one thing, and he believes in my politics. He is also fond of talking on the phone, and that is why each afternoon at four, while I am sitting at my desk at the GMHI, I close the door to my office, make a gin and tonic, and call Mack. At this exact hour, across town in the leafy Cherrywood neighborhood where he lives, Mack is at his desk, in his home office, fixing himself a gin and tonic. When we talk, we first go over the minor annoyances and triumphs of our day, and then we begin to discuss the political and cultural events of the world's day. At five o'clock Joseph comes home from the bookstore, leaving the evening retail hours to his assistant manager. Joseph is quieter than Mack, a kind and gentle man who is decidedly not fond of talking on the phone and is not exactly tolerant of disruptions in the daily routine. And so, when Joseph presses the Open button on the automatic garage door opener, Mack says goodbye and goes to the kitchen to prepare some cocktails and snacks for his partner of twenty-seven years, and I close up my office for the day. Someday, I would like my domestic life to be that way, as predictable and easy as Mack and Joseph's, but until then, I have a telephone and Mack and I have our conversation and cocktails.

Some may find it a bit surprising that I drink alcohol at the office, but the end-of-day cocktail is a civilized and well-deserved reward. We would do well as a culture to honor that sacred hour. Think of the productivity that we might inspire if the last hour of the workday was for cocktails: what a lovely, dangling carrot! I'm not talking about some forced social interaction in an unsightly break room or a mass retreat to the corner bar. I simply mean that each individual would pour himself or herself a generous drink while seated at his or her desk. How easy it would be to answer that annoying e-mail or return the awkward call if you had the perfect heft of a cocktail tumbler in hand. Think of the happy homes we might encourage if Mommy and Daddy didn't come home from the office washed out and sullen, but rosy-cheeked, with ears abuzz. I often wonder if my own father wouldn't have benefited from something as simple and civilized as cocktail hour. He was a sort of teetotaler, other than the four beers he permitted himself during Green Bay Packers games (one per quarter). Otherwise, he said, alcohol was for the weak. An emotional crutch, he said, and he was firmly against those. I said this to Mack one day, and Mack burst out laughing, almost choking on his cigarette: "Oh, I am all about emotional crutches. I have so many!"

Today, Mack answers the phone on the fourth ring.

"Hello?" he says.

"It's me," I say.

"I didn't think you'd call today, Zeke. It's Friday."

"Friday!" I exclaim. "I forgot."

Every Friday, I join Mack and Joseph for dinner, and so usually I do not make my customary happy-hour call.

"Right!" I say. "I'll see you at six thirty! What can I bring?"

"Just yourself," Mack says, as he always does.

I decide that I will talk to Mack and Joseph this evening about my mother's insistence that I begin thinking seriously about marriage. In fact, it occurs to me that I should set a target date for marriage, as the article in *Simply You* magazine suggests. This odd quest mirrors one of the classic drivers of the literary subgenre known as *chick lit*, in which a youngish (but no so young) woman, in a moderately successful but unfulfilling career (usually of an artistic or cultural bent), decides that she must find a life partner but experiences many travails and obstacles in her quest for said partner—married men,

87

bad dates, the blurting out of unpremeditated declarations, chunky thighs, et cetera. You may find it odd that a man of my age, particularly one with a little bit of money and decent looks, would have that same desire for domestic tranquillity. Ah, but even in the Preamble of the U.S. Constitution there is that phrase—*insure domestic Tranquility*—a charge to the newly forming federal government to keep the peace, the bliss, the love. It also had something to do with the suppression of slave uprisings and putting down economic revolt by the exploited working masses, but it is best if one looks at our nation's founding documents through slightly rose-colored glasses, focusing on the spirited high ideals of the language rather than the underlying injustices. Sometimes I wonder if the Founding Fathers, now held in such mythic light in our collective history, were ever plagued by unhappiness. Did Thomas Jefferson or Benjamin Franklin, understanding the ironies and inconsistencies of their new nation, ever plunge into black depths that threatened to bog down our new and emerging democracy? We now know that Abraham Lincoln was subject to great battles with melancholy; we can guess that Bill Clinton also had his share of the soul's dark nights. What else could project him into such strange, reckless obsessions as a rather unattractive and unstable intern?

Perhaps I've just illuminated why I, and so many millions of other Americans, will be so deliriously happy when this dreadful reign of George W. Bush comes to an end. He seems to be a man who sleeps well, who is unencumbered by something as pervasive as unhappiness—and that tells me he does not have the depth or complexity needed to lead our nation. How can you understand America's peculiar unhappiness if you, yourself, go about your day whistling "Camptown Races," joking with the custodial staff, and calling well-educated, honorable people by cute, offensive nicknames?

We are an unhappy nation and we crave leaders who can share our unhappiness. Our finest leaders are always the haunted ones. When the individual in charge looks untroubled and unaware of the dangers and chaos in the world, the unpredictable nature of the economy and domestic life, well, that is even more troubling than reckless and bad policy. That alone can send us into a collective and far-reaching darkness.

It is nearly four thirty. I drink the last of my cocktail and leave the tumbler of melting ice and twisted lime on the coffee table in the reception area, knowing Lara will wash it eventually. I cherish this small gesture, although I know how dated it is to have one's secretary scrubbing cocktail glasses. It is a small shred of domesticity that I share with Lara. I sort of want to believe she enjoys doing it, too.

Walking to my car, bound for the warm glow of my friends' table, I feel, as I often do after happy hour, light and alive.

9

Zeke is coming to dinner.

As i've said, I have dinner with Mack and Joseph every Friday. The way this all started is rather embarrassing, I suppose, but I never find honesty embarrassing; lies are embarrassing, the things we tell others to make ourselves appear more stable or happier than we truly are. In fact, I find that one is often relieved when an embarrassing truth manifests its bright and bushy head.

Anyhow, Mack dropped by one night several years ago to drop off some books I ordered, and when I didn't answer the door, he let himself in and found me sitting in the breakfast nook of my small kitchen, iPod ear buds in my ears. I was staring at a fetching, thirty-something woman in a J. Crew catalog, asking, quite seriously, what her name might be, and what brought her to the Cape at such a chilly time of year. I was eating a mess of scrambled eggs, green pepper, and hot dogs, doused in ketchup (cooking seriously for one seems wasteful, to me), and I did not see Mack until he slid into the breakfast nook across from me. I sat up, closed the J. Crew catalog, and removed the ear buds from my ears.

"What are you doing?" he asked.

I stared at him for a moment and then, without looking from his eyes, I said, "I was trying to get a date."

He burst out laughing at first, but then, seeing the seriousness of my statement, he eventually said, "Well, um, then, tomorrow, I want you to come over for dinner. Six o'clock."

With that, he left, the awkwardness of the encounter too much for even close friends to bear. There was nothing else to say. He had seen me at my intimate worst; unbidden, he had seen the skeletons in my closet.

I did, after getting up for a beer, return to my catalog. The model, like so many women from the pages of J. Crew and Eileen Fisher, seemed the sort of come-hither sophisticate who might enjoy a romp with a younger man on a weekend away from the city. Perhaps she was a high-powered editor staying at her grandmother's drafty old farmhouse, rattled by sea winds, where she had retreated to try and get over a failed relationship. But this particular model did not seem out of my reach; she was not glamorous, just well scrubbed and pretty, the sort of model you might find in the ads sent out by a very respectable department store, Macy's or perhaps Barney's. Does Barney's send out catalogs? There are so many things I do not know about New York City. In this way I am a typical Midwesterner. If you are a New Yorker, ask yourself, how often do you think about Duluth? Well, that is exactly as often as Duluth thinks of you!

When I lived all alone, before my mother and the twins moved in, I developed a minor obsession with catalogs, particularly those that featured women's clothing. For instance, I would come home from work in the evening and check my mail. (I did not have a cat or a dog that was eager to welcome me home. In fact, I very purposefully had chosen not to allow a pet into my life. Pets can lull one into a sense of not quite realistic domesticity, but in reality they cannot take the place of human relationships. So, until my life partner came to live with me, I vowed, or I with her, there would be no pets sleeping at the foot of my bed or in a basket on the floor.)

So there it is: I once had nothing waiting for me at the end of each day other than the mail. I immediately shredded all of the junk mail, of which there was a great deal. It still sickens me, the amounts of human energy and resources that go into the production, packaging, and delivery of absolute trash (for more information, see GMHI grant #56-888-2001: *The Coming Death of the Postal Service and the Coinciding Decline of American Imagination*). After I disposed of the junk mail, I looked at all of the legitimate bills—phone, utilities, student loans, insurance premiums, and credit card statements. These I would secure in a large binder clip with a label that said THESE MUST BE PAID. This is what Hemingway used to do with his bills when he was poor and lived in Paris. Once, when I was still young and easily impressionable, I read this literary tidbit in the introductory text of a famous *Paris Review* interview and decided that this would be exactly how I would organize my bills.

I then prepared to look over my personal mail. I began by fixing myself my second cocktail of the day. Then I removed my shoes, sat down in an old armchair I purchased at a neighbor's yard sale (and subsequently paid seven hundred dollars to repair and recover), and looked over my correspondence. Less of it than I would like, always, but sometimes there was a letter or a postcard from a friend.

I subscribed to five magazines then (and still do)—the *New Yorker, Harper's,* the *Progressive, Virginia Quarterly Review,* and *Esquire.* If one of those arrived, I often perused that while I enjoyed my drink. But mostly I just got many, many catalogs. These were the things I read while I sipped my pre-meal vodka tonic. For example, I would get the J. Crew catalog and begin to peruse its pages, first deciding on an outfit that I would wear—maybe a pair of weathered boot-cut khakis, brown oxfords, a crisp light blue tee, and a navy cotton blazer. Picturing myself dressed in this outfit, my face perfectly unshaven, my hair mussed just so, as if I'd just awoken from a nap in a hammock, I would imagine, perhaps, that I had just arrived at somebody's weekend home in Maine on a windy and cool Saturday morning. Who was waiting for me? The freckled redhead wearing a bikini on page nineteen? Or maybe the boy-hipped brunette in white capri pants and a green polo (page eleven), or the woman, a sage at fifty, walking barefoot in the sand, her short hair blown across her right cheek? Or did I spend the evening with the willowy blond on page twenty-six, the one in the purple J. Crew bridesmaid dress, the one with high heels in hand as she walks barefoot across the green, for some reason distant from the other wedding guests, alone and separate from the joy the others are so greedily drinking up?

Once I had my date for the evening, I would decide on an opening line, get up from my chair to prepare some supper, usually quite simple and quick; then, as I ate, I spent a long time staring at the woman I'd chosen. I learned her backstory—how old was she, what did she do, where was she from, was she single (not always, the naughty vixen!)?—and I shared something with her: a drink, a coffee, some dinner, a dance. I envisioned our whole evening together. Sometimes I drank too much and fell asleep in my easy chair after supper, still staring at the catalog, and the woman disappeared into a dream; sometimes I'd get discouraged and felt pathetic and offered the woman a kiss on the cheek and then got up from my chair and went to bed, lonely; and sometimes the woman I was imagining took off the outfit she had been modeling, or I would slip a strap from her shoulder, and then we would slip off to the bathroom, catalog and I, where we would consummate the relationship. It sounds a bit like the depressing and secret business of a teenage boy, but I assure you that all men are like this despite their public admissions. Such acts serve a physical purpose, and it is not a wholly unpleasant way to spend the evening. And, I supposed, it did keep me in romantic shape so that I might be prepared to give and receive both physical and emotional pleasure to my life partner someday.

Still, one might say that it is good for me to no longer live alone, and one might say that my mother and the twins have saved me from a rather pathetic and increasingly odd life. Who knows?

* * *

So this is how it comes to pass that now, on this fine evening, the world newly replete with promise and life, the green of leaves and the color of blooms, that I am dining on Mack and Joseph's screened-in back porch, the acceptor of their standing dinner invitation meant to save me from making my catalog fetish a daily ritual. When Mack brings a plate of mozzarella, tomato slices, and basil (drizzled with olive oil and capers) to the table to enjoy with our cocktails, I almost shiver with contentment, as if I am taking in Mack and Joseph's long, happy domestic bliss by osmosis. If I were to handpick my parents, this is the kind of couple they would have been.

Just then, the cat—Nancy—walks into the room. Joseph leaps up to feed her some tuna fish. Mack takes a sip of his drink and fiddles with a pack of cigarettes on the table, then asks me to help him with his lighter.

"I've been having these pains in my hand," Mack says. "It doesn't even work some mornings."

"Really?" I ask. "Is it numb?"

"Not really," he says. "It just doesn't work all that well."

"Have you seen a doctor yet?"

"No. No, I hate doctors. You know that," Mack says.

"You should go see Dr. Fish!" I say. "My chiropractor."

"You go to a chiropractor?" Mack says.

"Once a month for spinal alignment," I say, "whether I need it or not. I also go to acupuncture every six weeks and I see a Rolfer fairly regularly."

"Really?" Mack says.

"You should totally go see Dr. Fish," I say. "He's a miracle worker."

"I don't like chiropractors," Joseph says, coming back into the room with more wine.

"Why not?"

"I don't like that we—and by that I mean we Americans—seem to need entire staffs to help us combat our stress and illnesses," Joseph says. "Chiropractors, acupuncturists, herbalists, psychiatrists, massage therapists, homeopaths, personal trainers, yoga teachers, blah, blah, blah. What's wrong with working less and drinking more wine? There. I can save every American a shit-ton of money with such a prescription!"

"Don't listen to him," Mack says. "He's a nasty, bitter man. I'll go see Dr. Fish. Let's talk about something else, goddamn it."

"I'm getting married," I say.

"What?" Mack says.

"To whom?" Joseph says.

"Exactly," I say.

"You what?" Joseph says.

"I've made a decision. This is the year," I say, "for Zeke Pappas to move on. I have identified three women, all of whom I find deeply attractive, intelligent, and pleasant."

"You're kidding!" Joseph says.

"Not at all," I say. "The grieving widower is no more!"

"What brought this on?" Joseph says.

"My mother, to an extent. But she merely crystallized what I have been thinking for a long time. I'm lonely. I need to do something about it. My mother even suggested making a list of prospects. I've already been thinking about the women I'd place on the list."

"Jesus," Mack says. "Who are these women?"

"Are you sure they are women?" Joseph says, laughing.

"They are all women," I say, beaming. I forgot how good it feels to tell your family some good news: I got an A! I won the race! I'm in love!

I raise my glass. Joseph gets up for more wine, but Mack doesn't move. He just says, from behind his hand, "Oh, Zeke."

Even after I explain the logical approach I've taken to marriage, the methodical steps I have taken to prepare my prospects for my proposal, and the precision with which I have planned my eventual proposal, it is clear to me that my friends disapprove of my idea. I am sure, as I leave that night, strolling out into Mack and Joseph's tree-rich front yard, down the brick path that leads to my little car, that my two dear friends are a bit puzzled by my timeline approach to marriage. And I know it shouldn't matter whether or not two middle-aged homosexuals that I've known only for a decade or so approve of my personal decisions when it comes to marriage; after all, this is a cultural institution that they have been, unjustly, barred from joining.

Still, Mack and Joseph feel more like family to me than my own family feels, especially before my mother and my nieces moved in with me, and I want their blessing. I have spent many holidays with Mack and Joseph in the past, part of the motley crew of lonely Americans they bring together in their spacious dining room on Thanksgiving, Christmas, Easter, and just about every major summer holiday weekend. Five years ago, on Easter, for example, I was part of a dinner for twelve that included two penniless lesbian couples from Illinois, one orphaned college student, a recently divorced bookseller from Milwaukee, two single women in their late fifties, an alcoholic fly fisherman with a bad back, and me. It was the most delightful holiday I have ever experienced, maybe because expectations were so low. In my own unhappiness studies, I am always interested in the great weight that Americans put on holidays, as if they are failures if their holiday gatherings aren't perfect feasts rich with love and song. Perhaps it is because so many people work too hard, the only time they take for simple pleasures—drink, food, music, rest, conversation, reading, et cetera—is at the holiday season, and thus the pressure is simply too intense. I'm doubtful that the French or the Italians have such grim affairs. Perhaps we Americans, given the vastness of our country and the geographic distance that separates so many of us from our kin, feel a weighty obligation to be with the people, namely family, that we wouldn't normally choose to be with, especially not for four or five days of living under one roof.

I am standing at the edge of the yard now, near my car, staring up at the sky, and I realize that Mack and Joseph are still on their front porch staring at me, waiting for me to leave. They are good hosts, and they always escort their guests to the door, keeping a sort of vigil from the front porch until their guests drive off and away.

I turn around and call to Mack, "Get an appointment with Dr. Fish, first thing Monday, okay? He'll fix that hand for you!"

Mack waves the bad hand at me, as if he's agreeing to subject it to whatever rigors are necessary.

The sky has clouded over with the thick, overstuffed purple clouds of an evening thunderstorm and the wind has moved in with some significance. I turn and wave to my hosts one more time and then get into my car. I beam a smile. The thunder is loud enough to be unsettling; the lightning is certainly near.

My mood often darkens at the first rumble of thunder. I suppose that throughout human history, certain weather events, particularly storms, have made people sad—think of how many of our primitive ancestors perished in violent weather; in some way, my grief links me to a long, primal tradition. Valerie's death, in a storm, for instance, such a pure and elemental way to die, links me to this great and open past. (See GMHI Book Discussion Series #12: *The Weather as Divinity in World Literature*.)

When we were boys, Cougar was very afraid of thunderstorms. I had always loved them. It was the one thing Cougar seemed to fear as a child; in general, he was brave to the point of insanity. Heights, spiders, wild animals, or bullies—none of these things frightened him in the least, while most everything frightened me. But the first roll of thunder that moved in on a spring or summer evening was enough to send him scurrying under the bed, and I would stand brazenly near the window, awestruck, thrilled not only by the magnificence of the storm, but by the stunning and rare feeling of actually being braver than my brother. I believe that something magical dictates the weather; I do not know the scientific reasons behind thunderstorms—though I am sure they are easy enough to grasp, at least in basic principle—but I prefer they remain somewhat mysterious to me. This is sort of the approach many Republicans take to global warming or poverty: they know there's more to learn, but it would too greatly disturb their worldview to find everything out. I understand, with great compassion, the impulse that makes people turn off their brains to any sort of information that may rattle their spiritual and intellectual core. The more we know, the more we risk opening ourselves up to this American unhappiness that I speak of; conversely, the more we try to understand, change, or manipulate the political views of our fellow citizens, the more unhappy and weary we become.

Lightning illuminates the darkening horizon as I drive, and, for brief, green moments, I can see the hills of the rolling countryside that surrounds Madison. I think of Cougar in his final days, afraid of thunder, somewhere in Iraq, maybe in the middle of a sandstorm, maybe with shrapnel slicing open his skin. Do sandstorms come with thunder and lightning? I don't even know.

Thinking of storms, Republicans, and my brother, I find myself, tonight, parked outside of my boyhood home on the north side of Madison. I roll down the window, staring at my old front yard, and take a deep breath.

There's enough of a wind that you can smell the aroma of curing lunchmeat from the Oscar Mayer plant's lone smokestack. On windy days, the neighborhood smells like my father used to smell when he came home from work, as if my father's exploded heart flew off into the atmosphere and remains heavy above us like a nitrate-rich smog.

My father worked at the plant until his heart exploded inside of him after working a double shift making hot dogs. Cougar had been trying to get a union job at the meatpacking plant but had not had any luck. Times were tight. Quickly, the idea of pursuing vengeful justice became more interesting and important than the processing of cured meats. I don't blame him. I might have done the same thing in his position, had not literature and the humanities given me a sense of calling and purpose. He always seemed to equate the terrorist attacks on 9/11 with our father's untimely death. As if my father had been so wounded by them and the violence done to his beloved nation and had dropped out of the game, grief-stricken. It was as if Cougar went to war to avenge my father's death from a massive heart attack. I wonder, in truth, how many of the men and women in the current war are seeking vengeance for something completely distant from American foreign policy and homeland security—a ruined football career, a failed marriage, or a bankrupt farm. I do not say this out of a lack of respect for their courage or bravery, mind you, but because I think the depth of our nation's collective unhappiness is part of what propels us so easily and dutifully into war after war.

When my father died, the funeral was so sparsely attended that I was almost embarrassed for my father when Cougar told me about the head count. My mother said that the tragedy of the same week had overshadowed my father's death. People were so emotionally overwhelmed they couldn't bear to think of attending a funeral. But I think that my father simply had very few friends. He was an only child, a Greek immigrant who renounced Greece the moment he arrived in this country and embraced all things American. He never stayed in touch with his cousins in Greece, and he worked all day long. Maybe a dozen or so of the men from the plant showed up at the funeral, plus a couple of managers and a few of my mother's coworkers and three of our neighbors.

I didn't want to go. I hate funerals, as I've said. I also hate the Catholic Church, if you must know, and that was where the funeral Mass had taken place. (My father had converted to Catholicism when he married my mother; after his death my mother left the Catholic Church and opted for nondenominational, Jesus-based self-help.) Because I was a little vague internally, frankly, about my own reasons for detesting funerals so much, I lied and said that I couldn't, in good conscience, attend any sort of service at the Catholic Church. That was my excuse.

Cougar said I was a coward. Cougar said I was a selfish asshole.

Cougar said I thought about everything so goddamn much simply because I was too much of a pussy to do anything else but think and think all day long.

My mother wept as Cougar berated, but I still didn't go. I refused. It was a rather Joycean moment, like Stephen Dedalus refusing to pray with his sick mother, and I regret that so many key moments in my life remind me of something a purely fictional character once said or did.

The next day, I went and sat by the grave by myself, tracing my finger absent-mindedly in the fresh patch of still-black earth covered in hay. I stayed there a long time. I don't know how long, but it was dark when Cougar and my mother came and found me there, kneeling in the dirt. They helped me to the car. Cougar actually had to carry me. My legs seemed to have stopped working.

My father, a strange man, had an almost maniacal aversion to the past. He seldom talked about his boyhood in Greece, had never gone back to visit, and vigorously protected us from anything having to do with Hellenic culture—language, religion, or place. I am not sure what happened to him back in the homeland; I do know that Cougar and I were raised to be American boys through and through, with absurdly non-Greek Old Testament names (Jeremiah and Ezekiel!), and other than an occasional leg of lamb, or the liberal use of oregano in my mother's cooking, or our ability to tan, we were anything but Greek.

The evening after my father's funeral, I went inside the house and wandered around and found my way to the basement, to my father's workshop, where he kept his intricately labeled jars of bolts and screws, his pristine and well-organized pegboards. Everything sat untouched. I was not, and still am not, good with tools. I do very little with my hands, though this is where I used to like to go to think as a teenager. Standing there after my father's death, I realized that I was amid the only legacy my father left behind: a perfect workshop, well lighted, clean, organized. I moved from tool to tool, my fingers caressing the cold metal, the smooth wood. This was it. Here was the paternal legacy, the exquisite tool collection that I could not use. I couldn't saw my way out of a cardboard box. All of this was for Cougar, if he wanted it—and he never came home.

I stay parked outside the house for a while, in the darkness, the storm passing over and fading from the sky. I am trying to think of the last real conversation my father and I had, the last time we actually sat down and talked about something. I can't think of anything. He was alive for the first two and a half decades of my life, for nearly two of those decades we lived under the same roof, in the same small house, but I think that, for all of those years, we basically just stayed out of each other's way. We just made small talk.

After I moved out of the house, it was even harder for us to communicate. In recent years, I've admitted something difficult to myself: my father didn't *like* me. He thought I was an asshole, and he had thought so for a long time, maybe ever since I turned twelve. Maybe he was jealous of me for some reason; maybe he thought I had it too easy. I don't know. He didn't like many people. He complained about other people all the time—coworkers, neighbors, cousins, everybody. People were too dumb, too fat, too dirty, too arrogant, too liberal, et cetera. It was almost a bit surreal to realize that I had become one of the people whom my father vigorously disliked, who annoyed him simply by existing.

10

Zeke Pappas says, "I will."

WHEN I COME HOME that evening, my mother comes downstairs. Despite our many differences, when she sees me, she always has that instant of brightness that parents get when they see their children, unexpectedly.

"What are you doing up so late?" I say. "It's nice to see you."

"Waiting for you, actually," she says. "How are your friends?"

"Fine, thanks. How are the girls?"

"Exhausted," she says. "We went swimming at the YMCA after school."

"Nice. I bet they're getting good."

"A couple of fish," my mother says.

Some thunder rumbles outside. The storm renews itself.

"Anyway, sorry I'm so late," I say. "Just driving around."

"Not the best weather to be driving around in, honey."

"I know. Um, I was thinking."

"Oh, Zeke, have you been crying?"

"No!"

"Are you sure?"

"Yes. I'm very sure."

"I have some tea in a thermos," my mother says. "Come into the kitchen."

My mother pours two cups of chamomile tea, adds a spoonful of honey to each, and then we go to the dining room and sit. There is a small box on the dining room table.

"I have something for you," she says.

"What?"

"Your grandmother's engagement ring."

"Wow."

"I know," she says. "It's sort of pushy. It's just, I mean, if you do have someone in mind, well, when the time comes, you can offer her this."

I take the ring and look at it, a simple gold band with five tiny diamonds.

"Things were less flashy back then," she says. "But it's a very elegant ring."

"I know," I say.

"Are you mad?"

"No. No, in fact, Mom, I think you're right. I think I should get married. And sooner rather than later."

My mother and I sit in silence for a while.

Finally, she reaches across the table and touches my hand.

"Do you want some chicken tenders? I brought some home from work the other night and the girls don't want them. We had pizza after we went swimming."

"No, thanks. You go ahead though."

"Not me," she says.

"Did you eat?" I ask.

"I did," she says.

"I think you're losing weight," I say. "Are you?"

"Heavens, no. Don't I wish," she says. "So, who is the lucky lady going to be?"

"I have no idea," I say.

My mother gets up from the table, walks to the small desk in the living room, and returns with an envelope and a pen. She takes the *Simply You* article from the envelope.

"This is when we make a prospect list," she says. She slides the article over to me, along with the pen.

The article seems aimed at female readers, as most of *Simply You* is, but the described predicament is one I am all too familiar with: *Does it seem like you're ready for marriage, but you don't have any prospects on the horizon? Well, just like any good business executive knows the importance of cultivating contacts and nurturing networks, any woman who wants to find Mr. Right knows that she must do the same thing. Follow these simple steps, and you might just be head over heels (or engaged!) by the end of the summer.*

The article suggests that possible life mates are all around us, and as my mother works on a crossword puzzle from the morning's paper, I study the magazine's plan of attack. The article suggests you make a list of four people that you might want to know better:

Make a list of four people whom you know, but don't know well.

Pick one person you see every day, like a classmate, coworker, or that cute lawyer in your Spinning class. Sometimes simple proximity can gradually lead to romance.

I write the name *Minn (barista)* in this space.

Pick one person you really admire, a sort of dream date. Why not aim high? Is there someone you have a lot in common with, somebody you just have to get to know better? Set your sights on this potential Mr. Right by taking in something you'll both love (and love to talk about over a bottle of wine): a breathtaking hike at sunset, an indie film, a play, or an art gallery.

Here I write the name *Sofia Coppola*, the noted film director. Hey, the article says to "aim high." And I have been sending Ms. Coppola an e-mail message each week for the past eighteen months, for professional reasons. I certainly consider her an outside possibility.

Next, the writer continues, *pick one person you are curious about, somebody you sense might have a little crush on you. Find ways to be near this person. Flirt like mad.*

There is a space there to write someone's name, and that's where I write the name *Elizabeth Vandeweghe*.

Finally, you need to think of the obvious. Who is somebody you should have dated a long time ago? Who is the coworker, classmate, or "buddy" who may be burying secret romantic feelings for you?

Here I write the name *Lara Callahan*.

The article goes on to detail strategies for success, derived from the world of big business and corporate strategy:

- *Find an excuse to have face-to-face meetings. Every smart business-woman knows that face-to-face contact with clients yields higher results than phone calls or e-mail. Find reasons to talk to your prospects and engage them in conversation whenever you have a chance.*
- *Let them know you're open to a relationship. Nobody falls into a great new job without sending in a resumé. Your prospects need to know you're single and looking for love. Maybe let them know you go to the movies alone all the time, or how quiet your apartment seems in winter. Don't sound desperate, just independent and available.*
- *Set a reasonable goal, both short-term and long-term. Pick a date when you'll reassess your list of prospects. Maybe pick a date for your desired engagement, too. Again, the trick is to visualize success. If you feel like a wanted woman, men will sense it.*

In the margin, after this tip, I write the number "35" and the date 7.06.2009, my thirty-fifth birthday. Then I draw an engagement ring in the white space. And thus, my prospect list is born.

I slide the list across the table to my mother, who sets aside her crossword puzzle and begins to read.

"The coffee-shop girl?" she asks.

I nod.

"Who's Sofia Coppola?"

"Sort of a colleague," I say. The internationally acclaimed film director is certainly my loftiest prospect, but when I watch her films, I am convinced that she understands precisely what I am talking about when I talk about American unhappiness. I believe that if only I could get in touch with her, she would take a great interest, both personal and cinematic, in my *Inventory of American Unhappiness*. Maybe she would even turn the project into a film, her first full-length documentary. I write to her regularly in the hope that she, whom I consider the most beautiful woman in Hollywood (and yes, I am aware of how high that praise really is), will write or call or e-mail. Oh, what a day that would be, to log in to my account and see that name in my inbox. Sofia Coppola!

My mother continues to read.

"Elizabeth Vandeweghe?" she says. "Zeke, it's a bit soon for her to remarry, don't you think? There's a lot of unhappiness over there right now."

"You never know," I say.

"I suppose you don't," she says. "And Lara Callahan. Your assistant, right?"

I nod.

"Oh, Zeke," she says. "I'm so happy for you. This looks so encouraging." We sit in silence for a moment, sipping our tea. I look around at my house, full of tasteful furniture, original paintings, and hundreds of fine hardcover books. A pile of the girls' shoes is in a small wicker basket by the door. The coffee table in the living room is covered in Polly Pocket action figures and accessories. In one corner of the dining room, two Melissa & Doug art easels hold a collection of brushes and poster paints. The small side table that holds a bottle of fine single-malt Scotch and my favorite crystal tumblers also holds two American Girl dolls. My life has turned out in a way I have never imagined, and I make a comment like this to my mother and she nods.

"You know, Mom," I say, "I know we've had a lot of differences over the years. But you know, when I look around the house and see the girls' stuff everywhere, when I am safe in the knowledge that they are sleeping upstairs above us, clean, warm, well fed, and healthy, I have to say, Ma, we're doing this. We're making this work."

My mother smiles and she reaches across the table and takes my hand.

And then her smile turns to a grimace and her eyes begin to drown. Soon, she is weeping, shuddering at the table, and she lets go of my hand. She puts her palms flat on the surface in front of her.

"Mom," I say. "Mom?"

But she doesn't look up at me, and it's only then that I understand everything, what all of this talking has been about.

"My God," I say. "How long do you have?"

"Six months," she says. "Maybe less."

SUMMER 2008

11

Zeke Pappas is away from his desk.

THANK YOU FOR your response to *An Inventory of American Un-happiness*. Project director Zeke Pappas is out of the office on family medical leave and will return to the project in the fall. If you need immediate assistance, please contact Lara Callahan at lara@gmhi.org.

Theodore M., 28, cable installer, Morris, IL:
Ideas. Ideas make me unhappy. I get so many of them. I'm going to make a film about my great-uncle. I'm going to build a writing shed near the garage. I'm going to send a letter every day for the next year. But I don't follow through on anything. And I know that about myself, so it drives me crazy that I keep having ideas. I keep having ideas, but what am I doing this week? I'm re-watching *The Wire* on DVD. Starting over, season one.

Natalie B., 37, writer, Ames, IA:
There's a place over here on Lincoln Way, and it's called the Village Inn or something. A little family place, a step up from a diner, but not by much. And they have this big

banner in the window, something they had whipped up at Kinko's or whatever, and it says, "Free Slice of Pie on Wednesdays," and I think the deal is if you order a dinner you get a free slice of pie for dessert. I'm not sure if the pie is any good. I don't care if it is or not. My guess is canned filling, pre-made dough. But what makes me almost inexpressibly sad is that I think that probably works. I think a bunch of people actually go in for a free piece of pie. I don't like thinking about that. I don't really have the ability to take that sort of thing.

Wylie P., 39, gym teacher, Valdosta, GA:
I wish I knew.

Anna M., 31, lecturer, Rochester, MN:
The inability of undergraduate students to correctly use commas makes me unhappy. Seriously, I teach four sections of freshman composition each semester, and this about ruins my life.

Hal N., 36, stage manager, New York, NY:
Zooey Deschanel. The actress and singer. You want to know why? Because I don't stand a chance of ever shagging her. Or even talking to her. And I find that harrowing. I think she would be the first person to ever really connect with me, I mean really connect with me. I don't know why I think that. I just do. And the problem is I can't reach her, she'd want nothing to do with me, and I'd probably get arrested for stalking anyway. Wouldn't I?

Alexandria W., 23, waitress, Seattle, WA:
My boyfriend is a total dick.

Ron C., 24, waiter, Seattle, WA:
My girlfriend is a total bitch.

Brenda V., 43, engineer, Manhattan, KS:
When I'm alone with my thoughts, that makes me unhappy, because, you know what, there's some dark shit in there and when it comes out, I don't like who I am. Everybody likes me. I'm easy to like. That makes me unhappy because that's not the real me. The real me is a bitter, jealous, and unsatisfied asshole. I think of the day that comes out. What will my husband say? My mother-in-law? My kids? I think about the shit I'm capable of doing, if I ever act on what I really want to do, and my God, it's terrifying.

Brad V., 34, hardware salesman, Salt Lake City, UT:
The Debbie Gibson video I used to whack off to when I was like twelve or something. Every time I see that video, or, you know, hear that song in a doctor's office or something, my stomach turns watery, this deep pit of shame. I don't know. I don't know why I have that reaction, but when I think of that song, that video, Debbie Gibson in general, this self-loathing comes on and it doesn't go away for a long, long time.

Manuel P., 29, industrial consultant, Los Angeles, CA:
Judge Judy. Jesus. I can't fucking stand it.

Ginny O., 50, homemaker, Tampa, FL:
Real estate agents. Specifically, those professional headshots they put on business cards and in ads and on billboards. I can't even look at them without feeling such intense sorrow for everybody in the whole goddamn profession.

Wanda P., 37, sales associate, Cody, WY:
I guess when I see grownups dressed up for Halloween it sort of makes me unhappy. Unless they're real sexy sorts of costumes, like a slutty bee or a dirty cop or something. And I suppose it's okay if they're with their kids, or at

some drunken party or whatever. But I'm thinking about a secretary who dresses up as a witch, you know, standing there in the glare of the insurance office's fluorescent lights? Or a used-car salesman who is wearing devil horns? Or a postal clerk dressed up as a cowboy or whatever? I can't abide that. I can't think about it. It's about as sad as a guy who wears short-sleeve T-shirts and what he describes as "wacky" neckties. There are things adults must not do, you know?

Jenny, 33, blogger, New York, NY:
Early nineties ski apparel makes me unhappy. Anytime I come across an individual sporting an electric blue, hot pink, or neon green winter weather item (such as a dickey/turtleneck, windbreaker, ski jacket, gloves, or ear warmer) I wonder why, almost twenty years ago, they didn't have the foresight to have bought black. The neon colors are bright yet they make me feel dark—that contrast only adds an extra heaviness to the whole of it. At about the same time the icky feeling sets in, the thought that hey, maybe this guy or gal can't afford a new pair of mittens pushes its way into my mind. And then I realize that I am a judgmental jackass.

Jane G., 42, writer, Galena, IL:
I'm unhappy about my own slow disintegration, about humiliation, clinics, falling off cliffs, being stared at. Arrogant, dopey people make me unhappy, unless they're funny. It makes me unhappy if the people I love are unhappy. But I am not unhappy about animals or movies from the 1930s. Those I like.

Carrie, 33, legal analyst, Normal, IL:
These binders that line the walls of my office. They hold meeting materials for every damn meeting from the last ten years; the paper falling out of them is yellowing and often

printed in a font that I don't think exists anymore. We're always in the process of getting ready for another meeting and making another binder to put on the shelves. No one looks at the binders after the meetings are done, as far as I can tell, but we will never, ever get rid of them. On some very fundamental level I don't understand why we make or keep the binders, and since it is my job to make the binders, this makes me unhappy.

Michael, 35, photographer, Kiev, Ukraine
(via Madison, WI):
What makes me unhappy: Being alone in a country where I can't speak the language. Realizing another cabdriver scammed me and charged me four times the going rate. Hearing stories about my son when I can't see him. Getting to the end of another day without getting anything done. Skipping lunch, that sounds silly, but I've discovered that if it gets to about four P.M. and I forgot to eat that I just feel down, and I think it's my body telling me the fuel gauge has hit empty. Missing an opportunity because I once again ignored that dictum "He who hesitates is lost." Meeting someone I really admire and realizing that they have no interest in talking to me.

AUTUMN 2008

12

Zeke Pappas is back at work.

September 22, 2008

Dear Friend of the Humanities:

It's been an eventful summer here at the office of the Great Midwestern Humanities Initiative (GMHI). A number of our grant recipients completed long-term projects over the summer and held free public events all across the region. I hope you had a chance to attend some of them, from the Alley Stage Rural Play Festival in Mineral Point, Wisconsin, to the Backwoods Politics Symposium in Escanaba, Michigan, from the Reimagining the Rust Belt Conference in Cleveland, to the Catholic Worker Farmer Harvest Celebration in Story County, Iowa.

This year, the GMHI has also been the subject of a rather intensive federal audit, and while such processes do add a significant amount of stress and paperwork to our lives at the office, they are the cornerstone of the transparency and accountability that life in the twenty-first century demands. As we near our ten-year anniversary, we look forward to sharing

the results of the audit with you in our "Decade One" report,
which we will publish in 2010, a document of impressive
length and content edited and compiled by our longtime
administrative assistant, Lara Callahan, who has just been
promoted to the position of Associate Director. It's a well-
deserved nod of appreciation to Lara's lengthy, cheerful, and
excellent service to the cause of the public humanities in the
American Midwest.

Meanwhile, responses to our signature project, An
Inventory of American Unhappiness, *continue to pour in*
from across the nation, creating an impressive bolus of candid
information regarding our collective American psyche, so
bruised by a political system nearly destroyed in eight short
years, as well as a slipshod economy. We hope to publish our
first in-depth analysis of the Inventory *sometime next year, if*
funding permits. And planning is under way for our first-ever
"Midwestern Unhappiness Festival" in the fall of 2009, which
will replace the long-running Wisconsin Book Festival as our
signature event next year.

On a much more personal note, my mother, Violet Pappas,
has been immersed in a battle with stage IV lung cancer.
Thus, I was not as deeply engaged in the work of the GMHI
this summer as I otherwise would have been, and if I've been
difficult to reach, or conspicuously absent from our special
events, this is the reason. It is no wonder that in moments of
deep family tragedy, our intellectual and professional pursuits
seem like dross.

Still, autumn with its sad, purple afternoons, brief and
fleeting, finds me back at this desk, happy to have meaningful
work in a time of sadness. I'm writing this letter in the hope
that you will see how the humanities—our understanding and
exploration of our own role in the human narrative—challenge
and sustain us in times of trial and woe. Please help us continue

to do our work, so that citizens across the Midwest may live rich
and textured lives while the Lord grants them time.

Godspeed,

Zeke Pappas

GMHI Executive Director

Lead Scholar, An Inventory of American Unhappiness

"You can't send this," Lara says upon reading my letter.

"I most certainly can," I say. "It's an honest assessment of where we are as an organization and of where I am as its leader."

"Zeke, it's way too personal," she says. "It's beautiful at times. I was even moved by it, Zeke. It was poetic, eloquent. But I am your friend, a trusted colleague. I am not a donor or potential donor. In some parts it's a bit, well, depressing. At best. Unsettling, at its worst."

"Lara," I say, "it is absolutely appropriate for you, in your new role as associate director, to offer well-considered and well-crafted opinions about my choices as the executive director. However, I reserve the right to both respectfully disagree and to make all final decisions. And my decision has been made, and this is going to be our fall fundraising letter."

"Can we take out the 'Lord' line? Or change the word *Godspeed* to *sincerely*?" Can we at least do that, Zeke?"

"No. Absolutely not. A number of the humanists in the Midwest are rather devout. It will be refreshing to them to see a liberal academic invoking the Lord."

"But you're not religious," she says.

"Exactly!" I say.

Lara looks at me for a long time. Since I have been back in the office she seems to regard me with pity and panic. Apparently, the auditors have been hounding her for information during the summer while I was on personal leave. (We have a generous family leave policy at the organization, and I availed myself of it to care for the twins, and my mother, and to attend meetings with oncologists and surgeons and lawyers and such.) Lara is a little uncertain, I can see, thinking that perhaps I am not ready to be back at work. But that is precisely why I promoted her to associate director. She deserves to be compensated for the graceful and intelligent way she handled my long absence this summer. But I am back at work now, and I must be the leader.

"At least change a few things," Lara says.

"Lara," I say, "you are a warm and empathetic person, and you were moved by the letter, and I hope there are other warm and empathetic people out there on the mailing list who are also moved."

"Do you think that perhaps your intelligence has been crippled by grief?" she asks. "Could your understanding of human behavior be permanently altered by the tragedies your family has experienced?"

"Lara," I say, "I expect these to be sent to the printer and then to bulk mail, and that they will reach all twenty-five thousand, six hundred members on our mailing list. I want the reply envelopes to be green. I want to use recycled paper and soy-based ink. And those are, frankly, the only details you should worry about. I wrote the most honest letter I could write. I can do nothing else."

"You do know, Zeke, that this is a sinking ship. We'll be broke by Christmas. Have you been reading the newspapers? Do you know what is happening to the stock market?"

"I am a fundraiser, Lara, and well aware of the crisis plaguing our investment sector. I will raise the funds we need when we need them. Now, if you'll excuse me," I say, standing up and sliding on my brown twill blazer, "I'm going out for coffee."

This fall, my almost-sister-in-law, Harmony, has come from Michigan to help with the twins and to care for my mother so that I could return to work. Harmony is a real estate agent in Michigan, and there is no real estate to sell in Michigan right now. Or rather, there are no buyers and hence no sales. There is a glut of unwanted houses with upside-down mortgages on the market. So Harmony has some free time on her hands, and she arrived at the end of August, bringing with her a new and vibrant energy that my grief-stricken and tired household so desperately needed. She took April and May shopping for school supplies and new clothes. She took them to the zoo and the Wisconsin Dells and the science museum in Chicago, and then, when they went back to school, Harmony assumed the role of primary caregiver and housekeeper, and I returned to my office full-time.

A few days after she arrived in Wisconsin, Harmony and I met with my mother's lawyer, Phil Crawford, whom my mother met while working at the Old Country Buffet. Phil was a widower and lunched at the buffet each afternoon, which was across the street from his modest office suite, and he developed a friendship with my mother. I had my suspicions that their relationship might have included more than mere cordial friendship, but I did not ask, and I was grateful for Phil's compassionate guidance and his willingness to come over to the house for meetings. By the end of this summer, an outing as simple as a routine appointment at the University hospital, thirty minutes in duration, would be enough to send my mother to bed for two or three days. The exhaustion that came with staying alive inside a rebelling and failing body was taking its toll on her.

It was a simple estate, Phil Crawford assured us that afternoon at the backyard picnic table. My mother was sleeping, and Harmony had just gotten back from a run. I had just finished putting dinner in the oven, and so Phil and I and Harmony sat in the yard, while April and May played in a new playhouse I had bought them at Home Depot. It was a dazzling bright afternoon, and even with the humming static of the baby monitor (which we had placed in my mother's room in order to keep tabs on her needs), I could hear a stunning cacophony of birds in the scrappy box elder trees above us. I remember how lovely the day was, how lovely Harmony looked, perspiring in the sun, a glass of sweating iced tea resting on her stomach. I remember how happy the girls sounded inside their new playhouse, their laughter echoing off the plastic walls. I remember all of this because the news I was about to receive from Phil Crawford was so dark and unhappy in contrast to all the joy and beauty around me: all of my mother's possessions, the ones she had in her permanent residence (my house), were given to me. I could do with them whatever I wished. My mother's few financial assets—a savings account of four thousand thirteen dollars, a retirement account, a modest life insurance payout, et cetera—would be put toward her debts (she still had roughly fourteen thousand dollars in credit card debt) and then into a trust fund for the girls to be divided equally between them on their eighteenth birthdays. And finally, custody of April and May would go to Harmony and her husband, Malcolm, though I would be guaranteed liberal visitation rights and had the right to two weeks with the girls each summer, at my home or at a vacation destination of my choice.

Harmony began to cry at this news. She and Malcolm had been trying to have children for several years, and she did love her nieces. I didn't doubt that. It's just that, well, I have been a constant in the girls' lives for some time.

Didn't that count for something? I asked.

Phil Crawford supposed I could challenge the will in court, but he doubted that my mother's wishes would be overturned.

"Zeke," Harmony said, "Malcolm and I will be absolutely certain that you get to spend a great deal of time with your nieces. You can count on that!"

"When did my mother write this will?" I asked.

"Earlier in the year," Phil Crawford said. "When she first began to feel ill."

"I know it must be hard to accept that she picked me, Zeke. But I assure you those girls will have everything they could ever need or want. I assure you that you will be a huge part of their life, and that you will . . ."

Phil Crawford held up his hands. "Wait," he said. "It's a little more complicated than it sounds."

"I hope so," I said.

"Excuse me?" Harmony said.

"There is a caveat, Zeke," the lawyer said. "The will stipulates that if you are married at the time of your mother's death, or engaged to be married with plans to legally wed within one hundred twenty days of her death, you will be the legal guardian of April and May."

"That's in there?" Harmony asked.

"Yes," Phil Crawford said, "it is. It's not all that uncommon for people to add situational criteria to their estate plans. It's done all the time to prepare them for eventualities and whatnot. Your mother, Zeke, worried she might be unconscious or otherwise unable to change the will if your domestic situation changed before she died."

"So if he gets married, I get nothing?" Harmony asked.

"You'll be a huge part of their life, Harmony," I said. "I would grant you the same visitation rights and relationship that you would grant me."

"I'm not sure how much time your mother has," Phil Crawford said. "But Zeke, you're not even dating anybody, isn't that right? That's what your mother told me, just a few weeks ago."

"If he gets married," Harmony continued, "by Christmas, say, then he is the legal guardian?"

"Yes. That's right," Phil Crawford said. "If Violet is still alive when he gets married."

Both Harmony and Phil looked at me.

"Is there anybody?" Harmony asked. "You're not even dating anybody, am I right?"

"I have a few prospects," I said. "Actually, there is somebody I plan to propose to, as soon as possible. My mother's illness, of course, sort of delayed things."

"What if it's a sham marriage?" Harmony asked. "Then what?"

"The will specifies a legal marriage," Phil Crawford said, "which must last for at least three years or custody rights will revert back to

125

you, Harmony. Or at least you could contest them in a court of law. I suppose you could request that Zeke and his new bride sign an affidavit of sorts, affirming that they have a real marriage and that they plan to be married for a long time. I can add that language, if Violet agrees to it, to prevent a sham sort of situation."

Harmony sighed.

"He's a drunk!" she said. "He can't raise the girls alone!"

"A drunk?" I said.

"Zeke, here's what your mother told me," Phil Crawford said. "She worries about you raising the children alone. She thinks you are too introverted, too involved in your own intellectual pursuits to really raise a family, and, frankly, she also worries about your drinking, which she says is getting a bit, well, enthusiastic."

I sit there in stunned silence for a moment, staring at my hands. And then I look up at the lawyer, who, after a minute of no reaction, finally purses his lips, nods his head, and says, "I'm afraid that sums it up, Zeke. Your mother thought a woman, a good woman who loved children, would help you. You'd change."

"I see," I said.

"Zeke," Harmony said, "it's not in question whether or not you love these girls, or, frankly, whether or not they love you. They do. It's simply a matter of providing them some stability in a life that's been full of overwhelming sadness and chaos."

Harmony reaches over the table and squeezes my hand.

"Of course," I said. "Sure."

I asked Harmony to keep an eye on the roast in the oven that afternoon and went to the bookshop, beginning to weep in the middle of the new nonfiction display. Mack took me out back to the loading dock and made me a gin and tonic.

But that evening, despite the tension of the custody rights hanging in the air above us, Harmony and I were civil. We made dinner for the girls together—macaroni and cheese and pot roast—and then I sat in the bathroom with April and May while they took a bath. They sort of liked an audience in there, though I knew they would soon outgrow that preference. Still, it was the one time of the day when they seemed to open up to me, to ask me honest questions or offer me honest expressions of feeling. We often talked about Grandma in there, about the fact that this cancer was something she might not get better from. It was in the bath where they heard me tell stories of their late father and mother. Frankly, I had made up many of the stories, especially some heroic stories about Cougar, but if there is anything I have learned in my years as a public humanities scholar, it is that narratives, fiction or non, have a remarkable capacity to simulate feelings of actual relationships. The more stories we hear about the people who have passed away before us, the more we believe we are still in relationships with them. They seem less ghostly, a real and tangible presence.

Children, I have learned, have a remarkable intuition that is at once wholly credible and often baffling. As if they sensed the subtext in the air, that night April asked me where she and May would live once their grandmother died.

"Well, sweetie, we're trying to figure that out," I said.

"It think it will be fun to live with Aunt Harmony," April said.

"It probably will," I said.

"I think that's what we should do," May said. "You have work. And you're not even married. We'd rather go to Michigan."

I swallowed hard, of course, upon hearing this. It gave me some reassurance, I suppose, to know the girls would be wholly comfortable with the course of action their grandmother had prescribed for them. It also, of course, hurt like hell to hear that the notion of leaving me behind could be so easily digested by them.

That night, as I was finishing reading to them a rather uneventful book called *What Happens on Wednesday*, which they seem to love, perhaps because it is about the daily routines of an intact nuclear family, I had to resist the urge to cry. I kissed them both, and they kissed me, and I went into the hallway and down the stairs. Not five minutes later, April was standing in the living room and she said to me, "Uncle Zeke, the only reason May said all that stuff is because she heard what the lawyer said while we were in the playhouse. We were eavesdropping on you, and May said we should be really excited about moving to Michigan with Aunt Harmony so that you would feel better about it."

With that April turned and ran up the steps before she could see me burst into tears. I sat down on the couch and thought, Only seven!

And this is how the summer ended: with me learning that when I lost my mother, I would also lose the girls I had come to think of as my children—unless, of course, somehow, before all of this loss, I could gain a wife.

I have accepted Harmony's role in our changing family and I have accepted it well. This evening, after I come home from a day's work, pleased with the way my fundraising letter turned out but upset over Lara's obvious lack of confidence in my leadership, Harmony and I make dinner together and I chat idly about my job, to which Harmony says, "I still have no idea what you actually do."

Afterward, we wash dishes, bathe the girls, and tuck them in together. My mother has decided to sleep through dinner, though after we eat, I go into her room and wake her, making her take five sips of an Ensure chocolate shake.

By the time it's dark, the girls are asleep and my mother is asleep and Harmony and I go downstairs and we pack the girls' lunches for the next morning. A rhythm has already emerged in our temporary domestic partnership, and we end each evening with a cocktail before Harmony goes up to bed, and before I retire to my mother's room, where I will sit in her bedside chair and read. If she wakes up, as she often does around ten or eleven at night, I will bring her a cool drink and small snack, and I will stay up talking with her.

Tonight, however, it is a warm night for autumn, maybe one of

the last warm evenings of the year, and Harmony and I take our cocktails out to the porch, and Harmony decides we should bring out the
entire bottle of gin, the bottles of tonic, the limes, and the ice. She
arranges all of this artfully on a tray and we sit down in the darkness.

In the past few weeks, as the shock of my mother's decision has
sort of worn off, I have allowed myself to admit that Harmony has
always been a good aunt to the girls, having them to her house in
Michigan at least two times a year: two weeks in summer, two weeks
in January, and sometimes during Easter break as well. Harmony always flies out to Madison and escorts the twins back to the Detroit
airport and then flies them back home. She and Malcolm pay for
everything. The girls love their time there, and they love their aunt.
I am certain they will be well cared for and adored if they stay there
on a permanent basis.

"So work was good?" Harmony asks me.

"I think it was fine. Some days it's hard to focus, you know?"

"I bet," she says.

"Have you heard from Malcolm lately? How is he coping as a
born-again bachelor?"

"He's not big on the phone," she says. "He doesn't say much; he
just sort of says, 'That's interesting' over and over until we're done."

"That's interesting," I say.

Harmony laughs. "He is sort of a workaholic when I am away.
He just puts his head down and gets ahead at work."

"Makes sense. I was certainly much more of a workaholic when
I lived alone."

"Yeah, I can imagine. Your life has changed so much since everybody moved in, I bet. No more wild sex parties, for starters."

"No, true. Those are now held at the office. For the children's
sake."

Harmony smiles.

"I'm sorry it's working out this way. I do think it'll be fabulous
for me. For the girls. Malcolm is excited too."

"He is?"

"Well, no. He's sort of horrified and excited. But he was crushed when it turned out we couldn't have kids. We've been trying to adopt."

"Well, good," I say. "This will be so good for you."

"Who knows?" Harmony says. "Maybe we will be able to adopt. Maybe the girls will have a baby brother or sister to take care of."

I say, "How cool would that be?" though I am suppressing a torrent of envy. At that moment, I admit I am thinking, Not so fast, sister. Old Zeke might yet find a wife before it's too late.

Harmony sighs into the cooling evening and stands to make us two more drinks. She is a beautiful woman, a spitting image of her dead twin sister, Melody, but thirty pounds lighter, with better hair and skin. We have been through an emotional storm together these last few weeks, as my mother's decline grows more obvious and rapid. We've been absolutely exhausted by grief. For Harmony, I suppose the exhausting part has been shepherding our nieces through that grief. All of the memories of dead siblings haunted us that summer, and we were emotionally and physically spent. Tonight, as she sits out on the porch in low-waisted jeans and a long-sleeved shirt that shows off her flat stomach and her navel accentuated by a small diamond stud, our conversational intimacy and her obvious attractiveness give rise to what I admit is more than minor lust in my heart. I feel almost impossibly close to her. I know it is no time for lust, but men are never able to avoid it, I suppose, especially when they are emotionally vulnerable.

I also know that lust makes men say some terribly dumb things, which is exactly what I do this evening, though later it will become clear that perhaps it is not so dumb.

"Are you happy with Malcolm?" I ask, sometime in the middle of my third gin and tonic, or, as Mack would say, at some point when I am "deep in my cups." In my opinion, Malcolm is sort of a bore, and I recall Cougar disliking him immensely. He is older than Harmony by twelve years, a physics professor at a community college, pudgy and unkempt and, based on my limited experience, fairly dismissive of women.

"What?" she asks.

"Are you happy with your life in Michigan?"

"With Malcolm?"

"With Malcolm, with everything."

"What are you getting at, Zeke?"

"You could leave him. You could leave him and marry me, for the girls' sake. We could have a family of sorts, a reconstructed sort of nuclear family for them. Right here, in Wisconsin."

"Zeke!" Harmony says, and she twists her face into an expression that comes close to sorrow, and then, suddenly, her mouth twists itself again into a vast, white-toothed smile. I am not sure if she thinks I am kidding, a joke in bawdy poor taste, or if she is slyly pretending to consider my offer. "You're so twisted," she says.

She was intending to laugh it off.

"You're thinking about it!"

"No!" she says. "Not at all. Zeke, I'm married to Malcolm. I love him."

"No doubts?"

"Not at all," she says.

We sit in silence for a while. And then she reaches over and holds my hand for a moment, so that our joined hands are dangling in the air between us, between our red Adirondack chairs.

"You love them so much," she says. "Don't you?"

"I do," I say.

"I think it's hard for other people to see," she says, "but you're a good man. You're an exceedingly good man."

I am so moved by everything: her hand in mine, the onset of autumn, the lovely sweep of her short blond hair tucked carelessly behind her delicate ears. The slope of her calf, the swell of her breasts beneath her shirt. I begin to weep. One might, on looking back at, say, a hidden camera recording of the evening, protest and declare that my tears were forced and artificial. But they are real, those tears; I am genuinely moved by her and what she said. She kisses me on the cheek, and she goes up to bed. I check on my mother, sleeping a rattly and phlegmy sleep, and then go into my room.

And I guess Harmony's tears, well, her tears are real too, that night when she comes into my bedroom, locks the door behind her, undresses before me, and climbs into my bed. We move in absolute silence, all breaths and buried moans. I can feel her tears on my chest and she puts her face there when she climaxes.

Afterward, I flip the bedside lamp on and off a few times and she says, "Zeke? Is this crazy? I just wanted to comfort you."

"I want to comfort you too," I say.

"You did," she says, a smile taking over her face.

The next morning, I wake early, hoping, before the cold glare of dawn makes things seem real, that she will do it again. But she is already out of bed, and I put on my sweatpants and a T-shirt and go downstairs and find that everybody is awake and pancakes sizzle on the stove.

"Good morning," I say, to April and May, who are sitting on either side of my mother at the dining room table. My mother is in her robe and it looks as if Harmony has brushed her hair. April and May seem happy about this, and the trio returns my good morning.

"You look good, Ma," I say, but I don't quite mean it and she smirks in a way that tells me she knows I don't mean it. What one should say, what one means to say in this situation, is "Hey! You look like you're still alive!"

I excuse myself from the dining room. "I'm going to go and help your aunt cook breakfast," I say.

In the kitchen, I come up behind Harmony at the stove, pressing into her just enough to suggest that I enjoyed our night. She whips around, spatula pointed menacingly at my midsection.

"Please, don't ever mention this again," she says. "It's as if the rules were suspended for a night. It's as if all of the chaos, all of that tragedy, just sort of suspended reality for a while, okay? I think that's all that happened. We needed something."

"You think?" I say.

"It has to be this way, Zeke," she says.

I am impressed that her voice is even and her eyes are dry. She seems to have made a very intellectual choice the night before and has assessed it with the clear eyes of a historian the morning after.

"Fine," I say, brushing too close to her once again as I move toward the sink. Her hand touches my shoulder, a faint squeeze. As I go into the dining room, I play Van Morrison's "Comfort You" on my iPod dock, loudly. The twins complain. They don't care for the music. They want to talk to their grandmother. I turn off the music and sit down to breakfast, gorging myself on pancakes and sausage. I try and say goodbye to my mother after we eat, but she is asleep on the couch by the time we clear the dishes.

Just as I am ready to usher the girls into the Honda so I can drop them off at school before I head to work, Harmony comes out of the kitchen, hands the girls their lunch, kisses them, and then watches them as they go out into the yard.

Harmony looks over at my sleeping mother and then looks at me.

"You understand why we can never admit that happened," Harmony says. "Don't you?"

"Yes," I say. "And you understand that I may very well get married before my mother dies. Don't you?"

Harmony is good at many things, as I have learned the night before, but she makes weak coffee, and hence, once the girls are at school, I go straight to Starbucks. I want to see Minn behind the counter, and for the first time in days I am not thinking about Harmony or the girls or my dying mother. It's odd: when a loved one is going through the horrors of terminal cancer, anybody who has no connection to your world of illness and oncology and imminent death seems incredibly vibrant and witty and beautiful. Though in Minn's case, I remember, I always considered her to be all of those things.

She's not there.

This summer, caught up in childcare and medical appointments and the logistics of household management and the looming reality of death, I rarely went to Starbucks. If I did go, it was often late in the evening. Minn was never there. At one point, I inquired after her and a suspicious, goateed barista informed me that she was on a long vacation. I nodded and didn't tip my customary eighty-three cents.

When I walk into the Starbucks today, a man back at work, a man with a mission to marry somebody worthy and lovely and capable of motherhood in the next few months, I can feel the air in my soles, as if I am about to begin floating a bit above everything.

It is my favorite time of day at Starbucks, the midmorning, when the rush and mess of the before-work crowd have been tidied away, the after-lunch to-go crowd has not yet arrived, and the new slants of midmorning light give the windows a warm glow. A few students type away on laptops, a retiree reads a spy novel in a large armchair, and a familiar-looking white-haired man in a suit seems to be awaiting somebody at a corner table. The music is appropriate for autumn, yellow and grim—a female folk singer whose work I am unfamiliar with is singing about a move to Brooklyn. The man in the suit nods at me. I nod back. In a Walgreens or McDonald's, such a nod would never be exchanged, but in a Starbucks, such nodding makes perfect sense. This is community space, and I am glad to be part of it, though I'm unsettled by the sudden inkling that the man in the suit might be waiting for me. He begins to write, in tiny script, on the legal pad before him.

It does not take me long to confirm that Minn is not at the counter. I look at my watch. She should be present. I casually order my beverage from Wallace, the fellow with the horn-rimmed glasses and a brush cut, and as I am adding a splash of cream to my Americano, I ask, casually, as if I don't care (one must be careful not to appear creepy when one has a major crush on a service industry professional): "Where's Minn?"

"She transferred to another store," Wallace says.

"She did," I say. "Really? I thought she liked this store."

"She's managing the second shift at the Starbucks on the west side."

"Oh, right. Which one is that again?"

"In Fitchburg," Wallace says. "Highway PD."

"Right," I say. "That's a shame. She was very nice."

Wallace nods, as if he is afraid to commit to any more banter. His eyes shift to the person who has just come into the store, a young woman dressed in track pants and a tank top. I predict the drink in my head—nonfat latte with sugar-free vanilla syrup—and bingo, I am right. At the last minute, I predict, she will also order a cookie to go. Right again.

13

Zeke Pappas is unjustly accosted.

I GET BACK to the office with my still-steaming beverage. (Wallace cannot make a decent Americano to save his life—they're always too hot and without enough room for cream.) Two men in suits are waiting outside on the concrete steps. They rise when they see me coming toward them, my key already pointed at the door. One of them is very tall with blond hair cut in a style that used to be known as the Princeton. The other is shorter, squarer, with black wavy hair combed back on his head. They are both about forty-five years of age, both fit and tan.

"You must be Zeke Pappas," the tall man says.

"I am," I say.

"Can we ask you a few questions?" the other says. "I'm Josh Farnsworth and this is Temple Morris, and we're with the Department of Departmental Compliance and Oversight in Washington, DC. We spoke briefly, on the phone."

The men each hand me business cards that back up their claims.

"I've never heard of such a department," I say.

"We're housed in the Department of Homeland Security," Farnsworth says. "I trust you've heard of *that* department."

I nod. Just the mention of that chilling wing created by the Bush administration is enough to silence me.

"It's all pretty new," Morris says. "Sarbanes-Oxley, reform-driven kind of stuff. Fallout from all of the big scandals, the collapse of Wall Street. We're swiftly implementing new powers of oversight. Protecting the taxpayers."

"We just try and keep everybody honest," Farnsworth says, "at the domestic level, at least."

"Well, can that be done?" I ask.

"What?" Farnsworth asks. He is typing something in a handheld wireless device and doesn't look up.

"Well, isn't honesty something you have or you don't have? I mean can you *keep* people honest? Aren't some people genuinely dishonest?"

"Can we go inside your office?" Farnsworth asks.

"Sure," I say.

"It's unlocked," Morris says.

"Oh?" I say. "You've met Lara then. Good. I trust she offered you coffee or water?"

"We've spoken to Lara a lot over the summer," Morris says. "But she wasn't here this morning. We had a key made. Lara had it made."

"We're sorry to hear about your mother," Farnsworth says. "How is she doing?"

I nod. "Thank you," I say. "She is okay."

It seems odd that these men would have any knowledge of my personal life, and equally odd that they should have a key to our building, but it is possible, I suppose, that some federal regulation required us to give a building key to the Department of Departmental Compliance and Oversight. I find complying with federal regulations tiresome and it is Lara's responsibility to handle such things.

When we go into the office, two men and three women in business suits are going through files in the conference room.

"Auditors," Morris says. My face must look a bit baffled, because he is quick to add: "Nothing to worry about."

"I was under the impression the audit was almost through," I say. "I thought Lara had finished all of this business while I was away."

"I'm sure you run a tight ship, Mr. Pappas," Farnsworth says. "We're just double-checking a few things."

"Inconsistencies," Morris says.

I nod. I wish Lara were here, so she could advise me as to whether or not this sort of appointment had been a scheduled part of the audit. We go to my office and I take a seat behind my desk while Farnsworth and Morris sit in the only other chairs in the room, the ones in the corner by a small end table, arranged as if they were waiting for two old chums to sit down for tea together.

"Do you need a warrant of some sort?" I ask.

They chuckle. "It's not a criminal investigation, Mr. Pappas," Farnsworth says.

"Of course not," I say. "It just feels a bit unsettling."

"So tell me, Mr. Pappas, about the way the GMHI awards grants," Morris says.

I begin to give the usual answers. "We work with certain individuals and organizations to assess the cultural and social needs of the region, and then we ascertain—as best we can—how public humanities programming can meet those needs."

"And do you choose the grant recipients?" Morris asks.

"No. Not technically. The board of directors does that, in theory. Though, I suppose, they give me a great deal of latitude. They really listen to my input on matters dealing with mission, vision, and scope. Those kinds of things."

Morris nods.

"How do you let the general public know about available funds?" Morris asks.

I begin the litany of press releases and online marketing activities that our former marketing director, Jennifer Holbein, used to do before I laid her off.

"Now I handle a lot of that myself, sort of on a smaller scale," I explain. "There are not enough funds to give away anymore. We're in a redevelopment of sorts. A reinvention."

There are more questions about staffing, budgets, that kind of thing. One of the auditors—a woman of Asian descent—comes in and hands Farnsworth three files from our grants database. Farnsworth asks me to tell him a little bit about each project. Thankfully, they are three GMHI-funded projects I remember fairly well and not one of them was controversial by any means: a rock-and-roll history program in Detroit, a conference on Northern Ireland in Milwaukee, and a symposium, hosted at Illinois Wesleyan University, on the image of the prairie in American literary and artistic work. Morris makes very few notes as I am explaining the reasons why such projects were funded.

"You've also funded," Farnsworth says, "a project on the socialist movement in Milwaukee, yes?"

"Yes, it was a very important part of Milwaukee's history," I say. "The only major American city to ever elect a socialist mayor."

"Grant 88-009-2006: *Urban Utopias Reconsidered: What Almost Was and What Still May Be in Marxist Milwaukee*," Farnsworth says.

"Yes," I say. "That was it."

The truth is that I am only a little unsettled by this revelation. A little political controversy may be good for the organization if we can arouse the sympathies of the same rich leftists who donate to the ACLU and Amnesty International.

"And Bill Ayers once appeared at the Book Festival, did he not?"

"I believe so," I say. "We've hosted hundreds of authors over the past decade."

"I'm sure you have," Farnsworth says.

"Next year we'll be having a new signature event. The Festival of Midwestern Unhappiness."

"Nice," Farnsworth says. "Sounds like a blast."

"Zeke," Morris says, "if I may? Our job is to be sure that federal funds are not used for political advocacy."

"Of course. Would you gentlemen like some coffee?" I ask. "You sure?"

They both shake their heads no. I have finished most of my mediocre Americano by now, burning my tongue in the process, and I'm now feeling the fine flutter of three shots of espresso hitting my bloodstream. My right eyebrow is pulsing.

Morris writes something down in his notebook while Farnsworth gets up and peruses the books on my shelf.

"Could you tell me a little something about the sign on your door? *The Inventory of American Unhappiness?*"

"Oh, that's just a sort of thing I run."

"From the office?" Farnsworth asks.

"And with the board's full approval and backing," I say. "We examine our nation's swelling, collective unhappiness through the prism of individual woes and disappointments."

"Do you think the nation is that unhappy?" Farnsworth mutters, without looking up from the book he is perusing, Nicholas Delbanco's *The Martlet's Tale.*

"That's a rather rare book," I say. "It's signed, by the author, or else I'd let you borrow it. Have you read it?"

"Could you answer my question, Mr. Pappas? Do you think that the nation is unhappy?"

"Well, I am compiling all my research—our research—into something I, we, call *An Inventory of American Unhappiness.*"

"What's that?" Morris asks.

"It's an oral history and documentary project that examines the diverse histories of a generation in an attempt to find commonalities among our individual fears, eccentricities, obsessions, and dissatisfactions. It does so in the belief that such exploration is essential to a thriving democracy and a healthy human community."

"Fascinating," Farnsworth says. "Do you keep separate books for that?"

"Did you ask Lara?" I say. "She really is the puppet master around here. Makes the trains run on time, and so on."

"And the public response," Morris says. "How is it?"

"Well, as with any new program, we have our detractors. But I do think it's an adequate, if not innovative, public humanities project and that is what I am paid to produce."

"You think it's innovative?" Farnsworth says.

"Funds are limited," I say. "It's a low-cost project that involves many citizens and hopes to illuminate something about our collective history and our civic future."

"I see that you're a natural fundraiser," Morris says.

I nod. "Thank you."

"We were spot-checking your travel records. Your chair, Mr. Logan: it looks as if he spent eight hundred dollars on the GMHI credit card at a male strip club in northern Virginia," Morris says. He slides a yellow credit card slip over to me. "That credit card, as far as we can tell, is paid with federal funds."

"That may be," I say. "But, I assure you, H. M., Mr. Logan, always reimburses us for his travel expenses. He is our largest donor. So technically that is not an expenditure of federal funds."

I examine the credit slip.

"The Bus Stop?" I say.

"We checked it out," Morris says. "A gay strip club."

"Oh, I see."

"Don't you check your staff and board travel?" he says.

"I skim them. We're all trustworthy here. Lara handles reimbursement. She makes sure that Mr. Logan covers all of his personal expenses."

"That's fine," Morris says. "I would suggest that he find another way to cover up his extracurricular activities, however. For his sake, if nothing else."

"We've been trying to reach him," Farnsworth says.

"Mr. Logan gave us one hundred fifty thousand dollars last year! Certainly we can look into this matter without costing him his privacy or dignity, I hope."

"We've already made copies of the receipts," Morris says. "By the way, your machine is low on toner. Anyway, we'll ask Mr. Logan when we catch up with him."

"Ask him what?" I say.

"To keep his personal expenses personal," Farnsworth says. "Even if he does pay the organization back."

"Many times over," I say.

"Your brother was a vet?" Morris says. "Lara mentioned he died in Operation Iraqi Freedom."

"That's right."

"I was in the first Gulf War," Morris says. "The 'easy' one. Though it wasn't easy for those of us who were there, let me tell you something."

"What was your brother's name?" Farnsworth says.

"Jeremiah Pappas. We called him Cougar."

"What did he think of your work?" Farnsworth says.

"I don't see how that matters. Frankly, I doubt that he knew anything about my work at all. We didn't talk much while he was at war. We e-mailed, sometimes. But we basically wrote about our mother, the Packers, that sort of thing. He was a good man. But did he understand me? My work? No. No, I don't think so."

"Don't you think he would have hated your work?" Farnsworth says. "Frankly, me, I'm just curious. It's a personal question. Off the record? How did an American soldier, serving in Iraq, feel about your work? And that's a term—*work*—that I am using very loosely."

"No, I'm sorry," I say. "But I *do* have *work* to do and I don't see how this process is illuminating anything about the operations of the

Great Midwestern Humanities Initiative, which, by the way, have always been remarkably transparent and well documented."

"Doesn't it occur to you that your project might be responsible for unhappiness?" Farnsworth says. "Isn't art supposed to be uplifting?"

"Well, these are the humanities. There's a major difference between the arts and the humanities," I say. "Maybe art is uplifting. But, no, I don't think that art is *supposed* to be anything, do you? And the humanities are certainly not uplifting. They are the study of humankind's narrative—its tragedies and trials and sorrows and hurts and woes and continually broken spirit—how could that possibly be uplifting? They are, in an intellectual and spiritual way, however, exhilarating."

"Farnsworth," Morris says, "cool it."

"I just feel," Farnsworth says, "that you have an obligation to spend federal tax dollars in a way that celebrates rather than cynicizes."

"Seriously," Morris says. "You're an auditor. You're not allowed to have feelings."

"Did you say *cynicizes*?" I ask.

"One more question we have to ask," Morris says. "Have you ever associated with known terrorists? Have you ever knowingly diverted federal tax dollars to organizations that support foreign terrorists?"

"Do I need a lawyer?" I ask. "I think I need a lawyer."

"It's just a routine question," Farnsworth says. "We ask that of everybody, post–Patriot Act."

"They ask that when you open a checking account at the bank," Morris says. "Strictly routine."

"So just answer: have you?" Farnsworth says.

"Certainly not," I say. "I loathe fundamentalism of any sort."

"Very well," Morris says.

"Okey-dokey," Farnsworth says.

Farnsworth and Morris walk out the door to my office and I follow them. Morris knocks once on the open door to the conference room, and as soon as his knuckles hit the wood, the five auditors leap to their feet and walk out the door behind them, leaving a pile of shuffled manila folders and large stacks of grant applications littering the table and floor of the conference room.

14

Zeke Pappas is baffled but unbowed.

I AM FLUSTERED when Farnsworth and Morris and their squad of silent auditors leave the GMHI offices. I can't sit still. I go to Lara's desk and stand there for a moment, as if I can will her there. What does she know about this? Has she just let me be blind-sided by a team of aggressive federal bureaucrats? Why? Perhaps I have been too nonchalant about this whole process. Why didn't she warn me how serious and thorough and militaristic the auditors actually were?

I lock the door to the office (what good does that do?) and head across the campus toward State Street, walking rather frantically, unable, even, to take my time to enjoy the sights of the coeds who are donning, for the first time in months, their autumnal attire: tight dark denims, wool skirts, and tall boots, all of them looking regal and sophisticated and bright.

I have one friend who is more paranoid than I am when it comes to the federal government, and I need to ask him if he has ever heard of the Department of Departmental Compliance and Accountability.

When I get to the Pilgrim's Pages bookshop, Joseph is behind

the counter, working. The store is largely empty, though a few customers linger over iced coffee in the adjoining café. I recognize the
gray-suited man from Starbucks, who apparently is spending the afternoon moving from downtown café to downtown café.

I head straight to the counter.

"Hey, have you ever heard of the Department of Departmental
Compliance and Accountability?" I say.

Joseph appears to be absolutely taken aback. He doesn't say anything.

"I don't know what you are talking about," he says finally.

"Joseph, do you know anything about this new office of the executive branch?"

"I'm sorry. I'm not sure I know what you are talking about, sir."

"You don't know?" I say.

"I'm afraid I don't; I mean, I've seen you in here before but—"

"You mean you don't know me? Is that what you're saying?"

"I'm afraid so."

"You don't know me?"

Joseph glares for a second.

"Yes," I say. "You do."

"Sir, I really am going to have to ask you to leave in your condition. You're obviously very drunk," Joseph says loudly.

Now I whisper very quietly. "I know everything about you! I
know you drink gin and tonics all summer, but you switch to single-
malt Scotch when the first frost hits. I know your favorite musical
composer of all time is Gorecki and that you listen to his *Symphony
of Sorrowful Songs* once a day, and I know your eighty-two-year-old
father owns a chain of beauty parlors in Florida."

Joseph narrows his eyes and sort of points with his chin toward
the café at the gray-suited man who is now looking down and reading a mass-market paperback. It is most definitely the same man I
saw at Starbucks that morning with the yellow legal pad set before
him: white hair, a strong jaw, red tie with a gray suit. He has large

dark circles under his eyes, puffy bags of stress and sleeplessness. The only other man in the bookstore is a man in a suit browsing the staff picks, hiding his face in a copy of Simon Schama's *Landscape and Memory*. This, I can tell from the Brooks Brothers shirt and suspenders, is Mack Fences, and when I ask Joseph, "Hey, is that Mack?" Mack sets down the book, carelessly corrupting an end-cap display, and runs, literally runs, from the store.

I stare at Joseph for a moment. His face is blank.

"Sir?" he says, and suddenly I understand.

"Oh, I'm sorry," I say rather loudly now. "I had asked a staff member from the bookstore a question about an out-of-print title last week. I must have you confused with somebody else."

"Yes, maybe Rory?"

"That's it!" I say. "Rory!"

"That's okay, sir. What was your name again?"

"It's Pappas. Zeke Pappas."

"Oh," Joseph says. "Yes. I just called you some time ago. Your special order is in. Let me get it."

I do not recall ordering a book recently, but perhaps it is an old order that has finally come into the store. Occasionally my special orders are difficult for the staff to obtain.

Joseph reaches down to the shelf behind him and pulls out a copy of *The Divine Secrets of the Ya-Ya Sisterhood* by Rebecca Wells.

I certainly did not order that!

I look at him and he nods, gravely. The grave nod is a gesture any serious man must master, and Joseph has mastered it to the point that I trust him implicitly when he offers it to me and I know that someone, most likely me, is in a great deal of trouble. Incomprehensible trouble, yes, but trouble nonetheless.

"It looks like it's been prepaid," Joseph says.

"Yes," I say. "I believe it was."

Joseph slips the book into a brown paper bag and hands it to me.

I walk around the corner and head straight for the office. It is almost three thirty when I return to the office, and still no sign of Lara. It appears as if she has taken the day off without notice. If she doesn't arrive the next morning, if the mini-storm about my fall fundraising letter does not blow over on its own, I will call her and apologize and beg her to come to work. But for now, I am exhausted. She wins; I can't imagine her taking a day off when auditors are coming, unless she had an emotionally or physically dire reason! Perhaps she left me a message. I haven't checked voice mail for hours.

I go into my office and pull the copy of *The Divine Secrets of the Ya-Ya Sisterhood* from the brown paper bag and open the book. I look at the first page, and then, on the title page, I see these words:

THEY WANT TO KNOW ABOUT THE SORTS OF BOOKS YOU BUY. THEY WANTED ALL OF YOUR SPECIAL ORDER REQUESTS FROM THE PAST EIGHT YEARS. WHAT HAS HAPPENED? WHAT DID YOU DO?

Then, although there are a number of quick actions I could and should take—call Lara, call a lawyer, call our bulk mail service and have them send out the fundraising letter as is, I begin reading the *Divine Secrets*. It is a surprisingly pleasant book to read and I wish that I could do nothing else but read it for the rest of the afternoon. I wish I could read until the daunting feeling of unavoidable trouble leaves my emotional horizon.

When I get home from the office that evening, Harmony is quiet and efficient with supper. We eat burgers and potato salad, and she eats alone at the kitchen counter. My mother gets up briefly and drinks water and pretends to eat, but I can see she has no appetite. The girls crowd her, wanting closeness.

"Well, how was work today, Zeke?" my mother says, a wheezy whisper.

"It was rather interesting actually," I say. "It turns out I'm involved in a pretty thorough review process."

"What's that?" May asks.

I chew on my burger. "Well, it's like I'm cleaning my room and then somebody comes in and checks on it. Makes sure I did a good job."

"Why?" April says.

"Because the IRS had nothing better to do than harass a hard-working taxpayer," my mother says. In the brief hours each day that she is awake, she still watches Fox News, which seems like a horrendous waste of one's final months on earth.

"Who's the IRS?" April asks.

"It's actually not the IRS," I say. "A new program. Homeland Security."

My mother nods. "Well, at least they don't take our money," she says.

"Oh, they find a way to get it, Mother."

I am wondering if my mother is going to muster the strength for a political argument this evening. Frankly, even if she is capable of doing so, I feel exhausted.

Harmony comes in with my mother's pills. "Take these, Violet, and then I'll help you get dressed."

"We're going to the mall!" April and May shout together.

"Grandma rides in a wheelchair there!" May says.

"We take turns pushing," April says.

"It's a big show," my mother says.

"Do you want to come, Zeke?" Harmony asks.

"I don't like malls," I say. "You know that."

"A simple 'no' would suffice," Harmony says.

"Why don't you like malls, Uncle Zeke?" May asks.

"He's too good for them," my mother says, standing from the table with great straining. "But it's all some of us have."

"I'm going out for coffee," I say.

"Why can't you have coffee at the mall?" May asks.

"I'm meeting somebody," I say. "A very lovely woman."

My mother, inching off to the downstairs bathroom, stops in mid-shuffle. "A date?"

"Yes," I say.

I look at Harmony when I say it, but then the girls remind me I have promised to tell them a brand-new Lizard Leopold story.

"I'll meet you back here at bedtime," I say.

"Not if you're on a date," my mother says. "I can tell them a story, Zeke!"

"A Lizard Leopold one!" April shouts.

Lizard Leopold is a character I've created for them, and he's named after the great naturalist Aldo Leopold. Lizard Leopold often finds himself in high-stakes conundrums exacerbated by ecological recklessness on the part of humankind.

It occurs to me that in a few months, my Lizard Leopold stories may be told over the phone rather than cuddling in bed with my two little chickens. Perhaps a webcam chat would work. I could tell the bedtime stories over the Internet. But then, but then, I will miss their breaths slowing down as I read, their humming subsiding as they drift to sleep. I will miss the feel of pulling the blanket over them, covering the down on their warm and soap-scented forearms.

"Okay," I say. "If I'm not back by bedtime, girls, Grandma will do a Lizard Leopold story. You can have your stories downstairs here, in the adjustable bed."

The girls seem satisfied with this arrangement and Harmony begins to find everybody's jackets. My mother winks at me and continues her shuffle.

"Have fun," she manages to say, before she is wracked by coughs.

I head out to the bus stop.

My stresses at work, though possibly significant and urgent, still must take a back seat, I remind myself, to the simpler mission that's before me: marry somebody, in accordance with my mother's last will and testament.

In the blue light of the bus, on this, the first crisp and frosty evening of the autumn, all of the passengers look to me as if they are trapped in some giant, mobile freezer. They wear winter caps and thick coats for the first time in months, and their expressions are frozen and devoid of smiles, a motley crew of grimaces, pensive looks, and dour, soured expressions. Just a week ago they went coatless, bare-midriffed, sandaled. Now, this, the siege of winter already hinting at its arrival. It makes me feel as if we're awaiting somebody's death in that bus and I am thrilled to get off when my stop finally arrives.

I am in Fitchburg, one of Madison's sprawling suburbs. I walk to the green Starbucks sign glowing in the fading light.

Minn is there. She looks like an icon against the bronze and brown of the tile that lines the wall behind the Starbucks counter, a saint done in mosaic; behind her the lighted menu shines on the ends of her pulled-back hair.

"Zeke! What a surprise!"

"Well, I found you. I went to the Starbucks on the Square today and you weren't there."

"Oh," she says, almost with a hint of remorse in her voice.

"Um, well, how are you doing?" I say.

"Great. I was traveling some, and then I switched stores. How are you?"

"Well, my mother is ill. Terminally so. I haven't worked much."

"I'm sorry to hear that."

"Thank you."

"And here you are now, all the way in Fitchburg? I didn't peg you for a Fitchburg guy. Do you live near here?"

Two customers have come in behind me, so I step aside so that Minn can take their orders. In my head, I guess: yerba maté latte for the thin one, vanilla bean Frappucino for the stout one. I am correct. It is an easy one. Once they have their beverages, I say, "No."

"No? No what?"

"I don't live near here," I say.

"Oh, so what are you doing over here then?"

"Looking for you," I say, knowing that this will either sound creepy or sweet.

A smile, even the slight hint of a blush, colors Minn's cheeks. "I see," she says.

Now I have no idea what to say.

"I went back to work recently. And you have not been there when I go for my coffee breaks."

"And how did you know I was here in Fitchburg?"

"Starbucks intuition," I say. "My sixth sense."

"Seriously?" Minn says, still smiling as if she couldn't stop smiling if she tried.

"Yes, and Wallace told me you'd been moved."

She laughs and the can lights above her twinkle in the blue irises of her eyes.

Two customers enter the shop, holding hands. This strikes me as a poignant and weighty image but Minn doesn't seem to notice it on that level. Just two customers to her. But before I step aside for them, I make a guess, whispering it to Minn. *Doppio macchiato for the man, skinny latte for the lady.*

And I'm one hundred percent correct!

Minn tries to act normal in front of the customers, but first she gives me a dazzled look, her eyes wide, a smile breaking out.

I stand off to the side of the counter and peruse the *New York Times* while Minn makes the drinks. She seems calm in my presence, not at all creeped out by the fact that I had found her at this new Starbucks.

When she has dispatched the customers, happily, I watch her wipe down a counter for a minute. I can't think of what to say next.

She speaks. "So, yeah, I would have liked to stay downtown. But they needed a supervisor here. It was a big raise. This is an underper-forming store."

"Of course," I say.

A man comes in wearing a yellow ball cap.

"Double-cap, low foam," I whisper.

Minn smiles and looks at the man, waiting. He looks up at the menu board.

"Double-cap, low foam," he says. "And a chocolate chip cookie, to go."

Minn makes the drink and packages up the cookie while I look at the CDs. She seems impressed, and she opens her mouth wide when the yellow-capped man walks out into the evening.

"Holy shit," she says, laughing.

"I missed the cookie," I say.

Then she lowers her voice. A white-haired man is typing away on a laptop, glowering in the corner. I stare at the man and he returns to his busy typing. He looks familiar, as if he could be the man from the bookstore. Or he could just be a random old man desperately trying to finish his memoir before his first stroke. It's hard to know, and either way, I don't care. I'm here to see Minn, Farnsworth and Morris and the federal auditors be damned.

"Seriously, how do you do that?" Minn says.

"Intuition. I'm never wrong," I say.

"Well, I'm glad you're here. You're a special customer."

"Am I?"

"Nobody else can guess drinks like you can. I'm so glad you came into my new store."

"I'm not sure if I am correctly guessing the customers' desire," I say, "or if, in the act of guessing, I subconsciously suggest to them what they would like to order."

"Either way," she says. "Fucking-ay."

It is an expression of hers I find most likable, just the right blend of the vulgar and the folksy.

The next customer comes in and poses a rather difficult dilemma: he is a tall, thin man with gray hair and white skin, a little on the emaciated side, which could mean one of two things—either he is a vegan who does yoga and takes frequent walks, or he is a wired workaholic who subsists almost entirely on caffeinated beverages and cigarettes and never goes outside.

I guess the former and whisper my guess: decaffeinated soy latte.

"Wow!" Minn says when the man orders exactly as I had predicted.

"Pardon?" the man says.

"Oh, nothing," Minn says.

Another lull in the evening's business, and I lean into the counter again.

"Do you have a minute today?" I say. "I want to ask you something."

But the window just sits there, open, letting in flies, and Minn does not go through it. So I start talking again, not ready to order my beverage and let the conversation end.

"So did you ask for a transfer?" I ask.

"I didn't ask for a transfer," Minn says. "They kind of made me transfer."

"Wallace told me you asked for a transfer."

"That's what they made me tell people," she whispers. "They don't like word to get out about *underperformers*." She has a great voice for whispering. Damn. "But it was a no-brainer, really. It was a big raise."

"Good," I say.

Minn leans in close over the counter and whispers, "Four extra bucks an hour, provided I start eee-fucking-mediately, and that's why I took it. I need that money. That's a huge raise."

"That is," I say.

"Are you okay?" she says.

This is the sort of question that can shift the relationship from one of service worker and customer to one of true friendship. I pause, grateful to have been asked, weighing the best response, and then I say, simply, "I'm a bit troubled."

"Umm," she says, a sort of low moan of concern, vaguely sexual in nature. "Look, I have a break in"—she looks up at the clock behind her—"sixteen minutes. Do you want to grab a bite with me? We can go to the Noodles next door."

"That would be lovely," I say, my heart twittering. "I'll go and get us a seat."

The restaurant is not full. Two families dine nearby, the parents looking exhausted in their now-rumpled business attire, the children hopped up on the unlimited refills of corn syrup–laden sodas and the rush of carbohydrates. In addition to the families, there are several single, solitary diners, all of them in their mid-thirties, all of them wearing nice but uninspired business attire. They are reading free newspapers and fiddling with BlackBerries and cell phones, eating from large white bowls that look vaguely Asian in their design, but undoubtedly American in their girth and depth. These are the sales reps away from home, killing time before they retire to their nonsmoking rooms at the Country Inn & Suites. These are the single software engineers who have worked too late again, who have not gone grocery shopping in weeks, and who simply want to eat something dense and heavy that will help them fall asleep on the couch moments after getting in the door of their drab apartments with the new carpet. These are the recently divorced marketing specialists and law clerks, still not used to living in solitude and silence, longing for more social engagements—book clubs, Ultimate Frisbee leagues, open mike nights—to fill their barren evenings. This is the collective pulse of unhappy America, right there in the Noodles at six forty-eight in suburban Madison, Wisconsin. These are the people that I don't want to become. Oh, I think they have beautiful souls, all of that aimless yearning, all of that buried itch—but I know that is where I am headed; if I am not married in time, my own canvas will be a vast tableau of loneliness and banality, and I am terrified.

Minn has just walked into the restaurant and is looking from single diner to single diner until her eyes stop on me. She smiles.

We have to eat fast. She does not have a great deal of time and, in fact, has called an order in ahead so that it would be ready. She has taken the liberty of ordering for me—a giant bowl of macaroni and cheese—and she has ordered some whole-wheat Mediterranean pasta for herself.

The food is brought to our table by a slender young girl in a visor and knit shirt, and then Minn looks over the whole ensemble, which I admit looks quite pleasing, and she says, "I'm so sick of eating here. Fucking-ay."

"You come here often?" I ask.

"My apartment is just across the street."

"Then this transfer is a convenient one?"

"Well, yes. But I like to work downtown. I would live downtown if I could afford it, but I can't. So I like to at least work there."

"But you also ate at Noodles downtown," I said.

"I'm in a rut," she says.

"We all are," I say, "after the last eight years."

"I know, right? I'm so excited for the election, aren't you?"

"I try not to put hope in politicians," I say.

"I get that," she says.

"But Mr. Obama is hard to resist."

"I know. Right?"

"Right. I imagine. Have you ever considered a career in the public humanities?"

"No, can't say that I have, Zeke."

"I want to offer you a job," I say. I'm not sure why I say this now, but it occurs to me that my organization is ready for a change, and what better way to have somebody fall in love with you, swiftly, than to spend eight or nine hours a day together, working tirelessly and idealistically on a project that helps to build a better, more thoughtful world?

"At the humanities commission? Is that where you work?"

"The Great Midwestern Humanities Initiative. I'm the director."

"What do you do there?"

"It's complicated. But you seem so bright, and smart, and efficient. You provide excellent customer service, and, well, I just think you'd be very good at this."

"Seriously?" she says.

"Yes. I can start you at forty thousand. Plus benefits."

"That's it? This is a job offer?"

Her spine straightens and she sets down her fork, as if she is preparing to bolt for the front door.

"Fucking-ay," she says. Then she looks over my shoulder at the wall. "Wow. I'm sorry, but I have to go, Zeke. I'm already late. Can I think about this?"

"Sure," I say.

We stand. She juts her left hip out at me a little bit, hangs her thumbs from the waistband of her pants, exposing just a sliver of lovely pale midriff.

"You aren't just making all of this up in order to impress me, are you?"

"What? My God, no!"

"Because it sounds like a good job for me. But, but, it's also obvious that you're attracted to me."

"It is?" I say.

She leans in closer and whispers, "You have had a crush on me for three years, Zeke. I know when a customer has a crush on me. It's one of the only thrilling—and sometimes creepy—parts of my job."

I blush and sit down in my chair, my hand on my face.

"Has it really been that long?"

"I knew it!" she says, pointing at me with her fork so that a tiny piece of black olive hits me in the chest. She is smiling, excited.

"Hey. Do you want to get a drink tonight?" she says. "I get off at ten o'clock. We can talk about this job thing, if you're really serious."

"I am!"

"Meet me in the parking lot, here. Or is that too late for a meeting?"

I nod. "No, it's perfect. I often work late into the night."

"You know, you could just ask me out on a date," she says. "You don't need to hire me to spend time with me."

It strikes me as an incredibly confident thing to say, and it strikes me that Minn would be just the sort of woman who might, in fact, make a rapid decision to marry me and help me raise two adopted seven-year-old daughters.

I know I am ahead of myself, but there is significant joy in my heart. Minn almost skips out the door. Nothing is as uplifting as two people aflutter with the possibility of a new friendship. I struggle to keep my mind right there in the blissful moment. I try not to flood my mind with images of our first home, shopping at Target, her belly full and pregnant; later, a baby resting in her arms as I rub her shoulders. Slow down, Zeke. Slow down!

But did you not see the giddiness with which she leapt from the table? Did you not hear the joy in her voice when she pointed a fork at me and shouted: *I knew it?*

Minn Koltes, neighborhood barista, is now a prospect. I'm so excited, I almost forget about the engagement ring she wears on her finger.

I spend the rest of the evening watching Minn go about her work as I sit in the corner of the Starbucks and read the *New York Times*. As I read about the health care crisis, the devalued dollar, the continuing drop in employment rates, it is easy for me to forget about my unsettling visit from Farnsworth and Morris, as well as the confusing encounter I had afterward, at the bookstore with Joseph and Mack. Reading about the general woes of the world has always helped me forget about my specific, personal ones. Every so often, I look up from my newspaper, sip on my Americano, and catch Minn's eyes as she efficiently mans the Starbucks drive-through. When our eyes meet, she smiles, a warm and wide smile that I can only describe as hungry.

At the strip mall in Fitchburg, I have twenty minutes or so to kill while Minn closes down Starbucks for the night, putting the deposit bag into the safe and cleaning the restrooms. While she does this, I wander up and down the sidewalk of the strip mall—actually it's called New Prairie Lifestyle Center, and it houses the Starbucks, several "upscale" fast-food eateries, a boutique fitness center for women, a stationery store, a store called The Faithful Gardener (which sells gardening supplies and inspirational books), and Colonel J. D. Fitch's South Side Brew Pub, a vast warehouselike cavern at the end of the center. I decide that I might be well served by a quick vodka tonic—a personality drink, if you will—and start walking toward the large neon beer signs that are ablaze in Colonel Fitch's floor-to-ceiling windows.

In the center window of Colonel J. D. Fitch's, at a high table surrounded by five high stools, a group of middle-aged professionals is sharing a large deluxe platter of nachos. They drink pints of beer and I pause for a moment to consider the nachos; they look good, and I am suddenly hungry and think that it might be fun to take Minn somewhere loud and open like this suburban fern bar. We could sit back in a corner booth and make smug comments about the earnestness of the place, the absurdity of the wait staff, the mundane music, and the questionable fashion sense at work among the bar's patrons.

Apparently, I have stared at the nachos in the window a little too long, I suppose, thinking of hunger and of Minn, because when I turn my attention to the five people dining in said window seat, I realize that they are looking at me without really looking.

There are two men and three women at the table. The two men are looking at me now. The women sort of seem oblivious to me, all of them laughing, weighted by too much hair, too much makeup, tank tops with the zealous sparkle and flesh-baring cuts more suited to sixteen-year-olds. The men are both in their forties and are wearing the sort of wrinkled dress shirts and loosened ties that speak of a long, hard day doing something not at all meaningful. Neither of them will break eye contact with me. The taller of the two offers me a smile, while the shorter, darker, stockier of the two is glaring at me, holding his beer in one hand, his other hand spread out wide on the table before him. It takes me a minute to place the men, because, truth be told, they look like just about every other single man in the bar. But then it dawns on me like an anvil. This is Farnsworth and Morris, the two men from the federal government who stopped by my office earlier in the afternoon. I had not recognized them in this innocuous and insipid context. How did I miss them?

I decide that I must confront these people. I have to find out exactly what is going on here; it will do me no good to sit back and wonder what I am up against. Have they followed me here?

Still, just as I harden, become a web of tensed and sinewy muscles pumped full of adrenaline, someone touches my arm. Minn! Oh, Minn. The warmth from her fingertips seems to push through the pores of my skin; my racing heart slows. I can smell her—the sweetness of coffee, lotion, antibacterial cleaning products used at closing time at Starbucks—and I decide that no confrontation is worth it. Nothing should risk what I may be about to begin with this lovely, dark-haired barista, whom I have admired from afar for a long, long time.

We walk away from the window of the bar.

"Do you want to have a drink?" I ask.

"You don't want to go in there, do you?" Minn says.

"In there? That bar? No," I say.

"Good. I hate that place. It's obnoxious," she says.

I must look funny, as if I have just been offended, because then she says, "Oh, I'm sorry. You like it, don't you?"

"No. No, why?"

"You made a face."

"Did I?"

"Yes."

"Oh, no. Well, no, there was just a woman in there, at the table. Someone I used to know, I guess."

"An ex?"

"Yes. Of sorts."

"Was she in the window?"

"Yes, she was one of the women at that table. It's not a big deal."

Minn smiles. "That's what I hate about Madison," she says. "Always running into people you had hoped you wouldn't ever see again, aren't you?"

I turn around for a moment to see if we're being followed. Something is greatly amiss in my world, something greatly troubling is about to occur; I can feel that. But I can also feel, suddenly, Minn taking my arm, the perfect amount of warmth and closeness and heft, and I am not about to say anything so odd or scary or strange that it would make me sound unstable, paranoid, or obsessive.

"Is this okay?" Minn says, stopping her stride. I stop too. "Taking your arm like this? You seem tense."

"No. No, I love this," I mumble. "It's just that it's been an incredibly odd day."

"Did you say *odd*, or *hard*?"

"Both," I say. "I guess."

"There really isn't a good place to get a drink around here, you know? There is nothing here that's worth going to in this mall," Minn says. "I can't stand a shitty bar. There's nothing more depressing, is there? You want to just go to my place, have a drink?"

I nod. It's all I can do, for the smile on my face, a medley of sheer joy and anticipated bliss and unidentified fear and tension, has me nearly paralyzed. Oh, Minn!

* * *

Minn asks me to wait in the parking lot of her apartment complex—a new, suburban affair that attempts, unsuccessfully, to mimic the lines of Prairie-style architecture. "Give me ten minutes," she says, and disappears into the building's front entrance. The complex is an attempt at architectural originality on a severe budget, and that has never worked, though in Wisconsin, soggy with the moody ghost of Frank Lloyd Wright, such a feat is attempted again and again. While I wait in the breezy evening, I wish that I had a cigarette. I smoke rarely, if ever, but every so often, when my heart soars with anticipation and the wind of a late summer evening seems to blow air into my feet and my palms, I do want to smoke. I am reminded of the possibility I used to feel at the end of each school year as a young man, on those first spring evenings, when options appeared limitless and the forces of evil and despair, which I knew, for certain, existed, were so far from my reality that I did not need to even consider them. No need to even keep an eye out for trouble, for none was brewing and my life seemed ready to become the sort of exciting and charmed life I once imagined I not only wanted but also deserved.

She comes out to me in a simple black cotton sweater, jeans, and black boots, tall and high-heeled. She has put on makeup, and her hair is no longer pulled back in a ponytail but is loose and flows down toward her lovely olive shoulders.

"You look lovely," I say.

"Is it too much? It looks like I'm trying."

"Not only trying," I say. "Succeeding."

She smiles, does a playful curtsy, which makes my heart race, my tongue swell.

"I checked my inventory, Zeke. I have one bottle of red wine—a cheap Spanish red—plus four beers, and a little gin, a few fingers of vodka, and a new bottle of tonic."

"Sounds great. But what will you drink?" I say.

She finds this marginally hilarious. I like her laugh.

We go up to her place. She spends a few minutes making gin and tonics; Minn is pleased to find half a lime in a Ziploc bag. "I don't cook much," she says. Her apartment is tidy. I have never enjoyed spending time with a woman in a messy apartment or home. It reflects an inner chaos that's better to avoid in relationships. We sit in a loveseat by the window. There are three long and narrow windows, from which you can see, in the middle distance, the illuminated Starbucks sign.

"That's a little sad, don't you think?" Minn says. "My view?"

"Oh, no. No, that's more, um, coincidentally ironic—maybe it reeks a little bit of American suburban despair, like a Green Day video directed by, say, Camus. Except it's cleaner than that, tidy, I mean. You have better hair, and I'd venture to say you smell better than any of the band members in Green Day."

She smiles. We exchange some basic background information—how long have you lived here, do you like it, et cetera. We exchange a brief litany of music and film and literature admired and find some similarities on our lists: the Shins, *Hoosiers*, Jim Harrison.

"I love the way women feel lust in Harrison's work," she says. "Most male writers don't allow their female characters to feel lust, they only receive it. Harrison's women get horny all the time. I once met a feminist bookstore clerk who said that Harrison was a misogynist. I told her she was being a misogynist by believing that female characters should not want it as bad as the men."

I feel myself blushing.

She asks me about my work.

I try to describe the *Unhappiness* project, and the whole history of the GMHI, but describing it makes me remember the curious visits from Farnsworth and Morris. An ulcerous burning of caustic worry flares and blooms in my abdomen.

"Well, what do you do all day?" Minn says.

I try to tell her, but it seems dreadfully weird and dull. The more I talk, the worse it sounds.

"So you interview people about why they are sad?"

"Unhappy."

"I don't get it."

163

"It's hard to explain. I'd have to show you some of the interviews. Sometimes I just ask one question: *Why are you so unhappy?* Sometimes, if people will let me do a more in-depth interview, I probe deeper. Much deeper."

"Interview me," she says.

"Oh, you don't want to do that," I say.

"How else will I know if I want to work for you?"

"You probably don't."

"Like hell I don't," she says. "Do you have your video camera here?"

"I do. I always have it."

"Well, get it out."

"I don't know, Minn. These interviews can get pretty intense. A little heavy. A lot of people cry. I make a lot of people cry."

"I never cry."

I stand up. "Is this a dare?"

"Look, you are obviously so nervous to be up here, drinking with me, that you are really blowing it. You suddenly have nothing to say? In the coffee shop you always had something interesting or funny to say, but now that you're here with me, without a counter between us, you clam up? Get out your camera. Give us something to talk about, Zeke. Make me want to be your assistant."

"Okay," I say, a little wheezy word of agreement.

"My God, you're seriously blushing."

It is hard for me to keep from skipping, so I give up. I skip.

There is raucous laughter behind me.

"While you're skipping," Minn calls out to me, "Skip to the kitchen and get me some more beer. And then turn on that fucking camera."

An Inventory of American Unhappiness
    Minn K., 29, Starbucks barista, Fitchburg, WI.
September 24, 2008, 12:15 A.M.
    Should we begin?

164

Please!

Why are you so unhappy?

That? That's how you begin?

Yes. So, tell me: why are you so unhappy?

I'm not.

Really? Think about it for a moment.

Okay. Okay. Thinking. Nope, not unhappy.

You'd be surprised how many people, after getting over the shock of the question's directness, start talking. Often it's the only question I need to ask.

What if they're not unhappy? As in my case?

Well, they're lying. This is America. Everybody is unhappy. Perhaps not chronically, but certainly, at times, we're all unhappy here.

Not true. I'm happy.

Well, occasionally some subjects take longer to confess their unhappiness.

Right. Okay. What do you do then?

I switch gears in the conversation.

To what?

I say this: Tell me about your childhood.

That's not much better.

In my extended interviews, I find it's better than a direct question. People make a few general statements—well, I grew up here or there, my father was x, my mother was y, I had two or three or four siblings—and then, once the throat is cleared, they go right to the sadness.

I see.

So? About your childhood?

It was happy.

Really?

No. My father was a high-functioning drunk; he saved his real unraveling, his true anger, for my teen years; my mother was a shattered little bird. We had an enormous house in a suburb of Minneapolis; I stayed away from it as much as I could. When I was eighteen I left for the university in Madison and I didn't ever go back home, not even in the summers.

Did you visit?

My mother came to see me once a month. We would spend the night in the Edgewater Hotel together. I'd order a shrimp cocktail and some champagne through room service. My mother would buy me anything I wanted. My father was later convicted of fraud and tax evasion, but we had enough money back then. By the time that trial came up, he was already in jail for repeated frunk driving expenses.

Frunk?

I meant drunk, asshole.

I see. Did you enjoy your college years despite the trouble at home?

I did, I guess. I was far too serious. I had very few boyfriends, no one-night stands, almost never drank, not even a beer. I studied all the time. My grades were exceptional.

What was your major?

Anthropology. Minor in rural sociology. I've told you that.

And you finished your degree?

Yes. I've told you that too.

If I may be bold for a moment: why are you working at a Starbucks then?

Well, because I have a degree in anthropology. [*Laughter*]

I see.

This is strange. How many of these interviews have you done?

Five hundred, at least.

166

And nobody has punched you yet?

God, no. Why?

It feels very invasive.

I'm sorry. We can stop.

No. No, are you kidding? I love talking about myself. There is no burden of conversation here. I can just blather on and on about my own life, which is typical of my first dates. I don't have to ask you anything. I don't have to pretend to care what your father does for a living.

Did. He's dead. He made hot dogs.

Oh, I'm sorry. You said that.

There you go. That's why people like to do this. They just answer the questions, which is easier than asking them, for most people. I like to ask the questions.

Hey, Bub, then kick it back to me. [*Laughter*]

Let's continue. Tell me, do you regret majoring in a humanities discipline? Do you wish you were able to find work in your field?

If I stretch it I can actually link my degree with my work. I just think about the fair-trade coffees we sell—we really have become a leader in that sort of business model, I swear. I try to focus on the international world music and the globally minded literary selections we sell—that sort of thing. And there is no better place to observe human beings at work in the twenty-first century. Starbucks is the new epicenter of suburban life. I'm thinking of writing a book: *Lattes in the Midst.*

The mist?

Midst. As in, the "midst" of everything, smack dab between the dry cleaners and the Kinko's.

I think that's all very true, the things you say about Starbucks. You seem to look on the bright side of things. Are you an optimist?

Yes.

[*Long pause*]

Zeke?

I'm sorry. This is more difficult than I thought it would be.

What?

Conducting one of my interviews while on a date.

Oh, right. This is pretty much a date, isn't it?

Yes.

Well, let's do something else.

Minn and I stay up most of the night, drinking nearly all of the alcohol in the house. We grow affectionate and flirtatious. I recklessly hint, once again, that Lara, my associate director, will be resigning soon, and that Minn, without a doubt, should take her place. At one point, sashaying toward me with two fresh beers, Minn says, "How will you be able to focus on your work with somebody as attractive as me around?"

"I won't," I say.

"Good answer," she says.

"I'm serious," I say.

I consider trying to kiss her, and I'm about to, but she excuses herself and goes to the bathroom and does not come back. I can hear her throwing up.

"Don't choke on your own sick!" I call from the couch as I'm about to finally pass out. I love using the word *sick* as a noun.

Later, while it's still dark outside, I awake on her couch, cotton-headed, my eyes painful, my mouth dry. I find a water glass and fill it. Minn is asleep, with pillow and blanket, on the floor near the bathroom. I have to pee, but I don't want to wake her. I run hot water and pee in her kitchen sink, and then douse the whole sink with Dawn so it smells of lemons.

I carry Minn to her bed, resisting the urge to undress her, which could be interpreted as a tender kindness or mild perversion. I go to the kitchen and get a glass of ice water and find some aspirin. I bring them in to Minn and find she has shed her clothes and they are in a pile on the floor. She is tucked under a burgundy comforter. I don't peek at her naked body, though the thought does occur to me. I do, however, once again, notice an engagement ring on her left hand.

Just as I am leaving her room, she sits up in bed, holding the covers over her breasts.

"Don't try to drive home," she says. "You can crash on the couch, of course."

"I took a bus. I'll call a cab."

"I suppose you don't want to hire me now?" she says, not opening her eyes or smiling.

"I am as drunk as you, Minn."

"I want to see you again."

"Okay. Me too. I want to see you."

"Sure. You don't have to hire me, Zeke. But you have to be my friend."

"Okay, Minn. I want to be your friend too."

"Zeke," she says, "I'm engaged."

"It's okay," I say. "I saw the ring."

"Can I explain?"

"I'd rather you didn't," I say. "I need to pretend it's not true."

"We haven't picked a date yet or anything. He's in Africa. He's building water purification systems."

"A do-gooder," I say.

"Bring me my toothbrush from the bathroom," she says. "Please. With some toothpaste on it?"

"Okay," I say.

She's sitting up in bed when I come back and I hand her the red toothbrush, dotted with Colgate, and watch as she moves it around in her mouth. It's hard not to smile as she rolls her eyes around.

"A glass of water too?" she says.

"There's one on your nightstand," I say. "But I'll get you another!"

I go to the kitchen and retrieve a glass tumbler of tap water. She could have sent me to Alaska for fresh-caught salmon at that point, and I would have done as she asked. I was officially smitten; I was in love. I was ready to propose marriage.

I hand her the water, which she drinks and then sets the glass on the nightstand.

"Now," she says, "please kiss me good night."

I kiss her slow. I kiss her as long as she will let me, worried about my own breath, but unable to think of such a charming way to brush my own teeth.

And then I am under the covers too. Minn is naked and soon I am too. I don't ask any questions. When I leave in the morning, I see the engagement ring on the nightstand and decide not to wake Minn. Despite the urgency of my mission, it seems strategically prudent to allow her to make the next move.

When I get home that morning, my mother is awake, sitting in the living room, in the dark, watching television with the sound off. She is watching an infomercial for something called the Abomizer, an exercise machine, and when I walk in, we both stare at the TV for a moment, where a parade of models are doing exercises on an orange stage. My mother flips off the television.

"People are so stupid," she says.

"They are," I say.

"I can't sleep. I never can sleep," she says. "And once you start watching these stupid people . . ."

I flip on the light, but my mother shields her eyes so I turn it back off and have a seat in the dark.

"It's almost dawn," she says. "Must have been a good date."

"It was," I say.

"Phil Crawford told me that he spoke with you. About my will."

"He did."

"And Harmony seems to think that you're going to try to find someone to marry. Anybody."

170

"I wouldn't do that," I say. "But there is somebody, somebody I have known for a long time, whom, well, I really, really, sort of suddenly, love."

I picture Minn in her apartment, waking up naked, sliding on her ring, and walking to the shower. Is she smiling? Shaking her head? Is her head hung down in shame? Is she crying or laughing?

"Well, I hope you know what I was doing with that," she says. "I was trying to be impartial and do what would be best for the kids."

"Impartial?"

"Well, I love you more than Harmony," she says. "You know that. She's lovely. I think the world of her. But she's not my child, you know? I don't have that kind of connection."

I nod.

"I don't love her the way I love you," she says. "My decision was practical, not emotional."

"You do love me?"

"Zeke," she says, "how can you even ask me that? Of course." She raises her hands out in front of her. "Here, help me up. Help me to my bed."

I stand up and help my mother do the same.

"Do you want to go out to breakfast, Mom?"

"Well," she says, her voice already wearying, already fading to a wheeze, "that might be nice. How about when the girls get up, we all go?"

"They have school," I say.

"They can be late," she says.

"Right," I say. "Where do you want to go?"

"I'd like to go to the OCB one last time. Before I die. See my old friends."

"It won't be the last time," I say.

"Help me to bed and wake me up when you're ready to go."

Once my mother is back to sleep, the sun begins to rise. I make a pot of coffee and am soon joined by Harmony, who comes into the kitchen in her nightshirt and slippers, looks at my rumpled clothes, the same ones I was wearing at supper last night, and says, "You just getting home?"

"I am," I say.

"Unbelievable."

"What?"

"You get around, that's all."

"I was told by a shadowy albeit sexy figure that one of the nights, and I quote, *never happened*. So I can't be judged for a night that never happened, can I?"

"It's still a respect issue, Zeke. You don't hop around like that."

"May I remind you that only one of us is married."

Harmony glares at me but says nothing. I continue.

"The ethical thing to do, Harmony, is for you to leave Malcolm, marry me, and help me raise those beautiful little girls."

"That's insane. My sleeping with you," she says, whispering through her gritted teeth, "had nothing to do with those girls or with Malcolm or with my marriage. It had to do with three gin and tonics and the fact that I've always found you cute and that I was feeling incredibly overwhelmed and lonely and I thought you were too, and—do you get it?"

"Oddly, I do."

"Malcolm had an affair last year."

"Oh, I'm sorry," I say.

The girls get up then. I meet them in the living room. They are holding hands, an adorable habit they developed as two-year-olds. When they are sleepy and near one another, they take each other's hands. It is a precious, amazing, and almost instinctive thing that they do.

"Girls," I say, "let's go out for breakfast!"

The five of us fit easily into the booth at the Old Country Buffet, especially now that my mother is forty pounds lighter than she used to be, a shrinking bird of a woman. A few OCB team members come over to greet my mother, and to tell her how well she looks, which is absurd, and they tell her how brave she is, and how inspirational she is, and I think, She is just waiting to die! She looks terrible and scared! Why is that inspirational?

It's not that I don't acknowledge that what my mother is going through is extraordinarily difficult and sad. But it seems sort of demeaning to me to pretend that there is any sort of dignity to her fight. There's not. It's simply death, slow and painful and premature. It's an injustice, an outrage, a crock.

I take April up to fill her plate at the buffet and Harmony takes May. My mother stays in the booth, requesting that I bring her some sliced peaches and maybe some yogurt. There's a steady stream of OCB cooks and managers and bussers coming by the table to say hello to my mother, and I notice that quite a few of the customers stop and chat with her too. A few of the customers look stricken by sadness, and for the first time in my life, perhaps a clue to the density of youth, I realize that, through a job I considered demeaning and meaningless, my mother had a broad and vast world all her own.

I eat my breakfast rapidly, fueled by a lusty appetite that I hope deadens my sorrow. April and May and Harmony are engaged in a conversation about the differences between fruits and vegetables.

"Tomato?" May says.

"Vegetable," Harmony says.

"Not true!" I say, a little more loudly than I mean to say it. April and May look a bit scared. "I mean, I'm sorry. It's a fruit. It comes from a flower. That makes it fruit."

"Cucumber?" April asks.

"Fruit," I say. "Fruit."

After breakfast, Harmony and my mother go back to the house, and then I take the children to school and stop by the principal's office to let him know that the twins' tardiness was my own fault. At seven years old, they have already entered the reward and punishment system of public schools, and I do not want them penalized for having a pleasant—well, fairly pleasant—morning off with their dying grandmother. Then I head back to my office, the unpleasant aftertaste of lard and eggs on my tongue. I find some peppermint schnapps tucked away in my legislative relations file drawer—no, *find* is the wrong word, I knew it was there—and have a generous draw from the small bottle. Immediately I feel refreshed and reborn, a new minty beast, and I check my voice mail, find nothing, and go back into the lobby, seeking Lara. Finding her desk still empty, I pace my way back into my office.

I do not do well in meditative states, especially under stress. The office is entirely too quiet. I direct my web browser to Pandora, a streaming music site that has become increasingly important to my sanity, and I scroll through the stations I've created, finally deciding on the Van Morrison station. This makes me want a Bloody Mary, so I pause the music, go to the small staff kitchen where I keep enough ingredients (tomato juice, Tabasco, olives, pickles, vodka, pepper, and salt) to make exactly that. Returning to my office with a generous pint glass, I sit back at my desk and continue the music. If one cannot relax while sipping a cocktail and listening to Van Morrison, then one is beyond the state of relaxation. I am treated to the song "Wonderful Remark," which is one of my favorites.

In order to send my mind off in a different direction from my own pressing worry and woe, I check the e-mail account I use to get responses from the *Inventory of American Unhappiness* project's web page. I have three new messages.

To: inventory@americanunhappiness.org
From: melindalarson@justpress.com
Re: Inventory of American Unhappiness
    I'm unhappy because of the rain today. My unhappiness is always linked to the weather, and I am very hard to please, weather-wise. I hate rain and clouds, detest the heat, find the bitter cold intolerable, and consider high humidity a

174

plague. So, in fact, for nine weeks, each autumn, I find myself deliriously happy and then, near Thanksgiving, the first bitter winds emerge, the first snow hits, and there I am again, despairing. I'm serious. If there was one place on earth that had autumn every day, I'd move there. But there is nothing like that—there are places on earth that have summer all day or winter all day, and I suppose several places like San Francisco or San Diego, maybe, I don't know, I've never been, feel like spring all year round, but there is no place to go to be continually cradled in autumn's bosom. Thank you. This feels better.

Melinda, 37, Boise, ID

To: inventory@americanunhappiness.org
From: dobiegillis123456789@yahoo.com
Re: Inventory of American Unhappiness

Hey. This is a cool project. Um, okay, I guess that insincere people make me unhappy. And curlers. When I see old ladies in the CVS drugstore with curlers in their hair, and you can see their scalp, and they look so old and tired but they are still trying so hard, buying makeup, hair products, I think that makes me unhappy. Put on a scarf, you know? CVS drugstore in general, that makes me pretty depressed. Especially when I see somebody buying food there. Once, I saw this guy at the CVS drugstore and he was buying a can of Manwich and some white hamburger buns and a carton of chocolate milk and a canister of corn chips and I was like, oh, man, this is not easy to watch.

Doug, 23, Redford Township, MI

To: inventory@americanunhappiness.org
From: starboard555@wilsontech.com
Re: Inventory of American Unhappiness

This seems to be a very counterproductive, self-centered project. I stumbled across it while searching for a speech I

heard, years ago, given by a young Robert F. Kennedy. You, sir or madam, would be wise to hear that same speech:
   http://www.historyplace.com/speeches/rfk-mlk.htm
   Stanley, 66, Morgan, IA

I click on the link sent to me by Stanley of Morgan, Iowa. It is the famous speech that RFK gave in Indiana on the night Martin Luther King Jr. was assassinated. I hit Play and watch the speech. The moment Kennedy reveals the news to the crowd, and the collective gasp leaps from their throats, I start to weep. In his speech, Robert F. Kennedy quoted the playwright Aeschylus: "In our sleep, pain which cannot forget falls drop by drop upon the heart until, in our own despair, against our will, comes wisdom through the awful grace of God."

How amazing that once upon a time our leaders were so well versed in the humanities. Oh, even Bill Clinton was well read—for all his Bubba-ness, for all his lechery, the man's favorite author was Arturo Pérez-Reverte. Clinton was a Rhodes Scholar. Oh, if only intelligent and curious men and women could lead us. Maybe this is precisely why we are so unhappy, Stanley, you sixty-six-year-old crank from Morgan, Iowa. Because our nation has been hijacked by buffoons who send our brothers and sisters off to reckless, endless wars, because the nation has lost all capacity for critical reflection, you asshole. Because nothing has any weight anymore, Stanley, you fucking piece of shit.

I leave my office for some water and a restroom break and find Lara at her desk.

"Good morning, dear," I say.

"Good morning, Zeke."

"My dear, I may need your assistance in a few moments. I have that idea for a new position here at GMHI that I'd like to discuss with you."

"A new position?"

"Yes."

"Given our financial woes and the federal scrutiny we're under, you may want to hold off on that, Zeke."

"My dear . . ."

"Stop it, Zeke."

"Stop what?"

"Calling me 'dear.'"

"Fine."

"How much have you had to drink, Zeke?"

"That's quite enough," I say.

"Jesus, Zeke, it's not even noon!"

"My mother is dying!" I say. "My mother is dying!"

That evening, I arrive at the far west side Starbucks with a great deal of hesitation. I don't want to appear to be some sort of stalker; Minn knows how to reach me if she wants to reach me. At the same time, I don't want to appear callous. Minn and I enjoyed a perfectly acceptable night of drunken lovemaking in her bed, and I do not want to appear as if the episode meant nothing to me. Not only do I still very much want to hire her, I also want to marry her. I figure I will stop by her place of employment and discreetly let her know at least one of those wishes. (Marriage, I suppose, should probably not be brought up until a second or third lovemaking session, at least as a general rule, but I must say that given the extraordinary courtship and accelerated relationship that blossomed the previous evening, swiftness and boldness may work to my advantage. If a woman is to agree to marry me before my mother dies, it will have to feel, at this point, like an insane and unavoidable matter of fate. She will have to believe that we have a destiny, of sorts, and that we have found each other for some mystical and inexplicable reason.)

But I do not see Minn at the Starbucks, so I drink a cup of coffee at a corner table for a while, hoping she'll appear from the back room or the restroom, but she is clearly not working. I decide not to ask at the counter (why rally the suspicions of her coworkers?) and instead head over to her apartment complex. I ring the buzzer several times; I get no answer. I do not have her phone number or her e-mail address, but when I get home, I resort to that last-ditch effort of twenty-first-century communication. I search for her on Facebook, find her quite easily (a picture of her with someone else, a man with dark skin and dark hair, and they are standing in front of a setting sun), and send her a "friend request."

15

Zeke Pappas is happy to honor your request.

MY FAVORITE SORT of Facebook status update is the sort that is obtuse and unknowable. For instance, nobody on earth would know that my status update alludes to me kissing Minn at her request. A good status alludes to some sort of emotion, some sort of yearning, but it doesn't offer any sort of clues. It does not, for instance, report on the mundanity of one's evening meal. It doesn't compliment one's "hubby" or report on an interesting journey or event. It does not make a political statement or wallow in the morbidity of actual tragedy. It does not alert you to a good bargain at Costco. For fuck's sake! Instead, a good Facebook status reminds your network, and yourself, that you are sitting alone somewhere, full of yearning, that you have a desire that needs meeting or a wave of nostalgia that needs revealing or an unspoken sorrow that needs an indirect catharsis. Once, I remember a friend of mine posting only this, the word *Nostalgia!* Another time a friend of mine posted this: *Remember the month when I ate nothing but tangerines?* I do not want to know *exactly* what my Facebook friends are doing; I want to know what they are struggling to express, I want the unsayable said, the unknowable known.

It's late, nearly eleven o'clock at night, and I have yet to hear from Minn. What is the ethical expectation for a one-night stand? Do you have an obligation to "friend" her via social networking sites? Or is that awkward, that ability the one-time lover in question would have to monitor your every public movement for months and years following the tryst?

I feel as if I should go to sleep, as if I should give up on Minn, but all rules feel suspended tonight, the whole world feels as if it is upside down, without logic, unmoored. Before I turn in for the night, or for the morning, as the case seems to be, I look over my prospect list scrawled in those now well-creased pages from *Simply You* magazine and decide to craft my semiregular letter to Sofia Coppola, director, writer, and marriage prospect. I have written to her often over the course of the past three years. But now that I have a goal of finding a suitable and willing marriage partner with some haste, my inquiries to Ms. Coppola must become more direct and urgent.

Dear Ms. Coppola,

My name is Zeke Pappas and I am an oral historian and a nontraditional documentary artist based in Madison, Wisconsin. I am currently at work on a project called An Inventory of American Unhappiness, *which aims to chronicle the growing and peculiar epidemic of unhappiness that seems to plague so many of our citizens, despite our obvious blessings and the comparative ease of our daily lives to that of the citizens of other nations.*

Your film Lost in Translation *seems to me to encompass the phenomenon of American unhappiness in a way that no other filmmaker of your generation, perhaps any generation, has managed to do. It is for that reason that I am writing to you, in hopes of discussing the visual/film component of* An Inventory of American Unhappiness. *It is my belief that we are intellectual, if not spiritual, kin.*

It is my belief that your aesthetic vision and intellectual
mission are more in line with the American Unhappiness
project than those of any contemporary artist at work
today. That is why I beseech you to visit our website at
www.americanunhappiness.org.

I read over what I have written, making no change save replacing the word *beseech* with *implore* and then changing that to *encourage.* Two years ago, I used GMHI funds and hired a private investigator to find me Ms. Coppola's personal e-mail address. Part of our contract includes a stipulation that he must check her e-mail address at the end of each month and make sure that it hasn't changed. I try to limit myself to one message every month. Occasionally, when drunk, I send her additional notes. Sometimes I send her weekly messages and sometimes I just share a link with her: *Sofia, thought you'd love to see this.* Or sometimes I'll just say: *Hey, Sofia, will you be in Chicago anytime soon? Would love to tell you about my new project.* I assume Ms. Coppola has read these and must imagine I am somebody she once met and now can't recall meeting. Who knows what she thinks? I admit, late last spring, after watching the movie *Me and You and Everyone We Know,* I was tempted to remove Ms. Coppola from my prospect list and replace her with filmmaker and performance artist Miranda July, on whom I have an enormous crush. But persistence is one of my best traits, and besides, would Ms. July really be able to sustain a long-term relationship? Might she be too damaged? Simply put, I had too much invested in Sofia Coppola to give up so easily. Spike Jonze has made a grave error in leaving this beauty, this stunning and smart young artist, behind.

Before I hit Send I reread my missive one time for good measure, stop, and visualize Ms. Coppola opening and reading the letter (The Power of Intention!), and then, just as I am moving my mouse toward the appropriate icon, I turn up the sound on my computer to see what Pandora has offered me, and the song "Sweet Thing" begins to play on my Van Morrison station. It is the song that Valerie and I once considered our song, though, in her devilishly humorous way, if you were to ask Valerie if we, as a couple, had a song, she would give the deadpanned answer "Sure, 'Big Balls' by AC/DC."

I set my computer to sleep mode and turn off my desk lamp. I take a minute to stare out at the darkness of Commonwealth Avenue in these last hours of night. There, on the sidewalk, I see a woman dressed in a white hoodie, standing in the light cast by my front porch lights. Elizabeth Vandeweghe is staring at my house. I wave to her.

I go outside. "Hello," I say.

"I wasn't sure if you could see me or not," she says. "I saw that you were awake."

"I didn't see you until I turned off my desk lamp. Were you out there long?"

"Not long."

"What's up, Elizabeth?"

"Do you have a cigarette?" she asks.

"A cigarette. No, I'm sorry."

"That's okay," she says. "I probably shouldn't be smoking anyway."

"No. Probably not. Can I make you a drink?"

"No. I just really wanted to smoke. I felt the urge to do something reckless. I was feeling a little stir-crazy, so then I wasted a few hours on Facebook, which made me feel worse."

"I was on Facebook too," I say.

"How sad," she says. "Seriously? Two loners on Facebook, in the middle of the night, about fifty yards, maybe less, between us. We could have been actually talking."

I shrug.

"Or doing something reckless!" she says.

"Something reckless?" I say. "What do you have in mind?"

"You know, I almost walked up to Laurel Tavern to buy some

182

smokes. I almost left the girls sleeping in their beds and just went for a walk and smoked and smoked. Alone."

"That probably would have been fine," I say. "Mina is ten, right? She can call nine-one-one if the house catches fire, I'm sure."

Elizabeth laughs.

"Pretty sad," she says, "when my idea of rebellion is sneaking out of the house to walk two blocks and buy cigarettes. What am I, fourteen years old?"

I smile. "That's not sad."

"Sadness. Isn't that your thing? Isn't that what you study?"

"Unhappiness," I say. "It's a bit different."

"How so?"

"Well, sadness is caused by something sad—a sorrowful event of sorts. And it's a natural reaction. Unhappiness is simply the absence of happiness. We go about as if happiness should be our default condition, you see. When we find ourselves in some other condition, well, we are unhappy. Does that make sense?"

"Kind of."

"Hey, do you want me to go and buy you some cigarettes? I'd be glad to."

"No. No thanks," she says. "That would be too premeditated. It would dull the edge of the thing."

"Not enough recklessness?" I say.

"Exactly."

Elizabeth and I both look up at the stars, two neighbors, considering the night.

"Hey! I have some marijuana!" I say, remembering an Altoids tin containing two joints that my friend Rory left at my house a few months ago. He was convinced my mother would need and want medical marijuana as the cancer progressed.

Elizabeth smiles. "Yeah?" she says. I run inside.

A little later, I've turned all the lights off in my house and on the outside of the house, and Elizabeth has done the same. Afraid to wake the adults and children who live with us, we walk a half block down to the old cattle crossing that is now a pedestrian tunnel under the new rails-to-trails path. It's a clear night, so we decide to sit right there under the bike path and share the joint. Our houses are quite close together in this neighborhood, so she figures—with a window cracked—she'll hear her daughters if they awake. We are not that far away.

"This is sort of reckless," I offer. "Yes?"

"I know, right?" she says. "It totally is reckless!"

We smoke in silence; the act of passing the herb back and forth seems enough. Also, I cannot think of anything to say and can sense that she is enjoying the fact that I am not saying anything.

At one point, however, good and high, I ask, "Do you really hate your life, Elizabeth?"

And Elizabeth, taking a deep draw on the joint, holding it for a good long time, finally exhales and says, "Naw. Naw. I mean, look at this: my life's pretty surprising."

We laugh about that.

A few minutes later, I walk her to her door. She hugs me.

"Thanks," she says.

"Good night," I say.

Inside, the Van Morrison station on Pandora is now playing the Counting Crows, an odd leap in musical logic, but they are playing a song called "Rain King," which is on an album entitled *August and Everything After*. The music calls to mind my freshman year dorm room at the University of Michigan, where that album was played, along with Pearl Jam's *Vs.*, an extraordinary amount. Listening to the music, I can almost smell the dankness of the rooms in Alice Lloyd Hall, the fried chicken smell rising from the dining hall beneath my room, and I can see my roommates, Brad and Mark, playing Sega video games in the center of that gray and white room. When I think of college, it is hard to remember how sad and depressing it all was until I met Valerie. Whenever I think of Ann Arbor, I am always greeted by a wave of slight nausea and overwhelming longing. And then some days I see Valerie, plain as day, walking across the Diag in the first weeks of May, the ruffled hem of her sundress rustling above her bare knees, the sun new on her bare shoulders, and I think, Look at us, we were just kids, we were so young!

I log in to Facebook for one last peek before bed.

Josh Miller is watching *Casablanca* for the first time.

Wendy Hayes wonders if any parents have heard good things about Water's Edge Preschool.

Morgan Sterbaugh: I can't sleep!!! Too many espressos!!!

Yan Wu believes in miracles.

It occurs to me that Elizabeth may be online at this exact moment too, and, it occurs to me, if she has any chance of marrying me before the grim and unpredictably impending date of my mother's death, I have no choice but to accelerate my slow courtship. The beauty of Facebook is that courtship can be done around the clock, and so, using the iLike function, I send her a YouTube clip of Bob Dylan singing "The Man in Me."

And then I see that, although Minn has yet to accept my friend request, I have myself a new friend request, and when I click on my Friend Requests icon, I can see a small picture of my dead wife, Valerie Somerville—older, lighter, staring off into the distance, a photograph shot in profile.

16

Zeke Pappas has not been entirely honest.

OF COURSE, I KNEW that she wasn't dead. I've always known that! I never even received a death certificate, and I never heard anything from the police or Valerie's family or the Social Security Administration. Any fool would have suspected that he was the subject of some sort of poorly planned though elaborate plot, a cruel plot too, and I suppose I did suspect that, but I could never bring myself to say it. I suppose it was easier to play the young widower than it was to admit that my wife, whom I'd been unabashedly mad for, would play such a cruel trick as a way to escape our marriage.

Valerie's friends in Ann Arbor had a memorial service and they made a big show of it, calling me and asking me if I would read a poem that I had written for her, or asking me what sort of music Valerie might have wanted, but I steadfastly refused to play the game. I blamed the numbing quality of grief: no, I can't even think about it, I said, I am too distraught. I suppose maybe I was expecting Valerie to show up, not exactly laughing at what she had done, nor begging for forgiveness for her unimaginable lie, but simply to return to the life she had in Ann Arbor. I sort of suspected I might see her again, in a coffee shop or on the Diag, and I imagined the weighty awkwardness of that eventual encounter for weeks.

They held her memorial service in a small room in the Law Quad, which was Valerie's favorite place to study. It was the week that classes started. It was my last year in college. Afterward, Jeanette brought the "ashes" back to my apartment, which seemed to be the remnants of somebody's Smokey Joe charcoal grill locked into a cigar box. It was a warm week, and I was sitting in front of a window fan in my boxer shorts, reading Rilke.

I answered the door but did not let her into the apartment. I considered her an enemy.

"You should have come," Jeanette said. "Hal and Malcolm played 'Anna Begins' by the Counting Crows. Except instead of the name *Anna* they put in the name *Valerie*. Everybody was crying."

"Sounds very nice," I said.

"I'm supposed to see if you're okay," Jeanette said. "Everyone wondered where you were."

"I'm fine. I'm reading. I'm carrying sixteen credits this semester, all of them in literature and philosophy. Right now, I'm engaged in Fowles's *The Magus,* which is no small feat. Have you read it?"

"No," she said, looking down at the book in my hand. "It looks like you're reading Rilke, not Fowles."

"Well, thanks for bringing these back," I say. I was about to close the door when Jeanette put her arm out and blocked me.

"Don't blame me for this," she said.

"Blame?" I said. "There's no emotion more futile than blame."

"What?"

"'When the wine is bitter, become the wine.'"

"What?"

"Rilke."

I shut the door.

Strangely, Valerie never returned to Ann Arbor, not to my knowledge. Nobody even came to get her things. She simply allowed me to consider her dead and moved on to some sort of different life. Did she marry somebody else? Transfer to a new college? Attend graduate school? Leave the country? I have never really known what became of her, and so I was able to perpetuate the myth she created. She was dead; I was a young widower. I called my parents and told them what had happened. They had never even met Valerie. My mother sent me a copy of C. S. Lewis's *A Grief Observed*, with the touching inscription *Although I never met Valerie, my heart breaks for you. Come home soon. Love, Mom.*

The autumn crept on, for me, with the slowness of monastic life, partly because, for most of that fall semester, I lived like a monk. I read constantly, wrote papers of inexplicable ambition and length, and subsisted largely on tea and bread. For a course on Chekhov, taught by a lovely and compact woman from Oxford on whom I had a delusional crush, I wrote a forty-four-page paper; the assignment asked for five. For a course on Thomas Merton, I wrote a thirty-nine-page essay detailing the rise of a "New American Mysticism" that was linked to the environmental movement. Occasionally, I'd have a hundred dollars' worth of Chinese food delivered from Dinersty, a dozen small cartons in greasy paper bags, and I'd eat out of those for a week or so. I had no idea what to do with Valerie's (alleged) ashes and for weeks I wandered around Ann Arbor in the late afternoon, trying to decide on a spot: the Arb, the Diag, the Law Quad, the dumpster of the Fleetwood Diner? None of them seemed sufficient—neither sacred enough nor ironic enough. Valerie would have appreciated either tack, I was sure. I thought about honoring Valerie's twisted sense of humor by scattering the ashes in a most inappropriate place—an Arby's trash can, the floor of Blockbuster Video, the bathroom of the Brown Jug—but this seemed inappropriate even to me.

The river Seine seemed the only logical place, and the grand gesture of this maudlin trip seemed to be the only way to continue to pretend that I was a grieving widower and that Valerie was, in fact, dead. Paris was the closest thing to sacred ground our relationship had. Thus, during Thanksgiving week, I found a cheap ticket through the student travel office, a direct flight from Detroit to Paris. As painful as it was, I stayed again in the Hotel Cambrai, and on my first morning in Paris, I woke before dawn and executed my inevitable chore. I threw in the small wooden box as well. And then it seemed to me that she was really dead, and that there was nothing suspicious about the story of her death at all. I decided, well, that I believed it; everything, every errant or odd detail suddenly seemed wholly logical and true.

I had three days to kill after my grim Parisian errand was completed, and so that afternoon, I went to a small brasserie and drank too much red wine. I met a woman there, the first single woman I saw who spoke English, a thirty-two-year-old American named Emily who was getting over a divorce.

What happened with Emily in Paris was remarkable. We ravaged each other out of some strange grief. We were not tender with each other; we told each other very little, in fact, about ourselves. But we spent most of those three days together, in my small hotel room or in the flat she was renting. We drank, smoked, ate vast amounts of food, and screwed. I felt a little like Henry Miller, except we practiced safe sex. I didn't want the clap.

Emily and I had not even exchanged contact information. On our last night together, we agreed that what we had was nothing special, and to try and rekindle it in any way at any later date would be disappointing and mad. She walked me out to my cab, gave me one of the most memorable kisses of my life, and sent me off to the airport. I think of her now, of course, on occasion, and I wonder. But that story is neither new nor unique.

I returned to Ann Arbor with my appetite restored and finished my senior year of college in a decadent litany of books read, meals eaten, wines consumed, cigarettes smoked, beers drained, and women bedded. Something about my status, as a young widower still in college, had made some women feel both curious and generous by the winter semester. I even slept with a few of Valerie's old friends, usually at the end of a long tearful and drunken conversation about the unfairness of life. Those of them who knew Valerie was still somewhere, alive, probably slept with me out of pity. Never underestimate the aphrodisiacal value of pity.

After a few nights with each of these women, I grew distant and rude and accused them of seducing me (almost always a distortion of major proportions) and disgracing the memory of my dead wife. Something cruel and inexplicable had taken root inside my darkest places, and I was able to go from unbelievably sensitive to unbelievably mean and vindictive within one short week. By the time I graduated from Michigan that May, I had lost most of my friends, and moving back to Madison seemed like the only real option I had.

And now, in front of me, her picture, very much alive, older than she was then, but still her, the woman I said I would love forever.

I resist the urge to click Accept and then resist the urge to click Ignore and I simply shut down the computer, take three Benadryl pills and one of my mother's Vicodins, and go to bed.

17

Zeke Pappas is just browsing.

I WANT TO SPEND the whole next day in bed, trying to forget the friend request from Valerie Somerville that I received the night before. I awake with a headache and cotton mouth. It's bright in my room, past ten o'clock, I guess, and I know I should call the office and let Lara know I seem to be sick, but all I want to do is sleep. I feel feverish and thin, like a Dostoyevsky character who has committed a heinous transgression, and who awakes the next morning, finally feeling the full weight of his predicament.

Then there is a knock on my door. Harmony comes into the room, frantic. "Zeke, get up. Your mother. She's not acting right."

At the University hospital, Harmony and I sit on the only chairs in my mother's small room. The girls have gone to a friend's house for the afternoon. My mother is sleeping, and Harmony and I listen to the oncologist tell us that there's nothing more to do but make my mother as comfortable as we can. Harmony reaches over and holds my hand.

When my mother wakes, she is fairly lucid and we explain to her that the next step will be hospice care and a vigorous regimen of pain management.

"I don't want the girls to see me in that stage," she says. "They've had enough sadness for one life. I don't want them to remember me unconscious and wheezing, a bag of bones that shits herself and wets the bed. I'm not going to do that."

My mother wants to go to the hospice facility, not back home. She wants to die there. For her, she says, it's an issue of dignity. She doesn't want her son to have to help her die. She doesn't want him to wake up at night and change her sheets, bring her ice chips.

"This is a job for a stranger," she says.

I try and disagree with her, but as I talk, I see her side of the equation and I decide that there is no reason for me to try and be a hero.

"Let's have one farewell dinner with the girls," she says, "if I can manage that, and then I want them to go to Michigan and start their new life with Harmony and Malcolm. I don't want them waiting for me to die. It'll be easier on them if they have all of their new routines in place before I go. They don't need a funeral and a new school in the same week."

My mother's voice is weak, and when I try to interrupt her, she holds up her hand as best she can. I take it.

"Zeke, I don't know how much longer my brain has. This is what I want done. Let's not wait to discuss it until I have a stroke or something, okay? This is how I want things done."

That evening, after we leave the hospital, after Harmony and the girls order pizza and put in a new Hannah Montana DVD, I head for the Starbucks in Fitchburg in the hope that Minn has returned to work. What if I just tell her my situation? "Minn," I will say, "my mother is dying and if you agree to marry me, my nieces will stay in my home." A woman I don't recognize is manning the front counter, and two men staff the drive-through. Another woman, clearly not Minn, serves as the floater, currently helping her colleagues steam vast amounts of milk.

I ask the barista at the counter, a gray-haired and attractive woman of sixty, if Minn might be working.

"No," she says. "No, she's not here. She's out of town."

"Oh? Will she be gone long?" I ask.

"I think she went to Africa," the woman says, then calls out over her shoulder, "Hank, did Minn go to Africa?"

"I think so," the man named Hank lamely offers. "Or Chicago."

"When is she coming back?" I ask.

"No idea," the woman says.

It occurs to me that the woman could probably go back to the manager's office and consult the schedule and give me some idea of Minn's anticipated return. But it also occurs to me that this might be unbelievably creepy, even if I hint at the fact that I have an intimate relationship with Minn.

A woman walks into the Starbucks in a fetching coat, one I recognize as a wool cashmere plaza coat, charcoal color, from J. Crew's most recent catalog. I step aside and motion for her to go ahead and place an order, but just before she begins to speak, I loudly interrupt her and say, "A tall chai, extra hot!"

She looks at me, a bit dumbstruck, and says, "Pardon?"

"That's what you were going to order, correct?"

The barista behind the counter calls out for Hank, who comes menacingly to the front register and crosses his arms, tilting his head in a sort of gesture of disbelief.

"What?" says the woman in the J. Crew wool cashmere plaza coat.

"I guessed your order," I say. "You were about to order a tall chai, extra hot, weren't you?"

"No," she says. "What's wrong with you?"

I shrug. "Well, excuse me then. It's a small game I like to play. It can often be amusing. I am uncannily good at it."

Everybody gives me an annoyed stare and I head for the exit as I hear the plaza coat woman say, "Tall coffee, room for cream, please."

* * *

There is a sort of foreboding feeling that creeps into my gut as I make my way back to downtown Madison, and as I approach Park Street from Fish Hatchery Road, I make the decision to go and see Mack and Joseph at the bookstore.

Mack is pricing remainders at the front table of the store, and he stops to give me a warm hug and fetch me a cup of coffee from the back room. I don't have the heart to tell him it's undrinkable, so I sip at the burned and bitter swill.

"So what's new?" Mack asks.

"Well, a lot."

"Did you propose to any of your, um, prospects yet?"

"Well, no. It's complicated. The waters are muddy," I say.

Just then Joseph enters the store, holding a plastic bag.

"Zeke," he says, "I've been meaning to find you today."

Joseph hands Mack the plastic bag, which I notice contains a bottle of Maalox.

"What's the matter?"

Joseph crouches down a foot or so and begins to whisper, though as far as I can tell, nobody is in the store save Mack.

"These guys who came in the store the other day. The ones who were messing with you? And with me? You have to be careful, okay?"

"Why?" I ask.

"Because they're serious. I've been making some calls, and I think these guys are for real. I think you're playing with fire here."

I see Mack roll his eyes and move toward another part of the store. "He's paranoid," Mack sings, as he walks away. "He's crazy!"

"Trust me, Zeke. Just promise me you'll be careful. Call me immediately if they come and see you again, all right? I'll have more information soon. Real soon. This has something to do with Congressman Leatherberry. I've called an old college friend who works at the *Washington Post,* and he's convinced of it."

"Joseph! Don't do that! Don't get the media involved!" I say. "My friend H. M. can't be exposed."

"I'm only trying to help," he says. "Do you own a gun?"

"I don't," I say. "Jesus!"

"Neither do I," he says, "but I will try to get you one."

Joseph heads off to the back room, and Mack comes over and motions for me to follow him to the plush chairs in the store's atrium. We sit down.

"He's sort of crazy," Mack says. "I think he's overreacting."

Mack pulls a small flask from the pocket of his blazer. Vodka. He takes a sip and passes it over to me.

"It's not classy," he says, "but I figure you might need it."

"I do," I say. "Definitely. My mother is in the hospital. This is it."

"Oh, dear," Mack says.

"And I have nobody to marry, obviously, so I lose the kids."

"Shit," Mack says. "Goddamn it. What can we do?"

"Just sit with me," I say. "Sit here and get drunk."

"You've come to the right place," Mack says. "Why don't I get some glasses though? And some limes?"

My mom wants hot dogs for her final meal with the kids.

"Hot dogs?" I say. "Seriously? Hot dogs?"

"Hot dogs with ketchup and relish. You know, salt and fat and sugar, the perfect combo."

"I can make something nice," I say.

"Yeah, I can make a roast or something," Harmony says.

"We want hot dogs! We want hot dogs!" May says.

April adds, "And mac-and-cheese!"

"Perfect," my mother says, and the twins crawl up next to her on the couch, each of them taking one of her hands.

We are in her room at the Hospice Center, a quiet, plush building near the Fitchburg Starbucks, and my mother's room has deep-hued carpets, overstuffed furniture, a well-stocked kitchenette, and sparkling white linens on the adjustable bed. I'm sad to think that it's most likely nicer than any away-from-home lodging my mother has ever had.

The girls curl up with my mother under a blanket, and Harmony and I conference by the doorway.

"Why don't you stay here with the kids?" she says. "I'll head to the store, get some hot dogs and mac-and-cheese and stuff, and we can just cook in the microwave here."

"Fine," I say. "Do you need money?"

"Don't be silly, Zeke."

"Buy the good ones," I say. "Chicago Red Hots. Don't get the cheap ones."

"Okay," Harmony says, and before she goes, she gives me a quick hug. "Are you okay?"

"I'm terrible," I say.

I stand in the kitchenette and begin, out of anxiousness, to set up paper plates and plastic cups around the small table that's there. I hope Harmony remembers to get drinks and then call her cell phone.

"Maybe some wine?" I say. "Or beer."

"And some orange soda for the kids?" she says.

"Yeah. That's right. And get them the Dora the Explorer mac-and-cheese. They like that."

"Sure," she says. "Of course."

I can hear my mother talking to the girls and I stand there, frozen, listening.

"Is this the last time we get to see you?" April asks.

"I think so, sweetie," Ma says.

"Until we're all in heaven?" May says.

"That's right."

"And you get to see Daddy and Mommy!" May says.

"Wow!" April says. "That's right."

"I hope so," Ma says.

"Aunt Harmony said you get to see them."

"Good," Ma says. She is trying not to cry and I have no idea how she is managing it. Maybe the morphine helps. Her doctor has also put her on an antianxiety drug and an antidepressant, and I worry that the drugs suppress some of the natural synapses that fire in the brain to allow the body to die. The doctor assures me that that's not the case, but I doubt anybody has studied my hypothesis. It takes a humanist, an anthropologist or something, to figure out things like that, to ask these questions that go beyond the biological.

"I don't know," May says. "I'd rather have you here with us than up there with them."

"Me too," April says.

"You know," Ma says. "You know what? If I could make the rules of the world, I would live with you forever and ever. You two are more precious to me than anything on earth."

When Harmony comes back from the store, she finds all four of us sobbing on the sofa.

My mother is able to eat her hot dog. No bun, no macaroni and cheese, but she eats the hot dog with a fork, dipping it into ketchup and relish. The girls are able to "cook" the dinner for her, and Harmony pours my mother a small cup of beer, and my mother, when she is done, pronounces it "the best meal I have ever had in my whole life." And then she begins to lose the thread of what she wants to say. And her voice weakens to the point of being inaudible and we all four of us lead her to bed, and we leave her sleeping there with our kisses and our tears. Back home, I help the girls bathe and dress for bed, and we all three brush our teeth together, and I tell them they are brave, and strong, and wonderful. I tell them they will have new bedrooms, painted any color they like, at Aunt Harmony and Uncle Malcolm's place. When Harmony comes in, she sits beside me on the bed, and she verifies my claim. "Any color," she says.

"Any color?" they ask.

"Except for," I say.

"Except for what?" they all say.

"Poop brown! No poop on the walls!" I say. And, for the girls, the evening ends in a frenzy of hilarity and giggles.

My night ends on a somewhat different note. I am not surprised when Harmony comes into my room again that night and locks the door behind her. We are exhausted by grief. What we need is anything that is something else. Quickly, madly, we give that to each other, and then afterward we lie in bed, far apart from each other.

"I can't believe the life those girls have had," she says. "Only seven, and they've essentially lost three parents in a row."

"Good thing you're not superstitious," I say.

"Jesus, Zeke."

"Sorry. I feel so bad for them," I say. "I can't imagine it."

"I feel bad for you too," she says, propping up on one elbow, the sheet half covering her breasts. "You're losing everybody."

"You know whom I feel sorry for?" I say.

"Who?"

"Malcolm," I say.

She flops back down on the bed and stares at the ceiling.

"He's such a good man," she says. "He's damaged. He's super-damaged. He had such a rough childhood."

"We all did."

"True," she says.

"I know this must seem crazy, Zeke. I like you. Living with you has been sort of fun, in a bizarre way. The last eight weeks or whatever, as hard as they've been, they've been fun."

"Good," I say. "I'm glad they've been fun for you."

"I don't know, I don't mean it in a casual, wahoo, yippee sort of way. I mean it hasn't felt like real life. It feels like I'm somebody else."

"If you're truly happy, that should feel bad. Not fun."

"It's fun to escape sometimes," she says. "Take on a new role, you know? It's almost healthy for a marriage, I think."

"I suppose."

"I've always liked you, Zeke, and when this madness is over, I hope you will visit. You have to visit. The girls need you. They adore you."

"I know. That's why they should live with me."

"They adore me too," she says.

"That's true," I say. "Are you sure you don't want to leave Malcolm and marry me?"

"I'm sure, Zeke," she says. "That wouldn't be good for anybody in the long run. I do love Malcolm, madly. We're not great to each other, not all the time. But we'll be great to those children, I promise. They'll make us be better people."

"I don't think you should adopt kids to fix your relationship," I say.

"I know. I'm not saying that! Jesus! I don't know what's what, Zeke. I don't know why your mother has to be dying, or why I felt a need to be in bed with you, or why your mother chose me over you. But everything happens for a reason, Zeke."

"No, it doesn't."

We both get out of bed then, suddenly, and fumble around naked, in the dark, dressing. I go over and stand in front of her as she slides on her underwear, touching her hips with my hands.

"You're right," she says.

"About leaving Malcolm and staying here with me?"

"No. About things not happening for a reason. It just occurred to me. What a bunch of bullshit. None of this—Cougar, Melody, Violet—none of it happened for a reason, did it?"

I shake my head. "No," I say.

"Jesus," she says.

"You should know," I say, "that I still plan to be married before my mother dies. So this is your chance. If it's not you, it will be someone else."

She lowers her head onto my chest. "Let's get back into bed," she says.

"Why?" I say. "Have you reconsidered my offer?"

"No," she says. "I just don't know what else to do."

The next morning, Harmony and the twins load their luggage into the back of Harmony's Subaru wagon. They plan to come back with Malcolm for the funeral, and he will drive a U-Haul van back to Michigan with the rest of the twins' things then.

After I kiss the twins, attempting to keep the epic casual with a phrase like "See you soon!" Harmony comes and hugs me, giving me a quick kiss on the cheek. I take her hand.

"'All my pretty ones?'" I bellow, my thunderous voice echoing along the bungalows of Commonwealth Avenue. Harmony gets into the car and drives away and I keep on bellowing. "'Did you say all? O hell-kite! All? What, all my pretty chickens, and their dam, at one fell swoop?'"

Elizabeth Vandeweghe appears in her front door and she invites me inside. I shed many tears; I tell her everything that's happened.

Actually, that's not true. I leave out all of the fucking.

Late that afternoon, I am back at my office. Lara is not at her desk and I have no idea what is happening at the GMHI, but it feels good to be at work, pretending things are absolutely status quo.

The phone rings. It is Mark Siegel, a colleague of mine who runs an environmental nonprofit organization near the Capitol. We have met at several conferences, though I am never really sure if he is listening to me. He is handsome, an ex–football player (Yale). He often tells jokes that I don't get.

"Hi, Zeke," he says, once he is sure I recognize him. "I'm actually calling to do a reference check. Lara Callahan has applied for a position — executive assistant — at New Waters."

"She has?" I say. Mark says the word *actually* a lot.

"Actually, she said I could call you. Can you tell me a little something about her? What has she been like as an employee?"

"Disastrous," I say. "I can sum it all up in one word. Disastrous."

"Seriously? Why is that?"

"Completely unpredictable. A big drinker. A secret drinker. She can be great one minute, the next minute she's puking in the conference room trash can."

"Are you pulling my leg?"

"Look, Mark, she's attractive. I know what you're thinking. If that's all you're after, well, yes, go ahead and hire her, she's easy on the eyes."

"No, no. I thought she seemed very impressive, actually. Superprofessional. Bright. Experienced."

"Do what you must, Mark. I just want you to know you were warned. She's a complete pity case. She has children; she's a single mother. I can't bear to fire her and have those children end up out in the streets. But I can't, in good conscience, tell you that I would recommend her highly."

"Okay, Zeke. Thanks."

"Anything else?" I say.

But he's hung up.

My voice mail light is now flashing, so I check my messages.

I have two phone messages. One is from Farnsworth, and I delete the message without even listening to it. Fuck him and the midsize sedan he came in on! Is this the biggest problem the federal government has or something? How much is his goddamn room at Extended Stay America and the rental of a metallic pine green Saturn costing the taxpayers of this great and economically floundering nation?

The second phone message is from H. M. Logan. He is drunk and he is speaking very slowly. "Zeke, it's H. M. I keep getting phone calls from a guy named Farnsworth. Zeke? Zeke, he wants to know about my last trip for the GMHI. I went somewhere I shouldn't have gone. They found it on the credit card statement, Zeke! Zeke?"

H. M. for all his business acumen has never seemed to grasp the idea that I have voice mail and not an answering machine. All of his messages assume that I am standing there, listening to him, refusing to pick up the phone.

"Oh, and Zeke, I çalled some friends in L.A., as promised. I have Sofia Coppola's cell phone number. Zeke? Are you there? Anyway, I wanted to do this for you, before everything changes."

He leaves the number, repeating it five or six times in his slow, slurred way before my voice mail program finally gives him the boot. I return his call and leave him a message to meet me at Starbucks at ten thirty on Saturday morning. I then take Sofia's phone number and program it into my own phone. Even if I never work up the nerve to use the number, I feel somewhat powerful—nay, invincible—with that number programmed into my phone. I imagine, for a moment, myself as the victim of a hit-and-run accident in a strange city. A Good Samaritan pauses to help me, but I am near-dead. Panicked, as he waits for an ambulance, he picks up the phone he sees dangling from my blazer's inner pocket. He opens the phone, sees the name of acclaimed and absolutely breathtaking filmmaker Sofia Coppola, and he knows that I am somebody, that my life had some meaning. He calls Sofia, and she answers, but by now the Good Samaritan has become whelmed with emotion and he can do nothing but weep. Sofia listens to his weeping and this becomes the opening scene of her next film: a woman gets a phone call from a strange number, hears nothing but agonizing and soul-stirring sobs. For the rest of the film, she tried to find out the identity of that crying man, because she wants to comfort him. She too is alone. She too needs healing.

But, yes, I digress. Reverie.

I check my e-mail and find another response to my query *Why are you so unhappy?* I have been advertising on Google, and often, when somebody searches on any variation of the word *happy,* there is a link to my website on the side of the page, and if they follow it, they tend to send me messages like these:

To: inventory@americanunhappiness.org
From: sellmore@workathome.com
Re: Inventory of American Unhappiness

Hi, well, I know what make a lot of peoples unhappy! There boss! We can help you find a rewarding career working at home. No suits! No bosses! No meetings! No cubicales! No priar experience, no education neceserry! Visit our web site and SELL MORE, LIVE MORE!

Phil, 46, Crawford, TX

To: inventory@americanunhappiness.org
From: pfarmer@a2zconnection.com
Re: Inventory of American Unhappiness

So the other day I was walking around in Davenport, Iowa. I was there for a convention. It was a convention for people who make disposable restaurant products. That alone made me sort of depressed. I had spent three hours in a seminar called "The Meaning of Green." The whole seminar focused on how we can market disposable products as eco-friendly. There was a lot of sadness in the room, mostly over the decreasing use of Styrofoam. People were also pretty upset that plastic bags were getting such a bad reputation. "But they are so convenient," somebody actually said. "They make so much sense."

Anyway, this is not what I had in mind when I got a degree in marketing but of course I didn't have anything in mind. I was young. I figured that there would always be work in marketing. So that made me pretty happy. But what made me unhappy came later. I was wandering around downtown Davenport, which is, surprisingly, quite lovely. I'm serious. It's a nice little town. And there was this lighted walkway, a strange sort of architectural art piece you can walk down to the riverfront. Like an observation tower.

Very Asian, I thought. Very *Lost in Translation*. God, I love that movie. Anyway, when I got to the end of the long neon walkway, it felt very weird. A woman walking alone, at night, in a strange city, down a neon walkway that was empty save for me. And I got to the end and there was a casino. Not the river. The Mississippi River was behind all of that, but you couldn't see it, because there was a horrible, loud casino called Rhythm City and it had all this fake, shitty opulence. All these gang-bangers in Hummers as well as sweatpant-wearing people in sixteen-year-old minivans, and I thought, This is so outrageous, this is so unauthentic, this reeks and reeks of desperation and heartache.

I don't even know who is reading this. I don't even know why I wrote it. But it feels better. I am in an airport waiting for a flight to Erie, PA. I am giving a talk there at a seminar for restaurant managers. The seminar is called "Inside the Box: Why the Carry-Out Business Is Better than Ever."

I hate my life.

Peg, 34, Lexington, KY

As I've said, I rarely answer the e-mails to my inventory site. For one, it would be a time-consuming task. Two, one of the fascinating aspects of this project is that people unburden themselves of their unhappinesses without really knowing who (if anybody) will be reading it. If I were to make myself a sort of celebrity, in the sense that I become the guy who responds to all the e-mails, the sort of "unhappiness" guy who could easily become a celebrity in this strange age of YouTube/MySpace stardom, well, then, I would sully the project. I would ruin my life's work.

But I find Peg's e-mail so exhilarating and honest that I cannot resist.

To: pfarmer@a2zconnection.com
From: inventory@americanunhappiness.org
Re: Inventory of American Unhappiness
Dear Peg,

Thank you for sharing your story of unhappiness with me. I found it very moving. In fact, you mention a Sofia Coppola film. Ms. Coppola is actually quite interested in working with our project on a film component in the near future.

Anyway, ma'am, I found I knew exactly what you were talking about. Given our age, perhaps we are simply facing something that all humans must face. You know Jesus Christ and Alexander the Great, of course, both died at thirty-three. I'm sure you're aware of that. I'm sure you know what weight that age carries. But here we are at thirty-four! That historically and culturally significant age of thirty-three has come and gone! I do find that it's much harder to carry that kind of weight around in a Days Inn in Tuscaloosa or an Applebee's in Salt Lake City. I assume you know what I mean.

All good wishes,
Zeke, 34, Madison, WI
P.S. Will you marry me?

Yes, I am getting that desperate. Besides, one never knows, does one? But Peg doesn't respond.

One reason for my desperation, of course, is that I haven't heard from Minn—not via e-mail or phone or anything, and I am readily accessible via the web. So far, she has even ignored her online friend request. I decide to shift gears and begin work on an optimistic task: a job description for the position I am thinking of creating just for her: Program Officer for the *Inventory of American Unhap-*

piness. When she does contact me, I'll be ready to show her what I have in mind.

> **POSTING: Program Officer, *Inventory of American Un-happiness.*** The Great Midwestern Humanities Initiative (GMHI) seeks a Program Officer for the *Inventory of American Unhappiness* project. Candidate must have a profound understanding of the public humanities, as well as a degree (B.A. minimum) in a humanities discipline (i.e., anthropology, English, history, etc.). Ideal candidate will have training in oral history, but we will consider newcomers to the field who have a strong record of customer service and public interaction. Strong communication skills, oral and written, a top priority, as is a deep and unshakable intellectual curiosity. Zest for life, lust for living, love of people are all musts!

When Lara returns to work, I will hand her this new job description and ask her to place an ad for me in *Isthmus,* the weekly alternative paper, and perhaps on Craigslist. She will look shocked and perplexed, wonder why I need any more help than her able professionalism, but two can play this game she's started. If she wants to manipulate me by pretending to be unhappy at work, disappointed in me, and doubtful that I have the fundraising prowess necessary to keep our organization afloat, I can pretend to prepare for her departure.

I proof my ad one final time and feel a swell of delight in my chest. Certainly this is an adequate reason to track down Minn wherever she may be and offer her this once-in-a-lifetime opportunity.

Oh, I do love the hiring process! And so does H. M. Logan, a fact I know well. Perhaps I can convince H. M. to fund another position at GMHI and I can work with two bright and attractive women; H. M. worries about my loneliness, and I am sure such a move will be amenable to him, as soon as his paranoia dies down and he returns to a calmer plane.

It is time for a break. And thinking about Minn, and the possibility of her working alongside me, has me thinking about Starbucks. I decide to print out the job description I've just written up, and I place it in my pocket. Why not live expecting abundance? Why not expect that I will somehow find Minn, and somehow find a way to hire Minn, and somehow convince her to leave her fiancé, and why not simply set about making that hope a reality?

I will go and give Minn the ticket to a new life.

In the lobby, Lara's empty desk is as untidy as it's ever been, an avalanche of file folders and loose papers at the front of the old store, where the cash register must have been. Despite the mess created by the rummaging auditors, Lara's reception area remains pleasant, complete with fresh-cut flowers and a throw rug she purchased from Target with GMHI funds.

(Do not get me started on Target: nothing makes me more certain that it is time to end my decade of loneliness and marry! Oh, how I long to push a cart through those clean and wide, well-lit aisles with my wife at my side. We would add tastefully designed yet affordable lamps and bench seats and throw pillows into our lives; months before our first baby was due, we would nest. Saturdays would be a symphony of acquiring and arranging. I already know the trash cans I would have, the recycling center I would set up in the basement, and the laundry room organizer that would make the process of cleaning our clothes with lavender-infused eco-friendly detergent so effortless. Is that a summer breeze, my dear, or are you wearing freshly laundered pajamas? Please, permit me such longing. I am only actively manifesting the change I want to see in my life, a technique of visualization and focus I learned from the inspirational messages of Dr. Wayne Dyer.)

Just as I am leaving for the coffee shop, Lara comes into the office. She is dressed rather casually in jeans and a zipped-up hooded sweatshirt that professes her love of the Iowa Hawkeyes. Her hair is tucked back behind her ears and she is wearing a pair of trendy sneakers of turquoise and yellow. She is holding a box.

"Hi, Zeke," she says.

"Good afternoon, Lara," I say. "I was starting to worry about you."

"I've been in and out," she says. "I have plenty of personal days left."

"Oh, of course," I say. "I didn't mean that I was upset or anything. Anyway, I must say you look just as dazzling in your dungarees as you do in a business suit."

"What?" Lara asks.

"Nothing," I say. "Never mind."

"Okay," she says. "Zeke, I'm going to try and clean some of this up. The auditors sort of had their way with our files."

"Fine, Lara, it's your time. If you choose to work late, be my guest, but I have certainly never mandated it. Anyway, tomorrow we need to have a meeting. I will need you to set up the paperwork required—EOE, affirmative action, all of that stuff—necessary to do a new hire."

"A new hire?"

"Yes, a new hire."

"Zeke, didn't you look at the budget sheets I put on your desk?"

"Yes, that's why I am going to see H. M. Logan as soon as possible. He will fund this."

"Zeke! We barely can afford to make another month of rent and payroll!"

"Expect a miracle!" I say. "H. M. won't let us drown."

"How can you be so sure?" she says. "You're not at all nervous?"

"Not at all!"

"Did you call back Josh Farnsworth?"

"Ah, yes. I did."

"And?" she says.

"I was right," I say.

She waits for me to clarify.

"He's a jackass!" I say. I reach into my pocket, retrieve the job posting, and hand it to Lara. She takes it, reads it, and then looks up at me, dumbfounded.

"Jesus, Zeke. Zeke, this is serious! They are going to shut you down! You're broke! This is over. It's all over!"

This is when I take Lara's face in my hands, kiss her with conviction and gusto, a quick peck on the mouth. And then, to the sound of her gasping curses, I leave.

That evening, after another bus ride to the Fitchburg Starbucks and another baffled set of part-time baristas informing me that they have no idea where Minn has gone or when she'll be back, I trudge home from the bus stop, then up the steps to my front door, moving slowly enough that Elizabeth Vandeweghe happens to look out her window and sees me. She comes out her front door and calls my name, smartly dressed in what I'm fairly certain is a new J. Crew Super 120s Blair dress, shade: coal, made of four-season Australian merino wool, with a fetching scoop neck.

I meet her down in front of the house, near the driveway.

"Hi, Zeke," she says.

"Hi, Elizabeth," I say, adding, "You look quite amazing," which I believe is appropriate, since she is usually dressed in old jeans or shorts and T-shirts.

"Thanks," she says. "I had a job interview today. Trying to find something with benefits."

"Of course," I say. "In preparation for the divorce?"

How I wish I could hire every attractive woman I know!

I reach into my pocket and pull out a folded piece of paper and hand it to Elizabeth.

"Actually, we're about to start the hiring process where I work," I say. "That's the job description. Read it at your leisure."

"Really? That's kind of you. I don't expect any favors. I mean, I'll put together a great resumé and, no pressure, we'll just see what happens," Elizabeth says, visibly brightening with even the prospect of a new job.

"We offer excellent benefits," I say.

She smiles.

"Anyway, I just wanted to thank you for the other night. You were awfully sweet and I really needed a friend."

"Well, proximity often breeds friendship."

She nods.

"Actually, Zeke, the girls will be in Spring Green Saturday night with their grandparents. Do you want to get dinner or something?"

"Wow. Yeah, sure."

"Why did you say *wow*?"

"Pardon?" I say.

"You said the word *wow*. Is this weird? I mean it doesn't have to be a date or anything. Just two friends."

"No, no, it's not weird. It's very, no, I'm just surprised. Happily surprised. I've been wanting this."

"Why?"

"I think we should get married," I say.

Elizabeth looks at me as if she's just been shocked, electrically.

"I'm kidding!" I say. "Kidding!"

"I'm just glad you enjoyed—seem to enjoy—spending time with me," I say.

"Well," she says, "I do."

"Then it *is* a date. Six o'clock?"

"Sure," she says. "If the weather is nice, we can walk some-where."

She is barefoot and lovely as she walks away, and the new autumn light, a slightly muted yellow against a purpling sky, fills me with such joy that tears form in the corner of each eye.

That night, after I shut off my desk lamp and computer for the night, I stare out at the darkness for a moment and wonder if Elizabeth might appear on my sidewalk again, but she does not. But I like to imagine that she sleeps, or pretends to sleep, next door, perhaps, even, thinking or dreaming of me.

18

Zeke Pappas needs to focus.

THAT SATURDAY MORNING, while I drink the day's first cup of coffee, I look out my east side window and see Elizabeth, in running clothes, trying to get her children into the car and off to dance class. Being a single parent must be exhausting work, and certainly, perhaps, Elizabeth will soon long for a partner in that work, if she's not longing for one already. Still, it's very doubtful, given the fact that we have not even had one official date, that she would be willing to accept a marriage proposal this fall. But then again, my whole quest, the whole notion of proposing marriage to somebody by this imposed deadline, is fueled not by rational facts, but by magic. I must visualize success. And with Minn's chronic AWOL status, I must begin to think in terms of miracles, I must be the Brett Favre of courtship, making plays where no plays exist.

I have no doubt the recipient of my hasty marriage proposal will be shocked, but what I am hoping for, if I am free to admit my heart's deepest longing, is that the woman in question will be so moved, will feel a flood of inexplicable joy and unknown passion, that she'll accept, perhaps not right there, perhaps she will run from the room, screaming, laughing, or in tears, but she will accept. I can see it in my mind's eye.

Elizabeth is standing next to the minivan, buckling the kids into their car seats, and she looks quite amazing, her well-muscled legs rippling, the cheeks of her buttocks hugged by the turquoise running shorts. I watch her bend over and fiddle with straps, feel my blood surge, and have an idea.

I know after Elizabeth drops off the girls at dance class, she will, as seems to be her custom, go for a morning run. Upstairs I race, looking for the one pair of gym shorts I own, a red set of UW Badgers basketball shorts, quite baggy. Then I throw on a Mountain Dew T-shirt, some black athletic socks (I wish I owned some white socks, but I don't!), and the closest thing I have to sneakers, some navy blue Chuck Taylor high-tops.

When Elizabeth returns from dropping off her girls, she finds me standing in my front yard. Stretching.

"Do you run?" she asks.

"I do."

"Are you coming from or going for a run?"

"About to embark!" I say.

"Can I join you?" she says.

"Sure," I say.

"You can run in those?" she asks, looking at my sneakers. "Those have no arch support."

"It's all I run in," I say. "The only thing!"

Elizabeth then removes the hooded sweatshirt she is wearing with a quick zip, revealing a tight running tank top, purple. Her midriff is bare.

"Let's go," she says.

We go.

We begin with a walk down to the corner, then we cross Monroe Street, and as we hit the park near Lake Wingra, we break into a slow run.

"How many miles did you think you would go today?" she says.

"I'm flexible," I say.

The pace quickens. I feel a stitch in my side. We run through the path in the woods, which is matted with mulch. A tiny wood chip manages to slide into one of my Chuck Taylors, like a pointy toothpick. I keep going.

"Today I was going to go for six miles. The Arboretum loop. Have you run that?"

"Sure. Sure."

It's a little hard to run and talk.

She starts to pick up the pace again.

"You warm?" she says.

"Yes."

My ankles feel as if they may snap, and my heart is swollen with effort. I can feel it pounding in my rib cage.

Elizabeth gets a little farther ahead of me.

She hangs back, it seems, so I sprint to catch her and then blow by her. She runs faster. Soon we are laughing and racing through the Arboretum path, but then I fall over. I can't breathe.

"Oh, my God," Elizabeth says. I start to get up and stop when she stands over me and puts a hand on my back. "Are you okay?"

I am breathing very hard, but I manage a smile.

"I lied," I say. "I hate running."

She laughs so hard she nearly doubles over. "I thought so."

"See you tonight?" I wheeze.

"You bet," she says. "We'll celebrate. As of five thirty P.M. yesterday, I'm officially divorced!"

And then takes off running at a delirious speed, running so fast that she doesn't have time to turn around and see the delirious grin that spreads across my face.

I'm surprised by how much I like Elizabeth's sense of humor, which is something I hadn't really known about when she was just my married neighbor. In fact, I always had considered her somewhat humorless—she often looked tired and annoyed. When Rod would speak to me, small talk in the front yard, she always seemed impatient, as if the conversation was killing her. Perhaps she just was annoyed by her husband. Perhaps it had nothing to do with me.

Back home, I shower, taking a few extra moments to bask in a lustful fantasy of showering with my newly outgoing neighbor, and then I go off for my coffee meeting with poor H. M. Logan. Before I am about to ask people for money, I am flooded with many warm feelings toward them; I wonder, somehow, if this is an evolutionary trait, somewhat akin to the feelings dogs have for their masters just before breakfast.

I'm a bit late when I arrive at Starbucks, but H. M. is still waiting for me, a paper cup of coffee in front of him. He is wearing sunglasses, sitting at a corner table near the window, facing out toward the store. I wave to him, wave my index finger in the air to tell him I'll just be a minute, order a house blend with room for cream, and join H. M. at the table.

There must be thirty-five people in the Starbucks that morning, and the café is rich with the din of people hitting their caffeinated stride in the early hours of the weekend. Laughter, spirited discussions, exuberant exclamations into cell phones. It is quite uplifting.

I sit across from H. M. I do not like having my back to the rest of the café, mainly because there are so many beautiful women in trendy, neat apparel coming and going today, but I am late, and it would be bad fundraising form to ask to switch seats with H. M.

"Good morning," I say. "I'm sorry I'm a bit late."

"Look at me," H. M. says. He removes his sunglasses. Each of his eyes is bloodied and bruised, nearly swollen shut. He looks like a boxer after a tenth-round loss.

"My God," I say. "What happened?"

"I was beaten in the parking ramp last night, near the Hilton."

"Did you call the police? Who did this?"

"Zeke," he says. "What did you tell people? People are after me."

"Nothing, H. M. I asked you to have coffee so I could talk about finances. See, I need to hire somebody."

H. M. stands up and walks away from me, without a word. I watch him go out the front door. I hear a small clicking sound to my left, and I look, and suddenly, seated at the table next to me, is Farnsworth. Clipping his fingernails.

"Morning, Zeke," he says.

He slides the nail clippers into the pocket of his jacket.

"Are you behind that?" I ask. "What in the world are you after?"

"We're not violent people, Zeke," he says. "We would not ever do that."

"Why did he leave so suddenly then? He must have seen you."

"I'm offended that you would even suggest Mr. Logan was assaulted by somebody from the federal government. I think Mr. Logan has some other problems, much more substantial ones, than a bunch of midlevel Washington bureaucrats. Keep your eyes on the headlines."

"I have to go find him," I say. "He's probably outside sobbing. Look, don't drag him into this mess. The guy is an emotional cripple. Why wreck his life? What are you after?"

"Truth. Justice. The American Way," Farnsworth says. "So long, Zeke."

With that, he stands and heads for the door.

I notice the bulbous-nosed Clinton-esque figure in the proverbial opposite corner, scribbling away on a yellow legal pad. Before I leave, I stop by his table. I point at both my eyes and then point my two fingers at him, a gesture that I think means "I'm watching you, pal."

That afternoon, I'm unable to resist the impulse to make the drive out to the far west side Starbucks. But, alas, still no Minn in sight. Still no answer at her door. And just like that, my neighbor, Elizabeth Vandeweghe, becomes my number-one prospect.

19

Zeke Pappas is ready to make a move.

AT SIX O'CLOCK on Saturday evening, Elizabeth and I walk up the street to a new Belgian bistro that has been open for several months, but that neither of us has tried yet. Inside, we find a dark, oaky interior and are led back to a small alcove, where we have all the privacy we could ever want. I am wearing blue jeans and a gray cotton half-zip pullover over a blue oxford. She is wearing jeans, very flattering jeans, and a tight sweater of red cashmere. She also has on a feminine-looking brown blazer. She has a wonderful collarbone and her sweater is considerably liberal in its exposure of cleavage. Her blond hair is styled as always, simply, tucked behind her ears, a part on the side. She wears earrings but otherwise doesn't look like a woman who is trying too hard, which is good.

"Geez," I say, after the host leaves to fetch us some water. "I feel like a mob boss. Could this table be any more private?"

"It's nice," she says. "I don't want to see any of the other Monroe Street mommies tonight and explain what I am doing with you."

"They know you're separated, right?"

"Yeah. Most people don't believe it. They all think Rod is great." I smile.

"But I want to talk about something besides Rod. And kids. Okay?"

"Fine with me. Rod is a dick."

She laughs. "No. No, he's not."

"You should feel free to think so," I say. "You should feel free to move on with hate and bitterness. It's the only way!"

I like how she leans in and tells me I'm hilarious. "You crack me up," she says. "I don't think I know anybody else like you."

"Oh, I'm exceedingly common. But I'm going to try this beer I can't pronounce," I say. "It's thirteen dollars and I have to try a thirteen-dollar beer."

"Thirteen bucks?"

When the waiter comes by, I order two thirteen-dollar beers.

"Was that okay? That I ordered for you?"

"I actually prefer wine," she says. "But let me try this beer."

When the thirteen-dollar beer arrives, I find it delicious. As does Elizabeth.

Thirteen-dollar Belgian beers are quite potent, it turns out. Elizabeth and I walk, arm in arm, down Monroe Street and she suggests we walk to the lake. It's a cool night, and we huddle together out of both drunkenness and cold. The stars are out and when we get to the lake, she leaning in so close to me that I can feel her heartbeat, we sit on a bench and look up at the sky.

"I wish I knew the constellations better," she says. "I wish I had taken astronomy in college. I always was fascinated by the stars and planets."

"What did you major in?"

"French."

"Ah, the humanities!" I say.

"*Oui*," she says.

"Well," I say, pointing to a star ahead of us, over the lake, "that star is called Cyberius, and he is the guard dog of those stars called the Daphnes."

218

"Wow. Cool."

"And that cluster over there?" I say. "That's Plebius and if you look closely, the constellation that he is a part of—the Magodons—looks like a dragon."

"Yeah?"

"And there is Honduras, god of mischief."

"You're making this up," she says. "You asshole."

I smile. We watch the stars for a moment, laughing.

She cuddles in closer.

"This is really weird, don't you think?" she says.

"What?"

She sits up.

"This," she says. "You and me. I mean, we've lived next door to each other for like five years."

I look at her. Quizzically. "Is something wrong with that?"

"Well, you've always been the friendly, sort of quirky guy next door. A loner. I mean, the kind of guy, Rod used to say, that people talk about on the news after some unspeakable tragedy occurs. You know, *Well, he was a nice man. Kind of quiet. Kept to himself.*"

"He said that?"

"Well, like you said, Zeke, he's kind of a dick."

"Do you think I'm a psychopath?"

"No. Not at all. It's just that I never thought of you much one way or another. I liked you. I thought you were good-looking, but, well, women are different. I don't think we imagine everyone as a potential mate the way men do. Men look at every woman as a potential sex object."

"I'm offended by that," I say, smiling.

"You never once considered what it might be like to, you know, be with me?"

"Well, sure," I say. "You're attractive. You dress well. You have six-pack abs."

"I don't."

"Close. I've seen you running."

"Ha."

"So, is this *too* weird?"

"Not at all," she says. "It's nice."

This is when we start to kiss. We kiss well. We kiss long. Her hands roam, against my chest, my thighs. My hands roam too.

I kiss her neck.

"Kiss my ears," she says.

I do and she sighs little moans into my ears. An ear woman. Ear women tend to be fairly easy to please, sexually, in my opinion.

She runs her hands tantalizingly close to my rigid member.

And this is when I whisper in her ear, "I want to fuck you outside."

She stops.

"What did you say?"

"I said I want to fuck you outside."

She stops, shrinks back from me.

"Why did you say that?"

"Because it's true."

"That's a weird thing to say. On a first date."

"I just, I just thought . . ."

She stands up. "Tell me the truth, Zeke. Why did you say that? Why did you say it like that?"

I just look up at her.

"Don't lie, Zeke."

I can't tell her.

"You heard Rod and me fighting that night, you were listening, weren't you?"

"What?"

"You did," she says. She is sort of laughing now, in disbelief, so I decide, What the hell.

"Okay, I did. I heard you say, 'We've never fucked outside.'"

"And you tried to use that line on me? You thought that would have made me melt?"

220

I stop talking.

Elizabeth walks away. When I stand up, she kicks off her heeled boots and holds them in her hand. And then starts to run across the grass of Wingra Park, as fast as she can in jeans and no shoes.

I do try to knock on her door when I get back to Commonwealth Avenue, but she doesn't answer. I know my limits. I don't push it. I go home.

I wake up late on Sunday morning, hung-over yet again, and look out the window but see no sign of movement at the Vandeweghes'. I walk down to the independent neighborhood café for some coffee, but my triple-shot cappuccino is horribly done. The espresso tastes of ashes and there is far too much milk in my cup. I inform the assistant manager that Starbucks, of all places, knows how to make a cappuccino the right way, and perhaps they should consider going for training.

"Go fuck yourself," the manager says, which seems an overreaction to some constructive criticism. But, alas, it's a sensitive world, I suppose, more sensitive than I would ever imagine.

"This shit tastes like Kwik Trip shit," I say, and I open my coffee and dump it on the floor.

Exit Zeke.

The truth is, I thought Elizabeth would have taken my "fuck outside" comment as some sort of mystical confirmation from the universe that I was the soulmate she longed for—I really thought it was a winning play.

But, of course, it wasn't.

It's probably safe to say that I can move Elizabeth off my prospect list. This means that my other prospects require immediate attention. I hop the bus to Fitchburg.

Once again, Minn is not working at the Starbucks, but I sit and linger for a few hours, drinking a well-made cappuccino, picking at an overly sweet blueberry muffin, and reading the morning papers.

I wait until three, wondering if Minn might come in for a late shift, but, alas, she still is absent. I finish my muffin and the last of my beverage, neatly refold the newspaper so it can be used by another customer, and then walk over to the drab, suburban apartment complex where Minn lives. I pick a random apartment number and buzz, receiving no answer. Then I buzz a second one, and a sleepy woman's voice answers. "I have a registered letter for you," I say, "from the Madison Police Department."

"What is it?" she asks.

"I don't know, ma'am. But you have to sign for it."

"Come on up," she says, and the security lock unlatches and I am inside the complex. Minn's apartment is on the third floor, and the woman I've buzzed is on the second floor, so I take the elevator, hoping not to be greeted by a sleepy woman expecting a letter. I knock on Minn's door with a gentle rasp. I wait thirty seconds and knock again. After my third knock, quite forceful, I break the door in with my shoulder, which is surprisingly easy. No deadbolt. And I discover that Minn's apartment is completely empty, except for a black garbage bag full of packing materials, and the random dross of a hurried move—magazine reply cards, scattered pennies, one stray gray sock.

20

Zeke gets to the bottom of things.

MONDAY MORNING, after a brief and uneventful stop at the Hospice Center—Mother was sleeping—I find that there is a memo from Lara taped to the computer monitor on my desk.

> *Dear Zeke,*
>
> *Please accept my resignation as associate director of the Great Midwestern Humanities Initiative. I thank you for your professionalism and your generosity over the years, but I feel compelled to pursue other opportunities at this time.*
>
> *Yours sincerely,*
> *Lara Callahan*
> *Cc: Mr. H. M. Logan, Chair*

I take the letter, crumple it into a little ball, and hurl it across the office. This is madness. I certainly wish Lara were able to deal with her insecurities and disappointments in a less dramatic way. Perhaps I have not been completely sensitive to her needs as an employee, and possibly I have even blurred the line between professionalism and our personal lives. And yes, Farnsworth and his team of federal fucksticks, I'm sure, are unsettling to her. And yes, our financial situation is somewhat dire, but Lara has truly overreacted to everything. I need her help and stability now more than ever.

This makes me feel bad, because I do care about Lara very much. But in truth, it is absolutely essential that Lara stay on my prospect list because she is one of the only real marriage possibilities I have left. It is now Lara or nothing, and I'm not sure how much time I have left. If only I hadn't taken Lara for granted! I didn't give her the respect and attention a true marriage prospect deserves!

I check my messages. There are three voice mails from H. M. Logan, all of them begging me to call him and all of them from the middle of the previous night.

There is one e-mail from a fellow named Donovan Brass, the executive director for a group called ArtAttack, who wants to know if I can provide a reference for Ms. Lara Callahan, who has applied for the position of program coordinator with his organization.

I reply with the following statement: *Hiring Lara Callahan would be a debilitating and energy-sucking mistake. I wouldn't, if I were you, bring such obvious and soaring malaise upon your organization. Also, she stole from the organization on a regular basis.*

I hit Send.

I'm in the office, late in the day, still looking through Lara's desk for financial records and trying, futilely, to guess the password for our online banking system. I have no idea how to pay myself this month, and Lara left no instructions.

I hear the door to the main entrance swing open—a little bell lets us know somebody has entered—and I stand up to greet the visitor. Without Lara, the duty of reception falls to me. I sort of expect to see Farnsworth, or maybe even Lara, but it's Joseph.

His eyes are bloodshot and his face is unshaven and bloated. He wears a light gray hooded sweatshirt replete with food stains and he flops down on the couch in reception as if he's run for miles just to reach me. He's breathless. He takes a hit of his asthma inhaler, holds his breath for a minute, and then exhales slowly.

"What is it?" I say, a little annoyed by the drama.

"The Cynic Cessation Project," Joseph says.

"What?"

"The Cynic Cessation Project," Joseph says. "That's what it is. I've been on the phone and the web for twenty-six hours or something. I found a guy, a reporter from the *Nation,* who gave me this other guy to call."

"Joseph, what are you talking about?"

Mack walks into the office next. "Zeke, don't listen to him. He's crazy. He lives for shit like this and he's upsetting you for no reason."

Mack's voice rises a bit at the end of this sentence and Joseph and I both turn to him, surprised.

"Calm down, Mack," I say.

"This is who is harassing you!" Joseph bellows. "I'm sure of it. These guys, these guys are from that."

"From what?"

"The Cynic Cessation Project. It's a joint effort between the executive branch and Homeland Security, but it's privately funded. It's funded by the Heritage Foundation and the American Enterprise Institute."

"You're serious? How come we've never heard of it?"

"You will hear of it soon. Leatherberry's on the board of the Heritage Foundation, and this is one of his ideas."

"Jesus. Can they do this?"

"They have a mandate from the foundation to assess and then suppress instances of anti-Americanism, anti-capitalism, and anti-exceptionalism in federally funded programs or projects. They were going to start small, and so they started with you. If you want to know the truth, I think Leatherberry has been sleeping with H. M. Logan, and that's part of this somehow. There's been rumors about Leatherberry's gay lovers for years!"

"But Leatherberry's the guy who gave us the money in the first place."

"Exactly. Because he was fucking Logan! But if he comes down on you first, makes an example out of you, he can make Logan out to be some scorned, delusional liar."

"Jesus."

"You have to find H. M. Logan and find out everything he knows."

"You're amazing, Joseph. I don't know how to thank you."

"Are you kidding? This is great. This is validation that my fifteen years of paranoia, obsessive reading, code names, security systems, and everything else is all worth it."

"This is all speculation," Mack says. "None of it is confirmed. You're going to get yourself in trouble, Zeke. You should be focusing on getting yourself married if you want to keep those girls."

"How are you, Mack?" I ask.

"His hand is still messed up," Joseph says.

"That's too bad," I say.

Mack sticks up his middle finger. "I have to hold it like this."

"Isn't that convenient?" I say.

"As far as I can tell," Joseph says, "these are pretty rough guys. They talk the talk. It doesn't scare a seasoned anarchist like me, but Mack's just a sales rep. He doesn't like to know about this stuff. He doesn't want the truth. He can't handle it. Sales reps live for consensus and tranquillity. Room service and happy hour. But we booksellers are more like lone wolves, trolling windowless nooks and crannies, drinking bad coffee from stained giveaway mugs."

"Well, I don't know if there's anything I can do," I say.

"Fucking Heritage Foundation," Joseph says.

"They're going to close down your office," Mack says. "That is all he really found out. But I think it's because you maybe didn't keep track of your finances in the way you were supposed to keep track?"

"That's their excuse!" Joseph claims. "An excuse to silence all decent citizens in this nation!"

"Look, maybe I can get a job at your bookstore," I say. "I can just walk away from all of this. We're out of money anyway. Lara's resigned."

"No!" Joseph says. "Lara? She's one of your 'hot' prospects, right?"

"Probably the last one," I say.

"Too bad," Mack says. "What happened?"

"Incredibly long story," I say. "Look, why don't I just quit? Walk away from this whole mess, give the government back all its money, its building, its copy machine. Do you think they'd let up on me, Joseph?"

"Yes, they would," Mack says.

"Who knows?" Joseph says.

"And I could get a job at your bookstore for now," I say.

Mack and Joseph look at each other and then back at me.

"Well, Zeke, we should probably tell you," Joseph says. "Mack's been laid off, probably for abusing his expense account. Or for failing to conform to the sales projection worksheet format. Or because he can't use Excel. He can barely use e-mail. No matter, he's been canned."

"There's no soul in the spreadsheet," Mack says. "Anyway, it's not just me. The whole sales force in the Midwest has been laid off, and without my salary to keep things afloat, the bookstore is also out of money. Done. It's closing down."

"No!" I say. "Why?"

"Why?" Joseph asks. "Why? Because the age of entitlement, of excess, of intellectual preoccupations fueled by disposable income, of government funding, of private endowments, of leisure, of inaction, of self-obsession, of narcissism, all of that is over. Places like the GMHI are a casualty of that, and so, in some odd way, are independent bookstores. What you have left are things that make fiscal sense, which are really the things that fuel capitalism and war. All of the rest of this is bullshit, Zeke. We're all finished. You and me and every English major in a million-mile radius. We've finally become wholly irrelevant."

"Jesus," Mack says. "It's just time for us to retire. You need to hang around somebody other than two washed-up, middle-aged homosexuals anyway."

"But you guys are my best friends!" I say.

"It's an extraordinarily lonely and perplexing era," Joseph says.

"Zeke," Mack says, "we're not really your best friends, are we?"

I shake my head. "No! Of course not! Zeke Pappas has plenty of friends. You should see my Facebook page."

"Mack hates Facebook," Joseph says.

"Well, what are you and Mack going to do?" I say.

"We're moving to Florida, land of last resorts," Joseph says. "We're going to manage my father's chain of beauty parlors. He just opened three more in the Tampa area this year."

"Oh," I say. "Will that make you guys happy?"

"You're a good man, Zeke," Mack says. "But you ask all the wrong questions."

Lara lives on the near east side of Madison, on the first floor of an old two-flat from the early 1900s. She rents from a professor, a divorced historian, about fifty, who specializes in the Middle East and North Africa. His name is Hunter Moss and he occasionally accompanies Lara to social events and cultural affairs in town. She has told me, on several occasions, that he is not her type and that there is nothing serious going on between them, but I am sure Hunter Moss is interested in her in a sexual and romantic way. Still, as Lara's boss, I was never in a position to pry, despite my curiosity. I doubt that many women, if any, ever see me walking down the street and begin ruminating on the details of my sexual life; but Lara, a sharp, pretty single mother who does not appear to have had a serious relationship in a long time, must draw a great deal of speculation from the male sector. It's sad and obvious what we all long to know: has she felt any passion and longing for anybody since her husband left her years ago? And, if not, might one of us be able to restore such important elements to her life?

On her front porch, which she shares with Hunter Moss, two bikes are padlocked to the railing. A few leaves and stray pieces of litter blow around on the dusty surface. The lawn, which I look out on after I ring the doorbell—it is my polite custom to ring the doorbell and turn my back from the door while the person I am visiting prepares to be visited, i.e., dons a robe, straightens her hair, checks her makeup in the foyer mirror—is bare and spotty and the entire house, a washed-out gray, is in need of a paint job. Hunter Moss is certainly not a fastidious landlord.

Nobody answers the door. I knock again and swear I see a figure moving around behind the gauzy curtains in the bay window. So I knock louder. No answer. I am about to leave when my palms seem to fill with adrenaline and I reach for the doorknob and open the front door and walk into the house.

I shut the door behind me. Standing in the foyer, I can see that the house is a mess: the vast clutter that children bring into one's life—toys, books, crayons, multiple shoes and coats, a medley of large projects made from construction paper and cardboard—is everywhere.

"Goddamn it, Zeke," Lara says, walking briskly toward me from the kitchen. "You can't just walk into my house."

I don't like yelling, I remind her, and she screams in my face, a long, shrill shriek.

She looks lovely. She is wearing a close-fitting white tank top and black yoga pants and sneakers. You can see the surprising athleticism of her body. (Once, in graduate school, I took a fiction workshop in which I was chastised for having my protagonists always remark on the clothes and body of a woman when she appears on stage, but, do trust me on this, all men make an instant sexual judgment each time they see a woman—yes, she looks like someone I would want to sleep with, or no, not at this time.)

"I'm sorry, Lara," I say. "But I was very concerned."

I wish that it was winter and I was wearing a hat, gloves, and overcoat. A leading man, say, in a fifties noir drama, would certainly enter without knocking, then immediately begin to shed his outerwear, as if he were simply arriving at home, a gesture ripe with the sort of aggressive intimacy one associates with strong and forceful men of that bygone era. Alas, no hat, no coat, so I crack my knuckles.

"I'm fine, Zeke. I just think that, given the circumstances, I should resign."

"What circumstances?"

"We're broke, Zeke. Let's start there. You won't be able to make payroll next month. I don't work for free."

"Well, this is quite insane," I say. "Certainly you can't blame me for our country's delicate economic condition."

She looks at me, perplexed. "Zeke, this has been coming down the pike for two goddamn years. I try to talk to you about it every day."

"I know. I know! Wayne Dyer would call that scarcity thinking though, Lara."

"Zeke, please. I resigned. It's inappropriate for you to barge into my house and demand an explanation."

"Why didn't you answer the door?"

"I was doing tai chi."

"Seriously?"

"Yes. The kids are at school. I don't get much time alone in the house, so I thought I'd enjoy my day off. I start a new job next week. Despite your shitty references."

"Pardon?"

"Don't play dumb. Mark Siegel told me what you said. Luckily, he didn't believe any of it."

"I have no idea what you're talking about, Lara."

"What do you want, Zeke?"

"Tai chi, huh? I've been thinking about that," I say. "I could use something like that in my life."

"You know, I could sue you for that. For those false reference statements!"

"Do you find it centering?"

"What?"

"Tai chi."

"I do."

"Wow. Is it strenuous?"

"No. It's relaxing. That's the idea."

"Could you show me? How do you do it?"

"No."

"Don't leave me," I say.

"Zeke, I want you to leave now. This is so inappropriate."

"After all those years of friendship between us?" I say. "This is how we end things? A typed letter on my desk?"

That makes her back away.

"Zeke, look, I'm done. It's not just the way you treated me the other day, it's a whole lot of things. For one thing, I don't really even know what we do. I don't know what sort of career track I am on, answering the phones at an organization that gets increasingly obscure and broke with each passing year."

"I resent that. You seemed to value the work we did a few weeks ago."

"I've been doing some thinking. Soul-searching."

"Look, I want to start again. We could start our own organization, without federal money. Who cares what those auditors do? We'll start a private foundation. The Foundation for the Study of American Unhappiness! We'll do the Unhappiness Festival each fall, and we'll keep the *Inventory* project on task, and . . ."

"Stop it, Zeke."

"No. I'm serious! I'll pay you double."

"With what?"

"What do you mean?"

"What are you going to pay me with, Zeke?"

"We'll talk to H. M., Lara. We'll explain why we need his investment in our work now more than ever."

"H. M.?"

"We'll tell him we're getting married. We will get married."

"Zeke, you've gone nuts."

"Lara," I say, taking her hand, looking into her green eyes, which are remarkably large when you fixate on them in relation to her small nose and chin. She looks down but takes my other hand, moves just a faint step closer so I can feel some heat coming off the skin of her bare midriff. Oh, what a wonderful fashion trend, may it never die again! Ever since I saw Madonna's "Lucky Star" video as a prepubescent youth, I have loved the sight of a shirt rising just high enough to show a hint of skin. "Do you believe in retroactive sex?"

"What? What is that?"

She steps back.

"No, listen to me for a second. Retroactive sex is a guilt-free way of having sex. For instance, let's say there was someone you were friends with in college, maybe you had an intense attraction to that person and vice versa, but for some reason you never consummated it. Whatever. You were dumb and young. And you see that person years later—you can have total, no-strings-attached sex since you passed up your chance at it once before. It doesn't matter what your current situation is or whatever. The sex you engage in at the present moment is actually based on a past emotional response. So, well, the emotional repercussions are done. They're over. What you are engaging in is like a purely cathartic physical act."

"What?"

"Like a sauna, or massage, or something."

"Shut up. This is serious?"

"I'd like to think so. I sort of perfected this theory. But it's a widely believed phenomenon. I am surprised you never heard of it. It has plenty of useful applications—former students, say, for a college professor who resisted the temptations set before him in the

232

classroom and then meets the former co-ed when she is thirty-one, on a business trip for an insurance company. They could go back to her hotel, watch a filthy movie, smoke crack, whatever. It's an event happening, technically, in the present, but it's fueled by the past."

"That's not how it works," Lara says.

"Okay. Maybe you see your ex-husband's best friend, long after your marriage is over, and maybe he was single way back when, but now he's married. Right? But you can fuck him, right then and there. You still can act on something you held at bay due to social propriety, friendship, whatever. It's fine. It's a secret with no present-day complications."

"You're freaking me out," Lara says.

"Or in our case, you are no longer my employee and I am no longer your superior, so we can have the sex we would have had on that night in Omaha without any long-term emotional or logistical effects on our present situations or relationships. We get it over with, done, end of unfulfilled impulse, end of buried desire. Release of burden!"

"Omaha? This is crazy. You are such a sick man."

"Come on, when's the last time you had sex with somebody?"

"I don't know."

"See?"

"About two weeks ago, I guess."

"Oh? Seriously?" I say.

She turns away from me, crosses the room. I follow.

"Who?" I ask.

"It wasn't great. I probably won't have sex with him again."

"It doesn't matter anyway. That's the great thing about this. You can have sex with him again. Tomorrow, for instance. I, myself, had two possible opportunities for sex this week, but only one panned out and it ended badly. I don't know where she is."

"I can't believe this," Lara says. "I'm going to have to call the cops, Zeke."

"Certainly there's some sort of physical, or mental, attraction between us. All those years in the office, all of that forbidden pleasure we resisted because of professional ethics and our need for gainful employment, none of that is important now."

"Zeke. You're twisted. And you're lonely. And I have great affection for you, I pity you, losing your wife so young and now you work so hard, all of these years, on this insane project—but you're losing it. Let me say this clearly: *There's no money left.* And let me say this clearly: *I am not attracted to you and am not in love with you.*"

"Lara, let's at least talk to H. M."

"Zeke, H. M. is on the way to Mexico."

"Mexico?"

"Yes, he's been frantically trying to reach you. He's worried about things that apparently are about to be found out. He has a house in Mexico, his safe place in the event of this sort of emergency. He told me he'd find you before he left, but I guess he didn't."

"Stunning!" I say. "Jesus, how could he do that to us?"

"Zeke, calm down. You'll find some kind of job. So will I. We will be fine."

She goes off to the bedroom and comes back, holding something.

"Fine. Look," I say, "I am confident, very confident, that I can raise enough money to continue operations on a small scale, I'm sure. I mean, we may have to cut our grant program, but that seems a little nineteen-nineties anyway. *Grants?* Yuck! How passé! This is the era of the big donors, the fat cats, the private endowments, the windfalls, and I think . . ."

"All of that's over, Zeke. Do you read the news?"

"Lara, you have to marry me."

"Stop," Lara says. "I told you, I quit."

"What's that in your hand?" I ask.

"An electronic Taser," she says.

"Are you going to Taser me?" I ask.

"I hope not," she says.

"Where did you get a Taser?"

"My uncle is a police sergeant in Louisville. He doesn't think women should live alone without firearms. This was a compromise."

I drop to my knees.

"Lara, my mother is dying and if I am not married before she dies, then I lose the twins. They go to their aunt!"

Lara sighs and looks at me with maybe some real tenderness. She knows I have been good to her and she has been good to me, an intelligent, reliable, quick-witted assistant. She knows that she has survived difficult economic times because of my generosity. She's also known, all along, that her legs had something to do with it, and that maybe there is something more than professional tension in our relationship.

"Zeke, I'm so sorry."

"It's in her will. If I'm not married, Lara, by the time she dies, the girls live with their aunt and I am nothing more than an uncle who visits once or twice a year."

"Oh, no," she says.

"You have to marry me," I say. "I will take care of you. I will provide for you and your kids and my kids. Like the Brady Bunch!"

"Zeke, that's not how marriage works. I don't love you."

"I'm lovable though. I am!"

"You're odd, Zeke. I don't know if you are lovable in that sense of the word."

"Lara! I'm coming right out and begging you. Please marry me!"

"You don't even have a job anymore," she says.

"If I can secure my position at the GMHI, if I can prove my income is respectable, you'd consider it?"

"No, Zeke. I didn't mean that."

"What did you mean?"

"Zeke, I can't marry you," she says. "I don't love you!"

"Right," I say.

"I barely even like you," she says.

I nod.

"Don't cry," she says. "You cry too easily."

"My mother's dying. I lost my job. My kids are leaving me."

"Point taken," she says. "Weep away."

"You're being cruel," I say.

"Look, I'm going to take a quick shower and get dressed," Lara says. "Then I can go down to the office and show you a few things you might want to know, before they shut you down completely."

"I'm sorry if you felt threatened by me, Lara. I'm sorry you felt the need to get your Taser."

"I'm not afraid to use it, Zeke," she says.

"Is that a joke?"

"I don't know, Zeke."

"This is so surreal."

"It's okay, Zeke. It's okay to be in love with me; you can't help it. All of those years working side by side."

"We should be together, Lara."

"I mean it was inevitable that we'd have an awkward sexual encounter someday," she says. "I should have been more direct with you years ago. I am not at all interested."

"But what about at that conference in Omaha? We nearly kissed!"

"I know. This is the best job I could imagine having, moneywise. It allowed me to spend time with my kids when they were little, it gave us health benefits, it was easy."

"So what are you saying?"

"I might have led you to believe that I liked you more than I really do."

"You mean you prefer that we just remain friends."

"I made a vow to myself on my last birthday, Zeke, and it was this: I vowed to be more honest and direct. I read this great book called *Matters of Authenticity*; it had this subtitle like *How to Stop Pleasing the People Who Don't Matter*."

"I don't matter?"

"What I mean, Zeke, is that it's better if we just remain colleagues. And since I've resigned, that means our relationship is largely over."

I decide to switch tactics; as bruised as my ego is, I don't want to admit defeat. There's too much at stake.

"I know. I think you're right," I say. I feel rather faint and take a seat on the couch. "I'm a little nauseous."

"Okay," she says. "Zeke, please don't cry again."

She goes into the bathroom, shuts the door.

"I'm not going to cry!"

"Oh, you just looked like you might," she says, from behind the door. "I sometimes hear you weeping in your office and—well, I hate it."

"That's ridiculous! I have never wept in my office."

"You do. It's very unsettling when I hear it."

"Nonsense!" I bellow.

Sitting on the sofa, I pick up a J. Crew catalog and browse for a moment. One of my favorite models, a smiling, thick-haired brunette with a rather ample bosom (by J. Crew standards), is wearing the Seaside seersucker wide halter-top bikini. I stand up, swelling in my pants, my mouth dry and tasting of copper. My hand shakes. And then I push the bathroom door open a small crack (bathrooms in old homes rarely lock!) and see Lara's figure, naked behind the frosted glass.

"Zeke?" Lara says. "Are you in here?"

What an enticing image, the flesh of a woman, her curves evident and her details blurred, behind a steaming shower door. I unzip my pants and watch her for a moment, and then I undress, standing there in my boxer shorts, my pleasure growing evident. Lara turns to face me for a moment, and I see the darkness of hair between her legs, the curve of her breasts through the frosted glass. My heart is in my throat. I hear her scream, and I scramble for my clothes.

Lara slides open the shower door, just a small crack, as I try to zip my fly and pull on my T-shirt at the same time. She reaches outside of the shower and grabs a brown towel, then wraps herself in it.

And now I hear her shrieking a little bit. "Oh, God, Zeke, you are so pathetic."

I hear real disdain in her voice. I hear that she means those last two words. My heart crashes to my kidneys; my stomach gives way to water and cramps.

"I'm so sorry," I say, dressing hurriedly in the next room. "I completely misjudged your statement."

"What statement?" she shrieks.

"When you said you were going to take a shower, I thought that was an invitation."

"How could you possibly think that?"

"Lara, please. I am a desperate man."

"That's obvious," she says, coming out of the bathroom, wrapped in a towel, pointing the Taser at me.

"I need love, Lara. I don't have much time left!"

We stand there now, she still dripping wet, I half-dressed, fully aroused, crazy-ashamed, and suddenly weary.

She shoots the Taser at a potted plant to show me it works. It sizzles and hisses, the air suddenly dense with the smell of burning leaves.

Exit Zeke.

21

Zeke is digging deep.

THAT AFTERNOON, I stop off at the Hospice Center again and my mother manages to sit up in bed for a moment, but she is barely lucid. She asks me where the goats have gone and then she wonders aloud how my pregnancy is going, has a coughing fit, yells out Cougar's name, and then drifts off to sleep. I go out to the parking lot and make a few phone calls, letting my fading mother sleep. I call Peter Romano, a small-time mobster who also happens to be H. M. Logan's attorney down in Janesville.

Romano confirms that H. M. is out of the country, but that is all he will tell me.

"It turns out, Zeke, that H. M. and Representative Quince Leatherberry, Republican, Fifth District, Wisconsin, spent a weekend under assumed names at a resort called Sunbelts in the Caribbean with each other and about six male prostitutes from the Dominican Republic."

"I see," I say. I start to laugh. I can't help myself.

Romano doesn't laugh.

"And they're looking at the records of earmarks, special favors, that Leatherberry might have done for H. M. using federal money. And I am afraid the GMHI might be a prominent favor on that list."

"I see," I say. "Has this been leaked to the media yet?"

"Well, H. M. called me and told me about everything last night. He said he was leaving the country. But I didn't expect this," Romano says. "He was trying to get you a million dollars before he left, for your commie-faggot think tank or whatever he's been pouring money into, but his assets have been frozen. He's apparently also linked to some big Wall Street Ponzi scheme, I don't know. I know I'll never get paid now. That's what I know. He owes me forty thousand bucks. And counting."

"Okay, well, I appreciate the heads-up, Romano."

"H. M.'s main concern was that this not be damaging to his family," Romano says. "And I know H. M. was a weird little fucker, but I like his wife. I fucked her a few times. You'd be surprised, Zeke, how some of them older broads look naked. They treat a man well. And I like his kids. So, anyway, don't talk to the press about his, you know, predilection for male ass. Let's try and keep everything as quiet as we can, especially the ass play."

"You're kidding me," I say. "I think that's a moot point."

"Is it?" Romano says. "I hope so."

"Never mind. Anyway, Mr. Romano, what about the estate? Do you know how much money Mr. Logan might have left to the Great Midwestern Humanities Initiative? I know this sounds crass, but we're in a dire way and this story is not going to help our fundraising situation any. Perhaps, if he does do something drastic, which I hope he doesn't do, perhaps we will be in the will?"

"Zeke, I like you. You're as sick and selfish as I am."

"Well," I say, "is there any money left? I'm desperate."

"Zeke, H. M. is pretty much broke. The investments he does have are sketchy. Like I said, I think all the money he planned to will to the GMHI was in a pretty shady Ponzi scheme. He put his money in with some Germans in New York and he couldn't get it out when he wanted to. This isn't going to be a quick process."

"I see," I say. "Well, forgive me for asking about it so quickly and crassly."

"Happens all the time," he says. "Trouble on the horizon, crows and vultures darken the sky."

"Rather poetic," I say. "Did you think that up?"

"Did," he says.

"Romano," I say, "you didn't really have sex with his wife, did you?"

"Somebody had to," Romano says.

"I suppose," I say.

"All right, that's all I know, Zeke. Best thing you can do is avoid answering phone calls from any number you don't recognize if you don't want a reporter or some Senate page harassing you. Am I programmed into your phone?"

"Yeah. It's sad to see that two lonely homosexuals couldn't have themselves a little horny getaway without it becoming national news. Not that I condone married men doing things like this. I respect the institution of marriage immensely—in fact, I'm getting married this year—but, you know what I mean?"

"Well, Leatherberry is—was—pretty much a lock for attorney general if the Republicans win in November. He's a hard-nosed maverick. That's hot right now. Anti-immigration, anti-Arab, you know? His people are scrambling to keep this quiet."

"I see."

"They won't though. That meddling public radio know-it-all Don Gonyea has been calling me all day, looking for dirt."

"Give him my number," I say. "I love Don Gonyea."

I hang up the phone and go back inside the Hospice Center. For two hours I sit beside my sleeping mother, but she doesn't wake up, so I kiss her forehead and go into the hall. One of the nursing assistants is coming into my mother's room as I am heading out.

"Your mother talks about you all the time," she says. "You must have been very close."

"I suppose," I say. "We've gotten closer. Lately."

"It's always my son Cougar this, and my son Cougar that," the nurse says. "She is so proud of you."

"Thank you," I say. "That means a lot."

Later that evening, back home in my study, I sip on a glass of Scotch, and then another. I leave messages for H. M., expressing my support. I leave apologetic messages for Elizabeth Vandeweghe. And for Lara Callahan. I leave a message for Minn at the Starbucks, but the barista who answers the phone is not sure when Minn will be back. And then, when I go into the kitchen for fresh ice, more Scotch, I look up at the *Simply You* prospect list taped to the fridge. After fixing a new drink, I take my phone into the living room, settle into my favorite reading chair, and call Sofia Coppola.

"Hello?" she says.

I nearly fall over onto the floor.

"Ms. Coppola?" I say.

"Who is this?" she says.

I almost say, "You don't know me" but realize, just in time, that there is no better way to invite a hang-up from a celebrity.

"It's Zeke Pappas," I say. "Remember? I'm the director of the Center for the Study of American Unhappiness."

"Okay," she says. "How did you get this number?"

Again, I know that keeping her on the phone is of paramount importance.

"Giovanni gave it to me," I say, flailing to make a credible guess.

"Rabissi?"

"Yes. Exactly."

"Okay," she says.

"He thought, well, he decided it would be okay because he really liked my project. He thought you'd be interested in it. It's a film version of an oral history I've been working on for a long time."

"You're serious?"

"Yes."

"Well, this isn't a good time. I'm about to meet some friends for dinner."

"Oh, who's that?"

"Pardon?" she says.

"Who might that be?" I ask, and then realize I have made a colossal error.

"Why don't you call my manager?" she says. "You can discuss that with her."

"And who is that?"

I take down a name and phone number, write it on a Post-it note, and then quickly type it into my laptop's phone book as well.

"Okay, well, thank you," I say. "I'll be in touch."

"And tell me your name again?" she says.

"Zeke Pappas. The Center for the Study of American Unhappiness. Madison, Wisconsin."

"Sounds interesting, Zeke," she says. "American Unhappiness. A good title."

"You think so?"

"Sure. Call my manager," she says.

"I will," I say. "I most definitely will!"

"After dinner, I need to board a plane with my husband," she says. "I gotta go."

"Pardon?" I say.

"I'm leaving, after dinner, on a plane with my husband. His band is doing a European tour and I've decided to go along."

"Jesus," I say. "How can that be?"

And then Sofia Coppola hangs up.

I have had dinner some evenings in the past, alone in the house, tucked away cozily in my small breakfast nook with a nourishing dish of chicken and peanut sauce or rice and beans, with Sofia Coppola's beaming face dining across from me, smiling in the modest blue glow of my iBook. Our conversation is jaunty and allusively flirtatious. Our courtship is torrid and brief. We can hardly get through our meal, her foot moving up and down my calf.

After dinner, I take my laptop up to the bedroom and do a Google image search for Sofia Coppola. What will she be wearing tonight when she comes to bed? But when I Google her name tonight, a terrible thing emerges. I knew she'd been divorced from her celebrity director husband, Spike Jonze, but through Google I find out she is married again. Already! Again! It seems much too soon! And then I see that she and her husband, a French rock star, have a child!

How did I miss this? Where have I been?

My desire vanishes. And Sofia Coppola, regrettably, falls off my prospect list.

That night, I dream of Valerie. In my dream, she is asleep in a vast library, nude. I cannot wake her. Her red hair fans out on a wooden table where she rests her head. Her hair dances above her head, the only part of her moving, a halo made of fire.

I scream in her ear. The patrons of the library shush me. Finally, she looks up at me, and she turns white, her already fair skin going entirely translucent. Then she begins to scream. All the books begin to fall from the towering shelves. The patrons shush and scowl. I say nothing.

When I wake up, it's four o'clock in the afternoon and my headache is gone.

In the early weeks (and what ended up being the final weeks, as well) of my marriage to Valerie, I would often sit on an old wooden chair we had next to the futon on which we slept, and I would watch my wife sleeping. I was young and unable to predict the relentless nature of loss and failure that would dominate my early adult life.

When I gazed down at Valerie, sleeping, I had a sense of victory, a strange and warm feeling that my adult life would go easily and brilliantly, and that loneliness, despair, and, in fact, unhappiness were demons I had quelled—prevented—by marrying young. I would watch Valerie, sometimes for hours, until she stirred, and then I would pad across our drab, love-struck efficiency and make coffee, returning, just as Valerie woke, with two steaming mugs in hand.

I get out of bed and go downstairs. After making coffee, and drinking a cup in a state of absolute stillness, I move into my study, open my computer, and log in to Facebook. Once there I click on Accept. And I am now friends with Valerie Somerville, and I am now free to view her profile. She's in a relationship, she lives in Ely, Minnesota, she has posted only one profile picture, and she has one hundred thirty-six friends.

And then, within five minutes, she sends me a message on the chat module.

Valerie
Zeke!!!!
Zeke
Jesus.
Valerie
I know, right? Oh my god, how are u?
Zeke
I'm not dead.
Valerie
LOL. Don't you love FB. I'm so fucking addicted!
Zeke
Did you seriously just LOL at that?
Valerie
???
Zeke
You're sick.

Valerie

Zeke, you couldn't possibly have ever thought I had really died all these years later. I want to apologize.

Zeke

I consider myself a widower, if that's what you mean.

Valerie

Well, I'm alive.

Zeke

I know.

Valerie

I'm sorry. I want to start by saying I'm very sorry for what I did to you.

Zeke

Don't you find this is an inappropriate medium for such a weighty apology? I mean you faked your OWN FUCKING DETAH.

Zeke

I mean, DEATH!

Valerie

I wasn't a good person back then.

Zeke

But you were! I loved you so much.

Valerie

I loved you too. I got scared.

Zeke

Oh for fuck's sake.

Valerie

Look, Zeke, this is gonna sound weird but this seemed like the best way and least aggressive way to recah you and so I;m sory, okay.

[*Valerie is typing.*]

Valerie

But something important has come up. I'm getting married

246

and I need to be sure that you and I are totally divorced. Did you annul the marriage or what?

Zeke

Why would I do that?

Valerie

I had a lawyer look into it and we can find no public record of our divorce, but he did find our marriage certificate in the Washtenaw County courthouse. I sort of ignored everything the whole time.

Zeke

I'm not very good with details. Paperwork. You remember?

Valerie

I know! Me neither! I sort of figured it was, you know, taken care of. It was sort of meaningless now. But my lawyer here in Ely wanted me to find you to sign some papers. So you know everything is official just in case.

Zeke

I don't believe this. So we're still married?

Zeke is offline.

22

Zeke Pappas is reading the responses.

My last visit with Farnsworth and Morris comes the next morning. When I get to my office, I am told that all of the GMHI's assets, including its building and equipment, have been seized by the federal government—*frozen* is the word they use—and they tell me I have five minutes to select my personal items from my office.

Farnsworth hands me a box.

"What about all my books?" I ask.

"Bought with GMHI funds," Morris says. "Weren't they?"

"Some of them," I say.

"Pretend the building is on fire. Take only the most important stuff," Farnsworth says. "Technically, we don't even have to let you do that."

I have no idea if this is true or not. I have no idea what sort of rights apply to this sort of situation.

Five minutes later, I leave the office with a few framed pictures of the twins, one small picture of my brother, a signed copy of Rick Bass's *Platte River*, a handful of files, a baseball autographed by Kirk Gibson, and a small cactus. I also take a small stack of backup DVDs, which I conceal in my pants just in case they hassle me about the contents. I'm thankful that I've left my laptop and jump drive back at my home office, or I might have lost those too.

"We sort of hoped to nail you too," Morris says to me as I exit the GMHI building for the last time.

"But they told us to stick to the big fish," Farnsworth says. "Apparently, you aren't a big fish. They just don't want you to spend another dime of taxpayer money."

"Well," I say, "that's sort of understandable at this point."

With that, I close the door on a long and somewhat happy chapter of my professional career.

That afternoon, as I am on my fourth cocktail and in the midst of reloading the backups of my *American Unhappiness* blog and website onto a private server (to avoid the federal government shutting that down as well), a National Public Radio piece runs about H. M. Logan and Quince Leatherberry's affair. By dinnertime, my website, newly relaunched, becomes one of the most popular websites in the country, because Robert Siegel managed to ask a *Washington Post* reporter one simple question: *One of the most obscure projects that Logan was able to get funded with Leatherberry's help is something called* An Inventory of American Unhappiness. *What can you tell us about that project?*

And the *Washington Post* reporter responded: *Well, Robert, that's a really interesting one. Apparently, it's a project run out of Madison, Wisconsin, Logan's hometown, and it basically asks people to post a response to the question* Why are you so unhappy? *As of this morning, the website still seems to be up and is still taking responses.*

Some of those responses, which arrived on my laptop, were these:

Clarence M., 46, Duluth, MN:
It gets dark so early now. I can't stand it.

Michelle B., 53, Dodgeville, WI:
Brett Favre in a Jets uniform.

Minnie Z., 43, Salem, OR:
The way that Caribou Coffee tries to make their airport coffee shop feel like a Northwoods lodge.

Vivienne G., 46, Dearborn, MI:
Victoria's Secret ads that come on during prime time, especially when I see my husband is pitching a tent in his sweatpants like he's thirteen years old. You just don't feel very sexy after you try and compare yourself to one of those ads.

Kevin G., 29, Pittsburgh, PA:
The last of the leaves. The last of the leaves. Oh, oh, the last of the leaves!

Jasper X., 53, Arlington, VA:
Assholes like you who waste taxpayer money!

Moe H., 48, Dover, NH:
This woman I used to know, she now lives in Florida with a guy who beats her, and she doesn't want to leave. How about that for sad?

Lily F., 33, Royal Oak, MI:
I saw my third-grade teacher at the mall last week and she was using a walker and she was sitting all alone inside the Big Boy restaurant, drinking a cup of coffee with shaking hands, and picking at this muffin. And she made eye contact with me, through the window that looks out on the mall, you know? And she sort of smiled, like maybe she recognized me or something. And I didn't wave. I just kept on going down the corridor. I had something to return at Mervyn's. I had this shitty sweater my aunt sent me. I hated the sweater. It made me look shapeless. Old. I don't know what it is, but I am so unhappy. You're right about that. Who are you?

And so on . . .

Traffic on my website peaked after the Leatherberry sex scandal broke and the GMHI made brief national headlines. For a few weeks, it seemed as if I might be on my way to starting a for-profit rather than a nonprofit. Although my office was closed, my assets were seized, my paychecks stopped, and my staff disappeared, I was open for business in a way I had never been before. Americans rushed to my site to express their unhappiness, to register their many sadnesses and laments. With such web traffic, I thought, booming ad sales were the next logical step. Of course, economically and politically, it was no time to seek investors in a fledgling web-based business that traffics in unhappiness and woe, so I decided to wait for a few months, file for unemployment benefits, and allow the website to build as a word-of-mouth phenomenon of the newest order.

It's quite possible that my decision to try and chronicle the collective American unhappiness of a generation was nothing more than a weak-minded acquiescence to the prevailing sentiment of the past eight years. The artistic sensibility in the nation became wholly self-referential—the story of *my* life is what matters, not the well-crafted and distilled art of memoir, nor the carefully compiled story (and analysis) of the lives (and problems) of others—but the story of what I am feeling, right now, right this minute. And so, I became part of the problem, I suppose, the problem of indifference to the trials and tribulations of our fellow citizens and our brothers and sisters around the world. I wonder, sometimes, if Studs Terkel, our nation's greatest oral historian, who died just a short time ago, had begun his work today, in the first decade of the twenty-first century, would he have done things the way he did them? Or would he have begun with a blog about how he felt about his own job, whatever it might be? Would he have appeared on the quirky and likable public radio show *This American Life,* and would he have told some quirky and likable story about his own childhood, or his recent trip to Tehran, or his own job digging graves in Toledo? We have always loved stories, I think, it's just that we, as a nation and perhaps as a human race, recently stopped loving stories about the other; we began to love stories only about ourselves. We love stories in which *we* are the protagonists in search of truth. I do not want to judge this. But my feeling is that we can cope with the increasing smallness, rapidness, and indifference of our changing, violent world only by seeing ourselves as noble characters caught in the struggle. We are all, as Turgenev so presciently said over a century ago, either Hamlets or Quixotes, and we must be these kinds of people if we are to endure.

We see ourselves in a struggle of epic, or at least interesting, magnitude, and so we go about documenting it ourselves, not waiting for some future historian, anthropologist, or novelist to find our tale and tell it for us. YouTube, MySpace, blogs—all of these things are ways for us to make ourselves protagonists on a very crowded, violent, and unjust stage.

The next morning, I wake early, eager to check my website responses, and there is already a call on my cell phone. My first thought is that it's Lara, reconsidering my proposal, or H. M. begging me to join him at a Mexican villa by the sea, but it's not either of them. It's Claire Buchwald from Fitchburg Hospice Center and she gives me the news. "Hello, Zeke," she says. "I have some hard news."

"Okay," I say.

"Mother died today," she says.

"Pardon?"

"Mother died today," she says again.

"Ha! Is that a deliberate reference, Claire?"

"Pardon?"

"Is that a deliberate allusion?"

"To what?"

"Camus?"

"What?"

"When you said, 'Mother died today,' Claire, was that a deliberate allusion?"

"I'm sorry, Zeke. I don't understand."

"Camus! That's the first line of *The Stranger*!"

"Okay," she says. "I'll see you when you get here, Zeke. Do you understand what I've told you?"

It wasn't until I saw my mother that Claire's statement moved from the realm of accidental literary allusion to reality. It wasn't until then that I called Harmony and asked her if she would tell the girls and if they might get in the car and come, as soon as they possibly could.

23

Zeke Pappas is wallowing in November.

THIS PAST TUESDAY night, I sat alone in my living room, watching a newly elected president address the nation. Along with a reassuring fifty-three percent of my fellow Americans, I watched with significant joy and felt, for a moment, as if the whole of American history suddenly made sense. What, after all, is triumph without previous trials? And so, as I sat in my recliner, a man slightly drunk on gin and democracy, I wept. I wept not only because I felt, inexplicably, as if the darkness of the past eight years had lifted, but also because I was experiencing the whole event alone. I wanted, more than anything, to be with April and May, who were, I know, being raised by Republicans in Livonia, Michigan, and I wanted to be telling my beautiful and young nieces that this moment was for them, that even if we failed miserably to achieve anything in the next four years, this moment, this election, meant something for the future stability and peace of the world. Their generation might, as a result of this moment, have less hate in its collective heart than my generation, perhaps, and if that is not a triumph, I do not know what is. In truth, I even called April and May to offer this message via cell phone, but Harmony did not pick up on her end. Perhaps there were some sour grapes involved. I know, had the shoe been on the other foot, I would not have picked up a phone call from a McCain-Palin supporter on that night.

April and May had been here at the end of October—in fact, they'd done their trick-or-treating here, in their old neighborhood, and the next day they attended a simple but rather fine memorial service for my mother and their grandmother. They sat on either side of me, each clutching my arm, each crying onto my sleeve.

When one looks upon the death of a loved one from a humanistic rather than a faith-based perspective, one remembers the stories and the images and the rituals of the deceased, the way an oral historian or an anthropologist or a novelist might remember them. My house, where I now live, all alone, still smells faintly of my mother. Because she worked such long hours, she smelled, constantly, of biscuits and gravy and fried chicken tenders from the Old Country Buffet, no matter how many showers she took, no matter how much lilac-scented lotion and grapeseed oil she rubbed on her hands and arms.

When my brother was alive, my mother's main concern was my brother's well-being. After work, she often sat at her kitchen table, her laptop open, scanning the Internet for news of the war. She barely slept. She read Cougar's e-mails over and over. She wrote long, meandering letters to him that offered support and encouragement. She kept Fox News on all morning and wore an American flag pin on her sweater. She ate almost all of her meals at work, standing up, and some nights she didn't come home until ten or eleven, unless it was a Tuesday or Friday, her only days off. Last year, I remember that she asked for two days off in a row: the regional manager said no. Eleven years, and you can't get two days off in a row! This is not what the old union leaders gave their lives for in the early part of the twentieth century! This is not why striking workers risked getting their skulls bashed in with boot heels and clubs! Something I've recently admitted to myself is this: I desperately wanted my mother's life to be different, but now it's clear that it won't be different. This was it. Her story is written.

After my father's early and unexpected death in 2001, I thought my mother might find, in widowhood, a sort of melancholic but fulfilling freedom. But each time I tried to have a serious talk with her, urged her to find new, meaningful work or rest more than she did or eat better food, maybe even take in a lifelong learning program sponsored by the GMHI, my mother changed the subject. She only wanted to give me a rundown of my brother's life in battle: Cougar's got the flu and spent the day reading magazines in the sick bay. Cougar saw a man get his hand shot off today. Cougar ate a special fried chicken dinner last night. Cougar didn't get to sleep all night. Cougar has a rash on his thighs. Cougar's unit got a surprise visit from the Hooters girls last week. Cougar could use some energy bars, some Carl Hiaasen paperbacks, some moist towelettes: why don't you send him a package?

Once Cougar and Melody were both dead, my mother's attention turned to the twins, the orphaned daughters, and rightly so. She nurtured those girls with a warmth and tenderness and selflessness that warrant canonization, in my humble opinion. I assisted where I could assist, but she was the backbone of those girls' lives. I'm not saying this was in any way a bad arrangement; I only regret that my mother died without any chance to live for herself. Selflessness is both a virtue and a vice. In between mind-numbing and grueling wage labor, she cared for my father, for me, for my brother, and for my nieces. Then she got sick. Then she died. The humanist in me doesn't argue if this is fair or not, because it's obviously not fair, is it? Divine justice, spiritual struggle: this is the domain of theologians. The humanist in me simply wonders why some people have lives like this. What can we learn from them about our own lives? What can we do to prevent such lives, or is it futile to do so? Or even worse, is it supreme arrogance to do so, to cast judgments on the happiness of others?

My mother's service was sparsely attended, I'm sad to say, though I, against all of my long-standing anti-funeral principles, did go. I wanted to be there for April and May. We were a poor, huddled mass, and I, the mass's grief-stricken anchor, was devoid of answers. The pastor read from the Gospels. Whoever believeth hath eternal life, that kind of thing. My mother's favorite hymns, "Amazing Grace" and "Old Rugged Cross," were sung. Her coworkers from the Old Country Buffet were there, the ones who could get the time off, at least, and some of them were crying. A few of our old neighbors were there too, people we used to know on the north side of town, all of them grayer and paler than I remembered them. I couldn't remember their names; they were nameless to me, lost in a buried corner of my brain. People I'd seen every day as a child, now ghosts. The huge sanctuary of the vast church seemed ridiculously empty. The pastor's sermon echoed superfluously from the walls, an afterthought, an obstacle for him to hurdle before lunch.

And this is what I thought about that Election Day evening as I sat alone and watched history unfold. It was the first time in my life that I have ever longed for the company of younger people, for the hope I was feeling in my heart to be something I could express to somebody just making his or her own sense of a senseless world.

There were, I know, in Madison, many places I could go to feel part of the collective crowd—this was an election that was watched and celebrated in taverns and cafés and the student union. But I am now a man who lives alone, a man with only a few friends, with almost no family left, with, for the first time in years, no coworkers or colleagues, and it is time that I begin to live that way. Stillness, loneliness, the quiet and long hours of the evening in the latter half of autumn, these are now the things that will define a great deal of my days.

There, I've said that.

A few weeks ago, I drove to Ely, Minnesota, to sign some papers that Valerie had her lawyer draw up, and I officially annulled a long-dead marriage. I admit, for at least a few days, I considered the possibility of reconciliation. Perhaps Valerie was an answered prayer. Perhaps the fact that I was, at least technically, still married might reverse the terms of my mother's will, and the custody of the twins would revert to me, and perhaps, perhaps even Valerie would love me again, in a way she once did, long ago, and we would make a sort of family together. I thought about this possibility for a long time on the long drive, but when I arrived in Ely, Minnesota, I knew this scenario would simply not work. I knew that this strange and hopeless scenario was not something that could ever really happen. In fact, I only spoke with Valerie's lawyer; she didn't even come to see me. I found that extraordinarily offensive and hurtful, but in truth, perhaps I could not bear to see her again. Perhaps she did me some unasked-for kindness. A few weeks later, a Google search of the Ely newspaper informed me that Valerie had married a man named Sven Olson who ran a small resort in Little Marais, Minnesota.

This morning, the first Sunday morning post-election, I wake at four, and soon I am on the road to Chicago. This is something I do every fall, in the days of leaves and grayness. I go to the art museum there, and I find the small boxes made by the American artist Joseph Cornell, and I stare at them. This year, perhaps more than any other, I feel a kinship with Cornell, a man who seemed also destined for loneliness, devoting his life to collecting the unhappy scraps left behind by others and trying to distill them and make sense of them. In these boxes, in the small miracles of collecting and assembling, I see such love, such a profound desire to understand the world and its people, to preserve forgotten magic, and I know, from my research into Cornell's life (see GMHI grant #04-222-988: *The Miracle of Found Objects: Joseph Cornell and the Assembled Language of Loneliness*), that, ultimately, he failed. He did not understand the world and its people. He did not find an adequate expression of his love. I stare at the Cornell boxes each fall until, I swear,

I can hear voices rising from them, and then, each fall, there's me, a weeping man in a gray Filson Mackinaw cruiser heading for the exits.

Most of these late autumn trips to Chicago and the museum are tinged, from the outset, with a sort of melancholy. I usually take these trips when the very last of the leaves still cling to the trees, when winter is threatening to arrive with haste and indifference. I have been to Chicago many times in the late autumn and have found, always, something dour and forlorn about the vast and crowded metropolis as it inches toward winter. But today, when I am there, the very air in the city feels changed, as if it's been washed clean, the crispness of November as vital and bracing as any I ever remember. In my coat pocket is a small box. In that small box, my grandmother's engagement ring, one of the few things that my mother was able to leave me in her will.

Could it be possible that my entire subject matter, the very thing I have been chronicling for the last decade, has been lifted from the nation? Is it possible, I think, crossing Michigan Avenue at Monroe, on my way to the Art Institute? I look over at the edge of Grant Park, where just a few nights ago a multicultural, multi-aged throng of people waved American flags and danced in the streets. It was as if a long, long war had suddenly ended, and whatever jaded melancholy, whatever essential unhappiness we had shared, was lifted.

We were a nation that was living beyond its means, living inauthentic lives that we knew we could not sustain. We could no longer buy what we bought, use the oil that we used, plunder and destroy the countries we despised. We were exhausted. All of that dominance, all of that slickness and promise and debt, was absolutely exhausting.

Today, the city feels giddy. Not in the sort of way one might traditionally describe giddiness. Rather, we look as if we have emerged from one long, disastrous party. Hung-over, dehydrated, with bloodshot eyes and inexplicably profound headaches. It's as though a leader has emerged, carrying buckets of Gatorade and aspirin, to lead us back to sobriety. It's as if we have trashed our own luxury mansions, and a man has emerged who will clean up our mess, sell off the burden of too much real estate, and help us live a life that finally means something.

Perhaps I am overstating things. But what is undeniable is that on the streets, people are happy and beaming and friendly in a way I have never felt before. As I cross the street, I thank the yellow-vested crossing guard, an African American woman, standing out in the cold to direct traffic, and she looks at me and says, "Well, you're welcome! Have a great day!" And then, as I walk, a man stops me and says, "Excuse me, sir?" and I instinctively brace myself for the inevitable panhandle, but instead he says, in a voice marked by a hint of Haitian accent, "Excuse me, sir, but you forgot to turn the heat on today!" And then we both guffaw, as if it is the funniest joke we've ever shared with anybody. We clasp each other's arms. It was absolutely astounding! If I were a pundit, and paid to say such things, if anybody would listen to me, I would remark that American Unhappiness seemed to begin on September 11, 2001, and ended on November 4, 2008. It was as if we needed to have a great reminder of our deepest ideals, to understand that we truly were the most free and diverse and, yes, generous and remarkable civic experiment in the world. I am not sure if this is true. But today it seems true.

But now, this damp and gray Sunday morning in Chicago, the coldest morning of the season, all of that seems false: we, the legions of the unhappy, overeducated, skeptical, cynical, jaded, rootless, oppressed, drifting, navel-gazing, overly reflective, and underrepresented are suddenly a community, *organized*.

Perhaps I am overstating things. Perhaps things are not that good. And perhaps I should tell you the real reason I am here. Several days ago, I received, along with the rest of Minn's contact list, this e-mail:

To: Friends & Family List
From: Minn Koltes
Re: New Contact Information
Date: November 1, 2008

Hi all! I've been sent to an "underperforming" Starbucks store in downtown Chicago to try and turn the place around. Hey, it's a living! Come and see me in Chicago!

Yes We Can!

XOXO, Minn

In the signature area of her e-mail there was a list of new contact information, and I dropped Minn an e-mail, told her I'd be at the art museum less than ten days from now, on November 9, and I would like to see her again, briefly. Could she come? And she e-mailed me back this response: *Sure, 10 a.m. I will see you then. —M.*

At ten o'clock, Minn is standing in front of the museum, right under one of the two lions that flank the entrance. These are not the aristocratic, vigilant lions of the New York Public Library—rather, these are two dark lions that seem to me to be in mid-jump, about to destroy their prey. Brawling, working-class lions. Underneath one of these, Minn looks so tiny, an effect punctuated by her heavy winter jacket, the knitted gray cap she wears, and a pair of large black mittens. She looks so small. I have never seen her dressed in her winter clothes. The sky is so gray it seems to be made of stone. My grandmother's ring is in my pocket.

We hug. Minn looks at me, with something like pity, and says, "It's good to see you."

I want to say something dazzling and poetic—maybe I should say, "It's shattering to see you."

But I can just barely manage to say the words "You too."

She points across the park to a large maple. "When I first saw you walking toward me, you were right under my favorite tree. That's my favorite tree in the whole city. I liked seeing you under it."

I just smile. It strikes me as an exceedingly kind thing to say.

"I wondered where you went; you disappeared," I say.

"I know. That was shitty of me, but after we spent that night together, which I don't regret, I swear I don't, I kind of freaked out," she says.

"Of course," I say.

"But it was good," she continues. "It shook things up in a way they needed to be shaken. I've thought about you a lot. Really."

I smile at her and can't think of anything to say to that.

We go inside and get our tickets. I insist on buying and then we check our coats and we stand in the main entrance.

"What would you like to see first?" I ask.

"Didn't you tell me that you wanted to see the Joseph Cornell boxes?"

"Yes," I say.

"Let's start there. I have to be somewhere, later," she says.

"Of course."

The Cornell boxes used to be in a gallery and there were at least a dozen of them on display during my last visit, but today, I cannot find them, and so I finally stop at an information desk and I am told that there are only three Cornells on display right now—due to renovations—and they are down in the Touch Gallery, the kids' gallery.

"That's disappointing," Minn says to me as we walk to the staircase.

"Nonsense," I say. "Three will suffice. Besides, it's an excuse to get to see you. That's reward enough."

She says nothing.

"So how do you like it here?"

"I love it. I'm so happy here. I was at Grant Park on Tuesday. It was incredible, Zeke."

"Was it? I'm sure it was. I watched on television," I say. "I thought of you. I actually prayed for a glimpse of you."

"Oh, Zeke. Knock it off."

Walking down the stairs, I am seized by the desire to take her hand.

I take her hand. She does hold it for a minute, and then she lets go.

"Zeke," she says, "I'm seeing somebody."

"I know. You have a fiancé in Africa."

"I broke up with him, Zeke. You helped me realize that I had to do it."

"Well, isn't that good? You can hold my hand then!"

"No," she said. "There's somebody new."

"What? Already? You just got here."

"I work with him. His name is Allen. We actually got together on election night."

"Allen!" I say, as if the common name shocks me.

I picture her, Minn, in the post-election haze, dancing in the street with another man. Kissing him under a streetlamp. I don't blame them. I don't begrudge anybody such passion. I would have found somebody to kiss that night too.

"What do you mean when you say you *got together*?"

"Zeke, you know what I mean."

"Well, that's fairly new. Couldn't you just tell him the love of your life has come back for you? That he has an engagement ring in his pocket?"

"Zeke," she says.

"I'm kidding! I'm kidding," I say. "There's the Touch Gallery."

There are three Joseph Cornell boxes on display: one is a box made into the whitewashed exterior of a French hotel, and outside the hotel a giant green parrot perches on a swing. The other is an owl, gazing intently out at the viewer, from a knotted and deep, dark tree trunk. Then there is the final one, a soap bubble set, adorned with two soapstone pipes, a collection of odd seashells, and four small apéritif glasses. These tiny glasses are what get me.

I don't know how long we stand in front of these three boxes, but I can feel Minn's energy shifting, like she's ready to move on. "They are so remarkable," she says.

"It's this one," I say, pointing at the soap bubble set.

"Those glasses are just waiting for a celebration, for the glow of warm conversation, to be held up in the firelight of human intimacy, to hold the elixir of a great feast. What's desolate about them is that they are abandoned. That's what Cornell's work is about, to me, really, about our abandonment of joy, about our reckless inability to hold on to anything meaningful. This is an attempt to find meaning—no, to find magic—in our collective dross, in the castoff and the forgotten."

"I don't know about Cornell's life so much," Minn says. "Come on, let's go look at the special exhibit."

I follow Minn to an adjoining gallery, which features a special show on Paris and the work of Henri Cartier-Bresson.

Most of the pieces are photographs and small drawings or paintings that somehow relate to Paris. I cannot focus on any of them. I try to look at them, but I can't. Minn is looking at a series of distorted nudes, and instead of looking at them with her, I look at her, the profile fixed in concentration. The din of the museum at the day's opening grows louder as a school group of some sort—maybe college freshmen—wanders into the gallery. Minn's lips are open, barely parted, and so I kiss them, and for a moment, she kisses me back, I'm sure of it, and then a small bite of my lower lip and then she says, "No."

I wander to another wall. I randomly choose a picture to stare at, waiting for my heart rate to decelerate. It's a photograph by André Kertész, entitled *Paris, A Gentleman.* In the image you can see only the back of the gentleman, who is dressed in a black overcoat and black hat and black trousers, or at least it appears that way in the black-and-white print. He is holding an umbrella, which he clasps with both hands behind his back. He is an old man, slightly stooped, and he is observing the city move about him. It's obvious to the observer that he has stopped to rest, but to me, he looks as if he is suddenly paralyzed by a sense of loneliness. One looks at him and can tell from the slump of his shoulders, the odd and reflective tilt of his white head, that he is lonely and that he has been alone for a long time now.

I feel Minn come up alongside me.

"Are you crying?" she says.

"Hardly," I say, but it comes out very loud and high-pitched, because I try and say it mid-sob.

"Zeke," she whispers, "you are."

"Nonsense!" I say, my shoulders heaving a bit now.

"Zeke, what is wrong?"

"Nothing."

"Zeke, what is wrong with you?"

"Marry me?" I say.

"I don't believe this," she says.

Exit Zeke.

Outside, my damp eyes feel cold; the winds of November are coming off the lake with a new bitterness. I put my hands to my cheeks and try to dry them. I go and look at one of the lions and put my hand on its foot and stand there for a moment, shivering.

I see a cab approaching and I go to the curb.

I hail it and it stops. Inside the cab, I sit in the back seat, put my hands in my lap.

"Well?" the driver says, a thick Indian accent. "Where to?"

"Pardon?" I say.

"Where do you want to go?" he says.

"I'm sorry. I don't know," I say.

"You don't know?"

"No," I say. "I have no idea."

"You just want to drive around?"

"No, no. Not that."

"What do you want then?" he asks.

"'The *reducto absurdum* of all human experience,'" I say to him.

"Get out of my cab then!" he bellows.

"William Faulkner," I say. "William Faulkner!"

"Get out," he says. His bellowing continues.

I do as he asks. I get out of his cab, just as Minn comes out of the museum.

She comes out with my coat and stands at the top of the steps. She is dressed for winter again, and the sight of it is too much. It's probably the most heartache I have felt in a long, long time, seeing her hair tucked behind her ears like that, her knit cap pulled down.

I see her at the top of the steps, scanning for me.

When we lock eyes, I lift up a hand, expressionless. Minn lifts up her mittened hand too, and she takes my coat and drapes it gently on the handrail at the entrance. Then she turns and walks away, using the side staircase opposite me. I watch her for a long time, staring at the hem of her coat just above her knees, just for the sad thrill of it.

What makes me so unhappy?

People walking away, dressed in winter clothes, the sky the same gray as their coats, the branches of the trees around them, black-gray and skinned. And in my heart of hearts, I know that the tree Minn loves best will be bare by morning. Already, a gown of gold gathers at its feet.

24

Zeke Pappas writes his epilogue.

IT IS NO SMALL thing to be lonely or depressed. It is no small thing to feel complete confusion over the path that you would like to take. I do understand that, but I must say that my project has become very unappealing to me. Suddenly, the hundreds and hundreds of interviews I had done in an attempt to distill the nation's precise condition of discontent seem, well, trivial. Whiny, actually. The whole project seems to hinge upon my ability to make the subjects of my interviews whine, and, if I was lucky, a select few might weep. It seems to have gone stale while I was away from it, as many good projects do if you take a long recess from the work you have been doing so diligently for years. But no, this is more than mere staleness; this is more than the rustiness of my mental parts. This is a disturbing and awkward realization that I no longer care about the daily struggles of my fellow human beings. It's not that I do not understand, or even honor, the plight of humans, particularly in the middle third of their lives, trying to find their place in the vast and mind-blowing social order we have constructed in the millennia since we evolved from monkeys. The world is still disturbing, even with George W. Bush brushed off and sent packing into a dark history; many of my subjects face woes that are equally disturbing, or even more disturbing, in the era of Obama. I just no longer care.

In fact, I no longer care about anything really, save April and May.

I have just arrived, in fact, at my nieces' new home in Livonia, Michigan, a bland and nondescript suburb of Detroit that I once heard featured on National Public Radio as the least diverse, most segregated place in America. It seemed to epitomize, for me, the state of not caring. And as I made my way out of Madison this morning, I realized that perhaps I no longer wanted to live there among all that earnestness and intellectual idealism. Perhaps I wanted to live in Livonia, a few blocks from my nieces, the children of my dead and distant brother. Could that be all I wanted from this life? To be near my family? To be a stone's throw from the people I love, the few remaining? I considered this as I drove across the flatness of Illinois, past Rockford and Elgin, across the congested and gray Skyway, through the burning tire haze of Gary and the blighted midsize and rusted-out cities of western Michigan—Benton Harbor, Battle Creek, Jackson, where almost nothing of value is left. It is late December and gray piles of snow edge everything. The pavement is wet, the sun is occasionally obscured by thick, smoky clouds, and the air is chilled with a constant and deep dampness.

Livonia, where I now sit, idling in my Honda, is still today. Nobody is home at the home of Harmony and Malcolm, as I have arrived ninety minutes earlier than anticipated. I imagine that Malcolm is at work, and that Harmony and the girls are out shopping, perhaps picking up some of their Uncle Zeke's favorite snack foods and his preferred spirits. I know that April and May are excited for my visit. I imagine, and hold out some hope, that Harmony is too. Our meeting at my mother's memorial service was remarkably warm and cordial, as if she had slipped back into her regular life, Malcolm at her side, and I had slipped back into the life I had five years ago: a lonely bachelor who worked too much. But now I essentially have no work, and while the initial reality was depressing to me, it suddenly occurs to me that I could, too, live in Livonia, Michigan, a stone's throw from the twins. I could see them almost every day, attend their games and recitals and birthday parties, and this realization, so seemingly revolutionary to me, infuses me with energy. I decide to drive around for a while, to take in Livonia, where, perhaps, just perhaps, as it turns out, I might settle for good.

My impressions: There is no striving for anything in Livonia—justice, diversity, excellence, or intellectual prowess. It is a place content with its own safety and cleanliness, though it is mere minutes away from some of the most profound urban poverty in the Western world. I know that some of the men from Livonia must have gone off to war like my brother did, but it is not something often spoken of, certainly not with any sense of regret or despair. You do not see many bumper stickers in Livonia. Bumper stickers are always a good indication of the earnestness and striving of a place. And as I said, I am done with striving. It is as useless as everything under the sun, as it has been written.

The girls live in a modest colonial from the 1960s that is on a shady street with the rather pleasant name of Ladywood. Theirs is the seventh house off the corner of Newburgh Road. Nearby, there is an all-girls Catholic high school with the same name. It is a rather pleasant name, and when I say it, I feel as if I am saying the name of some old English manor featured in a forgotten novel where there is always surface happiness and order and an undercurrent of despair underneath the whole machine.

As I drive among the streets of Livonia, so geared toward the life of family, of stable and easy domesticity, I live a fantasy life of regrets, missed opportunities. I imagine them as if they had taken flight. For instance: Minn and I, in my mind, have an apartment in Paris (we simply *had* to leave the country) and the girls attend the American school near the Sorbonne. Or this: Lara and I own a coffee shop near the harbor in Kenosha, and we live, with my nieces and her daughters, in a huge, seven-bedroom apartment above it. Or perhaps Elizabeth and I live a quiet life in Ithaca, New York, and my first book has been published and has done quite well, and I am a tenured professor at Cornell, quite well respected and the holder of an endowed chair. The kids live with us and we all love Ithaca. We wear such lovely sweaters in the winter, and we ski, and at night, in winter, I drink brandy, expensive brandy. Or perhaps Ms. Coppola and I finally made things work, and we are living in upper Manhattan and the twins spend each summer with us there, ambling through Central Park, each one holding my hand as we make our way to the Guggenheim for lunch or to SoHo for some shoe shopping. Sofia, perhaps, invites over Scarlett Johansson one evening, and Natalie Portman too, and after much wine, it turns out they are very big proponents of the group shower. We shower together in a vast and well-ventilated bathroom!

Of course, it is hard to stop fantasies once they begin, isn't it? There is nothing wrong with the richness of this fantasy life. I am convinced of that: it is always so much more rewarding than reality.

But being wholly realistic, I must say this: I think Livonia will be an appropriate place for me to live. And just as I think this, I see the green warmth of an illuminated Starbucks sign, and I steer my Honda toward the drive-through, pull up to the speaker, and order. I decide, spur of the moment, to order a new sort of drink.

"Welcome to Starbucks," a woman says. "What can I get started for you today?"

"Soy mocha," I say.

"Whip?" she says.

"No," I say.

"No whip?" she says. "Seriously? Come on, live a little."

She laughs at her own coaxing and I laugh too.

"No thanks," I say.

I pull up to the window, my five-dollar bill in hand, and there is the barista, waiting for me at the open window. She is about my age, with lovely fair skin, large blue eyes, and a tangle of blond curls she wears piled up under her Starbucks cap. She takes my money and I motion for her to place the change in the plastic tip container. A strand of her blond hair springs out from under her cap, as if it's been electrified. She laughs and tucks it back under her cap.

"You sure about that whip?" she says, just before she's about to place a lid on my soy mocha. "It's pretty chilly today."

"Whip," I say. "Extra whip."

"Excellent," she says.

"I'm Zeke," I say.

She smiles. "Annie," she says.

As Annie goes to add whip to my beverage, I glance in the rearview mirror for a moment. An impatient, fat-faced man in a Chevy Suburban talks into a wireless headset, the glare of the day reflecting off of his wraparound shades.

"Annie," I say, "I bet the guy behind me ordered up a skinny vanilla latte and a pumpkin scone."

Annie pauses and looks at the computer monitor at her side.

"He did," she says. "Are you together?"

"No. No," I say. "Classic type-A sugar addict. Just a hunch."

It is just then that a cloud shifts and a rusty, weak beam of Detroit sun comes down upon my car. Annie's hair, coming loose from her cap once again, catches the light pouring in through the drive-up window.

"Soy mocha, extra whip," Annie says, handing the beverage to me over the small blacktop chasm between us.

Then, there's the two of us, Annie and I, laughing.

Perhaps I'll just leave you with that.

Author's Note

The events, characters, and situations depicted in this book are purely fictional, and they have no rooting in the various experiences I had while working for the Wisconsin Humanities Council between 2001 and 2009. My time with the state humanities council was an enjoyable and stimulating experience made richer by the dedicated, incredibly hard-working and caring, warm people (particularly Dena Wortzel, Michael Kean, and Esther Mackintosh) who make up the world of the public humanities and the National Endowment for the Humanities.

Acknowledgments

I wish to thank the John Simon Guggenheim Memorial Foundation, the National Endowment for the Arts, and Joen Greenwood (via Shake Rag Alley in Mineral Point, Wisconsin) for incredibly crucial fellowships and support while I was working on this project. I'm also grateful for support from Iowa State University's Center for Excellence in the Arts and Humanities and the College of Liberal Arts and Sciences. My students and colleagues at Iowa State have all been remarkable and helpful, especially Steve Pett, Charles Kostelnik, Marissa Landrigan, and, of course, Big Bad Ben Percy, whose insane work ethic keeps me on task and whose sense of humor keeps me from self-pity. Similarly, my colleagues and students at Warren Wilson's MFA program have taught me a great deal about craft and the writing life, and for that I am grateful. Thanks to Dr. Peter Kish, chiropractic genius, as well as my pals Coleman, John Fetters, Julian Goldberger, Perrin Chiles, Darragh Kennan, Jessica Kennan, Joe "Blessed Are the Cheesemakers" Burns, Katie "The Cheesemaker's Wife" Burns, Natalie Bakopoulos, and Jeremiah Chamberlin. Thanks to Lorrie Moore, for crucial encouragement in a dark time, and Charlie Baxter, for a million kind words and one harsh letter. Thanks to Becky Saletan for her faith and good humor. Thanks to Jeff Bean, the teacher who started everything. Thanks to copyediting genius Barbara Wood for the kind of eagle eye that is so necessary after eleven drafts. And finally, thanks to my wife, Amanda Okopski, who always supports the quitting of day jobs but never supports quitting on a manuscript; to my agent and unflappable friend, Amy Williams, who stayed with me in the desert; and to my editor, Adrienne Brodeur, who arrived with fresh horses and cold water, just in the nick of time.

About the Author

Dean Bakopoulos is the author of the novel *Please Don't Come Back from the Moon,* a *New York Times* Notable Book for 2005. The recipient of a Guggenheim Fellowship and a National Endowment for the Arts fellowship, he is also a playwright with the Alley Stage theater company in Mineral Point, Wisconsin. He teaches in the MFA Program in Creative Writing and Environment at Iowa State University, as well as the MFA Program for Writers at Warren Wilson College.